Acclaim for Ashley Schaller

"This is a terrific story that rockets along from the opening page to the genuinely surprising ending. Skillfully developed characters, prose, and scenes all contribute to the sense of being in the hands of a confident storyteller."
 —**DANIEL SCHWABAUER, award winning author and creator of** *The One Year Adventure Novel*

"*Inception* meets *Rise of the Guardians* meets *Sandman*. This is the book I've been yearning for since high school. It has everything a reader can ask for—an intriguing world, lovable characters, fast-paced non-stop action. I can guarantee you're going to have a hard time reading it in more than one sitting."
 —**HOPE BOLINGER, editor and author of 20+ award winning books**

"*R.E.M.* is a story full of emotion, adventure and high stakes. A story that will not only make you fall in love with the characters, but may also make you crave a coffee. *R.E.M.* is a beautiful story with a fantastic and unexpected ending."

—**JENNA TERESE, YA author of** *Ignite*

"A whirlwind of imagination, *R.E.M.* will keep you up late into the night. A dream-world thriller perfect for fans of *Inception* and mysterious, protective heroes. Schaller delivers non-stop action and just the right touch of romance."
—**C. F. E. BLACK, author of** *Blade of Ash.*

"With engaging characters and fantastical situations, Schaller's *R.E.M.* delves through grief and sorrow to discover a second chance with love and joy."
—**CATHY MCCRUMB, bestselling and award winning author of** *Recorder*

"An amazing, thrilling adventure that kept me fully engrosed and clinging to the edge of my seat. And that twist! Perfection!"
—AJ SKELLY, author of The Wolves of Rock Falls series and *Of Flame & Frost*

R.E.M. is the first place award winner of the One Year Adventure Novel's 2017 Student Novel Contest.

R.E.M.

R.E.M.

ASHLEY SCHALLER

Quill & Flame
PUBLISHING HOUSE

Published by Quill & Flame Publishing House, an imprint of Book Bash Media, LLC.

www.quillandflame.com

Cover design by Emilie Haney, www.EAHCreative.com

To the girl who fears the darkness. Look to the Light. He will guide you.

Chapter One

I squeeze my eyes shut and count off the seconds until I reach sixty. Then I deliver a good pinch to my thigh through my leggings.

Yep, that hurts.

I peel my eyes open.

But the scene hasn't changed. How I wish I could wake up and discover everything is a dream. It's not, it's not, it's not. The truth echoes through my core with every pulse of my heart.

Mr. and Mrs. Johnson still stand beside an open grave, tears turning his nose red and her cheeks black as her mascara runs. A harsh breeze stings my cheeks, effectively drying any tears I could produce.

Macy slips her hand into mine, fingers tight around my own as if I'm all that keeps her from tumbling into that open pit with its reek of fresh earth. I squeeze back with just as much force, so she'll know I'm here. I may not be family, but the loss of her brother hits me as hard as if we'd shared blood.

She offers a wobbly smile before her eyes fix on a point over my shoulder.

I turn and follow her gaze.

Beck. Our other best friend comes toward us, black ringlets bouncing around her shoulders. Her eyebrows dip low, and her eyes hold a softness identical to the downturn of her glossy lips. I slip my hand free from Macy's and step out of the way so she can hug Beck. They cling to each other while Beck pats Macy's shoulder and murmurs words of comfort. Does she even hear them? They sound like meaningless nonsense to me. How can this hole in my heart ever really "get better?"

I hang back, arms crossed over my middle, and turn to face Luke's grave so I won't be invited into the embrace. Plumes of white roses stand on either side of the black pit. They should have chosen sunflowers. Or at least something cheery with a splash of color. That's who Luke is. *Was.* But I'm not family, and I didn't get to help make the decisions.

A lump settles in my throat, and I press a hand against it, but that does nothing to ease the tightness lodged there. With each breath, the deep ache grows, twisting a hole in my core.

"Gwen." Beck steps away from the embrace and squeezes my hand.

I can't bring my numb fingers to respond.

With lips clamped into a thin line, Beck releases me and takes up residence on Macy's other side. Macy lifts a gloved hand and dabs at the tears leaking from her already discolored eyes.

The pastor steps to the grave and opens his Bible. His lips move, suggesting speech, but all I can see are Luke's parents. Mrs. Johnson blots the mascara running down her cheeks with a crumpled tissue, and Mr. Johnson wraps an arm around her shaking shoulders. They both stare at their son's casket with bloodshot eyes. Fresh tears spill down my own cheeks. Is it possible to run out? I almost wish I could.

A gust of frigid wind whips through the graveyard, rattling the surrounding trees. I wrap my black coat tighter around myself, fighting off the burst of goosebumps prickling my flesh. The winter chill shreds through the folds of my coat, making the fabric no more effective than water-logged paper.

The pastor drones on.

I stare at the casket without really seeing it. Instead, Luke's face floats before my mind, every freckle, every blond hair. I've known him almost my entire life. From catching worms to first crushes. He's like another brother...*was* like another brother. The pastor's amen draws my gaze up. I echo the word, my raspy voice blending with the other graveside attendants.

Amen.

So final.

I inhale a sharp breath, but the lump in my throat swells.

Macy squeezes my hand once more before stepping forward with her family. The Johnsons look so incomplete without Luke standing beside them. Macy tosses a single rose onto the mahogany container holding her only sibling and steps away, shoulders back, spine straight, head held high, like the ballerina she is. Only those of us who know her well will be able to spy the small quiver of her chin.

Mrs. Johnson nearly folds over, probably would if not for her husband catching her close. Her wails blend with the wind. I press my eyes shut, and my damp lashes cling to my skin. If I hurt this much, how much worse must their pain be? Luke always knew how to draw a smile from anyone. He'd hate these tears.

I lift my eyes and take in the broken couple before me. Mr. Johnson whispers into his wife's ear and steers her toward their waiting car. Macy chokes out a goodbye and joins the huddle of her family. Her family minus one.

With a headache throbbing, I trail Beck to her cheery yellow Bug. My boots crunch over shriveled leaves leftover from autumn. Luke's favorite season. Why does everything have to be a reminder of him? I shiver and tuck my arms over my chest, covering the hole left there. I pull my gaze away from the shattered leaves and focus on the bright vehicle in front of me. A faded flower sticker is pasted to the back windshield, and the license plate hangs from the vehicle's rear, one pothole away from tumbling to the pavement. Beck climbs into the driver's seat and starts the car. I reach for the other door handle with trembling fingers. The image of a demolished automobile bursts into my mind, and a tremor shoots through me.

I swallow.

It was an accident.

I'll be fine.

I slip into the passenger's side and lean my head against the cool window. Balmy heat blasts my chilled body while the car warms up. Beck backs out of our parking space.

My breath hitches. I'll be forced to face a world without Luke. The peeling seat pokes at me, and I brush aside an annoying piece of upholstery, taking the opportunity to swipe away an escaping pool of snot.

"You okay?" Beck bumps aside an empty coffee cup before maneuvering us out of the parking lot and onto the road. Something rattles ominously within the Bug's engine.

Fine. Perfect. Never better. I could snap any one of the replies, but I don't. Instead, I turn away from the sickly-sweet scent remaining in the Styrofoam cup and inhale a few clean breaths near the frosted window. How can she drink that stuff?

"Gwen, you okay?" Beck sneaks a look at me.

I shake my head before resting my forehead on my palm. "No." She's only lived here a year. She doesn't know Luke. Not like I do.

Did.

She offers a sympathetic smile before guiding the Bug down my street. My house grows larger the closer we get. How many times did Luke drive me down this same street? My heartrate picks up until my pulse seems to be fighting to break through my skin. I can't breathe. I tug at the turtleneck of my dress and chug down a series of breaths. Beck applies the brakes for a stop sign, and the Bug creaks to a standstill.

I clear my throat and release my seatbelt. "Actually, I think I'm going to walk from here."

Her dark eyes focus on me, styled eyebrows pinched together. "You sure?"

"Yeah." I need air. Now. I fumble with the door handle and scramble into the frigid January day.

"Gwen?" She leans over the console.

I raise my eyebrows.

She brushes a tight curl out of her face. "It's going to be okay."

Yeah, because losing someone you love will just stop hurting. But that isn't what she wants to hear, so I force down the lump in my throat and nod before pushing the door closed.

She offers one more syrupy-sweet smile before her tires grind over the asphalt, and she takes off.

The click of my boots against the sidewalk fills the empty air. I snuggle deep into the collar of my borrowed coat. The bitter wind tugs at the dark strands of my hair, whipping them against my cheeks. I shiver and increase my pace. A few small snowflakes drift from the ugly gray sky to perch on the tip of my nose.

Luke loved the snow.

An ache deep and raw throbs inside my chest. I glance to the right. Was it only last week he'd walked beside me, showing off a new card trick? By the end of the sidewalk, he'd coaxed me into learning the illusion. The pang in my chest burns deeper, and I do my best to shove thoughts of Luke from my mind. I can't cry. Not here. Not where someone could see me. I try to ignore the rust spotted white car loitering at the corner, try not to see the woman walking her pink-dyed dog while she casts curious glances my way. I suck in a shuddering breath and brush past the elderly gentleman shuffling down the sidewalk, hands pushed deep into his coat pockets.

A wobble attacks my chin, and I clench my teeth. I will *not* cry.

Not yet.

My house looms up ahead, offering shelter from the prying eyes of passersby. I skirt past the discarded Christmas tree at the curb of the driveway and jog the last few feet to my porch. I dig into my pocket and pull out my keys. It takes a little jiggling, but I persuade the bright red door to let me in. I spill into the foyer and fumble with the buttons on my mother's coat, intent on getting out of my funeral clothes.

"Gwen?" Nana's voice carries through the house, rising above the noise of her opera music floating from the kitchen's stereo system.

Tommy, my little brother, looks up from his cars lined up along the living room rug, stuck in traffic. Three cars are piled on top of each other. A wreck.

My eyes burn, and I struggle with the buttons, desperate to escape the coarse fabric. The stench of the casket spray wafts from the material. My stomach turns.

The music clicks off, and Nana shuffles into the foyer. Her wrinkled face softens when she sees me. Without a word, she steps forward and frees me from my wool prison. I choke on a sob and fall into her waiting arms.

"Oh, Gwendolyn." Nana runs a hand over my hair and whispers soothing words in Spanish.

I am loved. She is here for me. I soak in the calming sound and take a few deep breaths of the lavender detergent clinging to her shirt. Nana's arms tighten around me in a fierce embrace.

"I'm going to change," I say when my breathing steadies.

She nods against my head and lets me go.

I trot up the staircase and hurry to my room. My seven-year-old sister sits outside my door with her knees pulled to her chest. She rubs a fist against her eye.

"Maria?" I squat in front of her. I scan her for injuries, but nothing stands out other than a few marker scribbles across her skin. A fight with Tommy maybe?

Maria launches into my middle, sobs racking her small frame. I cup her head and rub her back while her tears dot my dress.

"What's wrong?" I stroke her dark hair.

She mumbles something into my shoulder.

I ease her back a bit so her mouth isn't covered. "What?"

"My heart hurts." A soft hiccup follows her words, encored by another onset of tears.

I pull her onto my lap. She rubs at her nose, mucus tracing an outline along the sleeve of her unicorn shirt. "I miss him." She leans her head against my shoulder, chin trembling.

I hold her tighter and inhale her peppermint shampoo. The scent smells like Dad and the peppermint candies he's forever sucking. Maria refuses to use any other kind while he's deployed. "Me, too."

Another dab at her running nose. "When are things going to go back to normal again?"

My nose stings, and I swallow. "They won't. Things are just going to be different now."

A fresh burst of tears erases the audibility of her next words.

"What?" I brush away a clump of hair sticking to her watery cheek.

"I don't want different." My sister turns her face into my neck. "I want Luke."

Once again, something I can sympathize with. "I know." I hug her close.

After a minute, her quaking breaths steady, and her body relaxes against mine.

I wipe away the liquid slipping from her eyes. "It's okay."

Maria moves to a corner of the hallway, scoops up a sock monkey, and holds the offering out to me. "I want you to have him."

The thing has mismatched red button eyes and a mouth which has been sewn together so many times it twists into a crooked line. Freaky, but well-loved. I reach for him and pull the creature to my shoulder. "I'll hold on to him, but only for a little while."

Nana pulls herself up the stairs and holds a wrinkled hand out to my sister. "Come help me in the kitchen."

Maria scampers to her, long scraggly hair bouncing around her shoulders, and the two disappear downstairs.

I inhale a deep breath and move into my bedroom. The purple walls soothe, and the air smells clean without a hint of the grief which has trailed me since the church. My drum set sits in front of the window, and my fingers itch to hold my drumsticks, but first things first. I take a second to just breathe. When my heartbeat slows, and the throbbing behind my eyes eases, I peel off the dress and stockings borrowed from my mom's closet and slip into my favorite pair of ripped jeans and black t-shirt. There. This is me. I slide onto the circular seat behind my drums.

I beat out a rhythm matching the one pounding in my temple. My drumsticks trace the scars on the well-worn drum set. It's my diary. More memories are stored within its structure than I can count. Some good days, others not so great. Like today.

For once, playing doesn't ease the tension in my shoulders. The thundering of the drums galvanizes the pounding in my skull until the pain pulses in torturous waves. Memories of Luke showing off his drumstick twirling skills doubles me over. Raw sobs claw at me until they burst out in sounds barely qualifying as human. I hurl the sticks across the room. The innocent pieces of wood smack against the wall before rattling to the ground. How is it that the action does nothing to release the pain digging deeper in my chest?

I push away from the drumkit and move to the light switch and flick it off.

Darkness swathes my room, save for the little light trickling through my curtains. The faded interior does nothing to soothe the invisible agony inside me, but somehow, it's still welcome. I tug my sleeves over my fists and curl up on top of my comforter. I tuck my covered hands under my chin and pull my knees to my chest. The ache still doesn't diminish. I shut my eyes and lay there, listening to the ticking of my clock.

A soft knock sounds against my door. "Gwen?" The barrier muffles Maria's voice.

"What?" I dare to lift an eyelid.

My little sister pokes her head around the door. "Nana wants to know if you want dinner."

I nod and maneuver into a sitting position. Every muscle within my body protests, as if they should be allowed to be dormant from now on. A dull headache throbs against my forehead.

Maria skips down the stairs in front of me, singing a song she made up earlier in the week.

"Unicorns are pink and blue,
Unicorns are purple too,
Unicorns smell like glue,
Unicorns!
For me and you!"

I trail after her, one hand against the wall for support. Frame after picture frame lines the wall. Luke's lopsided smile managed to make it into more than a few of the photos.

Nana sits at the head of the table, and Maria slips in beside Tommy. I lower myself into a chair across from the twins and run a fingertip over the smooth handle of my fork. To my right, is the empty chair my older brother Elijah should be sitting in. The second empty chair at the end of the table belongs to my mom. I try not to picture the newly empty chair at the Johnson's dining room table.

Across the kitchen, the clock on the microwave marks Mom's anticipated arrival as long overdue. My heart skips.

What if right now her car is smashed on the side of the road? What if she never comes home? Goosebumps flash across my skin, and I rub the earrings lining my ears. How long until sirens sound, announcing another home ripped apart?

Nana follows my gaze. "Your mother called. Her shift ran late. She'll be home soon."

I exhale and blink back a sudden burst of moisture filling my eyes. How long will this panic at someone's delayed arrival last?

Maria pushes at the beans on her plate, nose wrinkled. "She's never home."

It hasn't always been this way. My attention travels to the photo of my dad propped up on the counter, looking so unshakable in his uniform. Three months. Twenty-two days. Until he's home. And then Mom will be able to relax and not feel like she has to work so hard. They say every military wife has a coping mechanism. Work is Mom's. If I were fancy, I'd count the hours and seconds until his deployment will be over, but I'm not, so I content myself with checking one day off the calendar at a time.

Nana spoons a scoop of rice onto Maria's plate. "Your mother is very busy. She works hard for you and your brothers and sister."

Tommy picks at his meal. "She promised to take us to the library yesterday—"

"But she 'had to work,'" Maria finishes.

Like Luke promised he would take me to pick out new music today. Now that promise won't come true either. I swallow hard and force my voice to work. "I'll take you tomorrow."

In unison, the twins swivel toward me.

Nana eyes me for a long moment before raising her faded eyebrows at the duo. "What do you say to your sister?"

"Thank you," the twins chorus to their beans.

After a few bites, Tommy dares a peek up at me, an excited gleam coloring his dark eyes.

I maneuver my lips into something resembling a smile.

A tear slips down Maria's plump cheek.

"What's wrong?" Nana wipes away my sister's tear.

"Luke likes to come to the library, too." Her chin dimples, and a quiver runs through her jaw.

My nose stings, and I blink furiously against the watery sheen fighting to take over my vision. I stab my fork into my beans and hold it there. Like the pressure will somehow help me regain control.

"He did love the library." Nana keeps her hand pressed to Maria's face, eyelids closed, showing her blue eyeshadow in all its glory. "Just because Luke is gone does not mean you should stop enjoying the library. You understand?"

Maria nods, eyes solemn.

An egg-sized lump settles in my throat, cutting off my oxygen. Still, I sit unmoving, waiting for Nana's next words.

"We loved Luke, and we miss him, but that doesn't mean we must stop living." Nana's gaze moves to take in both Tommy and me.

"Okay." Maria runs her sleeve over her face.

Tommy and I both nod.

"Good. Let's eat." Nana takes a bite of rice.

When plates are scraped clean, the front door creaks, and Mom struggles inside with her arms full of groceries.

"Mommy!" Maria's eyes light up, and she pushes away from the table.

"You're home." Tommy races to Mom's side and takes one of her burdens, though the bag is almost as big as he is.

"Hey," I say, tugging my sleeve further down my wrist.

Mom kisses Tommy's dark hair before her eyes find mine. Studying. Searching. "Sorry I'm late."

Nana dishes a plate for Mom and passes it my way. I slide it to Mom's end of the table. She tosses her keys onto a stand in the foyer, sheds her coat, and smiles at us. The smile doesn't hide the bags under her eyes or the way her curly hair has frizzed from her ponytail. She straightens her scrubs and takes a seat. Finally, we're together as a family. Well, except for Dad and Elijah, but Dad's deployment is creeping to an end, and Elijah will come home for the summer.

If only Luke could be here, too. Why can't he just be away at college? Why does he have to be *gone*?

The ache in my chest pinches tight.

Mom's dark eyes study me, worry shadowing them. I force a smile for her benefit. I'm fine. Everything's fine. Mom's lips twitch in reply, a smile as fake as the one I model. Part of me longs to shout all the feelings swirling inside my head, but somehow the torrent of emotions won't churn into words, so I stare at her, silently begging for help. Sympathy swirls through her gaze, but maybe words don't exist for moments like these. Words can't fix broken hearts.

Chapter Two

After the little ones are tucked in bed, Mom comes to my room. I pretend I can't get enough of scrolling through my phone.

"Gwen?" Mom pulls her white cardigan tighter around herself.

I swallow hard and blink away the moisture threatening to spill over. "Yeah?" I force the word through my tight throat. The images on the screen blur in front of me.

"Are you okay?"

"I'm great."

Mom eases onto the comforter. "I know it's hard, babe."

I bob my chin even as my face contorts into what most would consider the first form of the "ugly" cry.

She presses a kiss to my temple. "It's going to be okay."

The simple words unlock the dam, and the tears I've been holding back spill out in a hideous river. My shoulders heave as I sob into my mom's arms. She strokes my back and lets me cry. When the wailing transitions to shuddering breaths, Mom pushes me back and cups one hand around my cheek and uses the other to brush a few strands of hair from my eyes.

"Better?"

"A little."

Mom's lips tilt up in a gentle smile. "It's not going to get better in a day. It's going to be hard. But, it *will* get better."

I nod again, new tears cutting off my ability to speak.

"Hey, I tried to call Dad."

I glance up, chest lightening.

Her brow wrinkles, and she rubs my arm. "I couldn't get through."

We rarely can thanks to spotty connections and military tape. "Okay." I try to smile for her sake. It's not her fault, and knowing her, she tried for longer than I would have.

"I'll try again tomorrow. I promise." She presses a kiss to my forehead. "Try to get some rest."

"Yeah." I slide my phone onto the nightstand and lay down.

Mom pulls the blankets back and tucks me in like I'm the twins' age.

"Night," I whisper.

"Goodnight." Mom kisses me one last time and turns out the lights before heading to her own room.

Behind my closed eyes, all I can see is the smashed metal that was Luke's car after the accident. My pulse races at the memory. For several minutes, I lay trying to fight off the picture, but in the end, my mind refuses to give me something more pleasant to focus on. I roll onto my side and fumble for my phone. The warm glow lights the room. I snag my earbuds and slide them into place. A few quick taps, and a soothing melody soars through my earbuds. I focus on the music. Regulate my breathing to match the pace. Force myself to focus on the melody. Anything to block out the mangled mess that was Luke's car.

I struggle through a week of school. It's like no one knows what to do with me. A few kids wave, but most duck their heads and scurry to class. I've become the weird girl. The one who's mourning a brother who wasn't even hers by blood.

Macy is, of course, not here, and she's already gotten all her required credits, so I'd be surprised if she even comes back. Beck is no help at all. She's away with her family, visiting with her grandmother. So, I'm forced to navigate these halls on my own. Ironic that it was my idea to even come. Mom and Nana wanted me to take a few days off, but the driving need for normal sent me running for the familiarity of school.

I fall asleep in algebra class and then bawl my eyes out in biology. The teacher finally has me go lay down in the nurse's office until Nana shows up with the car and a steaming mug of tea.

She dictates her day thus far to me as we pull out of the school parking lot. She's taken the twins to school, gone to an aerobics class, watched one of those cheesy soap operas, and mopped the kitchen floor. When the school is a good mile behind us, she pulls over and faces me. "How are you?"

I fiddle with the plastic lid covering my tea. "Fine."

She raises her eyebrows, waiting.

I swallow hard and shake my head. "Not fine."

"There's strength in admitting that."

I fall back against the seat, craning my head toward the ceiling. "I'm just so tired." I fall into bed by eight and then pull myself out when my alarm goes off. Most of the time, I have to take a nap halfway through the day.

Nana squeezes my knee. "That's to be expected."

"I'm just ready to…" I flick the lid on my tea.

"Ready to…?"

"To feel better."

"Oh, Gwen. It's not that simple. You just need to give yourself time."

Time. Not an answer I've ever liked. But I nod. I catch sight of my reflection in the side mirror. For a moment it blurs, but I rub my eyes, and it comes back into focus. Bloodshot eyes. Hair swept into a messy bun and not the cute kind. I need sleep. A shower.

Nana pats my knee one more time. "So, we have the whole afternoon to ourselves. What shall we do?"

I can't help but grin and meet her eyes. "*Pride and Prejudice?*" I, of course, mean the movie from 2005. None of the other versions come close to topping it, plus it has a killer sound track.

She pulls back onto the road. "I think I still have some Christmas candy stashed away."

I smile into my tea.

When Saturday dawns gray and overcast, I don't even both-er rolling out of bed. My skull pulsates, a constant accessory to my days now. The light sweeping through my curtains eggs on the throbbing. I groan and pull my pillow over my head.

My muted phone vibrates against my nightstand. I reach for it. Incoming call. Even though I know the number by heart, I let it go to voicemail. A few seconds later, my phone buzzes, notifying me of a new message. I slide my thumb over the screen and hit play.

Elijah's recorded voice crackles through the speaker. *"Hey, sis…I just wanted to see how you're doing. I'm sorry I can't be there. I guess…call me back when you get the chance?"*

I clutch my phone to my chest like it might actually do some good to ease the ache in my core. My phone buzzes again, and a text from Macy lights the phone.

Need 2 talk. Meet @ my house.

I throw my blankets back and pad over to my closet. I pull on jeans, a tank top, and my signature combat boots before hurrying down to the kitchen. Nana stands at attention, overseeing the bacon frying in a pan, and Mom catches a jar of jam before Tommy's elbow can send it crashing to the ground. I do my part by steadying Maria's hand to keep a gallon of milk from drenching our wood floor.

"Mom." I hold the edge of the island, waiting for my mother's attention.

She exchanges a few words in Spanish with Nana, discussing the menu for the week.

"Mom."

She turns my way, bumping into my little brother and his newly completed PB&J. She steadies him with one hand while raising questioning eyebrows at me.

I hold up my phone. "Macy texted. She wants to meet at her house."

Mom pushes a banana into my brother's hand. "Want me to drive you?"

"Nah, I'm good." I turn and head for the door. I stop long enough to throw on a dark sweater before jogging down the porch and onto the sidewalk. Warm sunshine greets me, and a cool breeze pulls at my hair. Once I get moving it won't be too bad. I shoot off a quick text to Macy, letting her know I'm on my way.

After stowing my phone in my pocket, I pop in my earbuds. Above the thrum of my music, a new sound rises. My heart skips a beat, and my pulse doubles in pace. Sirens. Is someone's family about to be shattered? I send up a prayer and hurry onward. Anything to put some distance between me and the sound that rules my nightmares. A dog barks at me from behind an aged fence, but I scurry past undeterred. For now, it's the wailing ambulance that is more threatening.

It takes fifteen minutes to get to Macy's house. The two-story structure lies stuffed behind overgrown bushes.

My lungs constrict. How many times through the years have Luke, Macy, and I made chalk creations on their front step? Or swam in the pool out back? I blink and run the back of my hand against the tip of my nose. The sting is just from the cold. I should have grabbed something heavier than my sweater. Right. If I keep telling myself that, maybe the lump in my throat will shrink.

A rusted white car sits across the street, adding further desolation to the scene.

I stuff my hands in my pockets and cut through the front lawn. The dead grass crunches under my boots, but I stomp through the foliage and step onto the leaf strewn porch. The front door swings open on the first ring of the doorbell, revealing a pale Macy. Her long blonde hair hangs in tangles around her shoulders, and purple bags circle her eyes. My best friend's lower lip trembles, and I pull her into a hug. She leans her head on my shoulder and sucks down several shuddering breaths. All I can do is squeeze her with as much force as she's inflicting on me.

Macy pulls away and dabs at the tear leaking down her cheek. "Come on in."

I step over the threshold and turn to shut the door. The white car's engine sparks to life, but the vehicle remains stationary. The tinted windshield shadows the driver's pro-file, and no amount of craning on my part reveals a face. Weird. I make sure to turn the lock.

The house smells like a failed attempt at baking. A pic-ture of Luke smiles at me from a hall lined with family photographs. An answering twinge tugs at my own lips. His smile has always been like that—contagious.

Macy rubs her hips with shaking hands. "D-do you want anything?" Always the perfect hostess. Just like her mom trained her to be.

"I'm fine." I slip off my shoes and trail my friend to the living room. Four cardboard boxes in various stages of packing sit around the room. Luke's name is scrawled across the front of the one closest to me.

The tv hums in the background, flashing a news story of a teen girl nearly killed in a collision with a drunk driver. They even show a picture of her mangled car. Macy flinches, snatches the remote, and turns the screen to black.

"What's all this?" I toe the closest box.

Macy drops onto the gray sofa with a heavy sigh. "Mom's already going through Luke's stuff." She dabs a hand against the pink tip of her nose.

I lower myself to the cushion beside her. The sunlight streaming through the front window highlights the paleness of her skin. Her sweater is also hanging loose on her petite frame. "I'm so sorry."

The doorbell rings.

Macy swipes at her leaky mascara. "That's probably Beck."

"She's back?"

"Yeah, they got in last night." She stands.

I tug her back down. "I'll get it." I peer out the window. The white car still sits across the street, engine running.

The doorbell rings again.

Beck.

Right.

I pull the door open. Beck brushes past me and hurries straight to Macy. 'Cause I'm not worth greeting. "Nice to see you, too," I mutter under my breath and push the door closed.

I turn to join my friends, and my foot bumps against a pair of Macy's discarded ballet slippers. I nudge the shoes aside and step into the living room. Coco, Macy's gray and white cat, rubs against my calf.

"Hey, girl." I bend to greet the feline. She leans into my touch, curling her striped tail around my wrist.

Beck unwinds her scarf and lays it on the open cushion beside her. Her hand entwines with Macy's, and Beck rests their joined fingers on her tight-clad knee. The two strike up a whispered conversation. With the couch full, I help myself to the shaggy rug and run the fluffy strands through my fingers. My hand bumps against a wicker basket piled high with yarn. An unfinished red sweater rests atop the pile. Something cold slips through my core, and I reach out a trembling hand to stroke the piece. Every year since first grade, Mrs. Johnson has made us each a Christmas sweater. Me, Macy...Luke. She'd already begun the process for next year.

"What's all this?" Beck studies the boxes.

Macy pulls her hand free from Beck's and tugs her sleeve over her fist. "Mom's been cleaning out the house. Going through Luke's things. Getting rid of the stuff she doesn't want to keep."

"What about your dad?" Beck unbuttons her coat.

Macy plays with the ends of her hair. "He's buried himself in work. I'm not sure he's even noticed. So, yeah. That's what I'm dealing with." She bumps a lock of hair behind her ear.

"I'm so sorry," Beck whispers.

Macy bobs her head.

I peer into the box beside me, and my throat constricts. A pair of drumsticks poke from a pile of graphic t-shirts. A yellow note is pasted to the wooden objects. Luke had been so proud of them. Never mind he couldn't keep a beat, no matter how many tutoring sessions I gave. His twirling skills were all he'd wanted the sticks for. He'd toted the prized possessions around all summer until he'd mastered several tricks.

"Everyone deals with grief in their own way," Beck says.

"Yeah, I know." A husky tone colors Macy's voice.

I twist the drumsticks so I can read the note attached to them. My breath catches around the lump swelling in my throat.

For Gwen.

Macy leans forward. "Gwen, Mom wanted you to have those."

I swallow. "Thank you." I pull the gift out of the box with shaky hands. "Have you asked your mom to wait?" Coco flops onto my lap, offering her chin for a gentle stroke.

Macy bobs her head. "Yeah. She wants someone else to use his stuff. Someone who needs them. And I mean, there's not much point in keeping them..." She lifts her brother's Bible from an end table and traces the faded words engraved on the leather. "So, I feel selfish asking her to."

"Maybe you could just keep a few things." Beck lays a hand on her arm. "Maybe a couple t-shirts. I found this lady online who can turn old t-shirts into quilts and stuff. Think your mom would go for something like that?"

Macy rubs her sleeve under her eye. "Maybe."

Beck whips a tissue from her purse and passes it over.

The doorbell rings.

Macy rolls the tissue between her fingers. "Who is it?"

Beck moves to the window. "It's Austin Taylor."

Sweat collects on my palms, and I worry my lip between my teeth. What is he doing here? I run a finger over the studs lining my ear. Is he just a concerned coworker showing up at Macy's house to make sure she's okay, or is there something else?

Macy smooths her hair and draws in a shaky breath. Beck hurries over and starts dabbing at the mascara darkened tears staining Macy's white cheeks.

"Can you get the door, Gwen? Please?" Macy's voice is a raspy whisper.

"Sure," I squeak. My knees tremble, but I force myself to move to the foyer. I run my sweaty palms down my jeans and jerk the door open.

Austin flashes a smile, sunlight catching in his golden-brown, dreamy eyes.

Heat flames anew in my cheeks. "H-hi."

"Is Macy here?" Austin cranes his neck to look past me.

I move my chin in an unfortunate imitation of a bobblehead.

He makes an awkward attempt at a laugh before he holds out a cardboard tray filled with three Styrofoam mugs. "Here, I brought these."

I blink, mesmerized by the dimple in his left cheek.

"Gwen?" Austin leans forward a bit, forehead knotted in a frown.

He knows my name. My heart stops and then surges. Warmth tingles through my fingertips, and my knees shake. "Y-yes?" And here I thought he didn't even know I existed despite having three classes together.

"For Macy." He holds out the tray again.

Get it together. "Right. Thanks. That's very thoughtful."

Our fingertips brush.

I jerk back.

Austin fumbles, but manages to keep hold of his gift.

"S-sorry." I push my hair behind my ear.

His smile doesn't dim. "No problem."

This time I don't drop the drinks when he passes them to me.

He drags his fingers through his hair, a color somewhere between blond and brown. Caramel? "Tell Macy I said hi."

"Right. Yeah. Of course." Shush it, Gwen.

"Oh, and hey, are you all right?"

I squint at him.

His cheeks turn the tiniest hint of pink. "I mean, after class the other day..."

Crap. He saw me in biology. Well, I mean of course he did. The whole class did. I'd bet the entire school knows by now. "Yeah. Fine. I'm fine." I'm doing that bobblehead thing again.

"Good. Well, bye." He raises a hand before he turns away and moves toward his car.

I wave limply at his back and step backward into the open door, and hit my shoulder. Hard. I bite the inside of my cheek to hold in a squeak and watch until he's gone before I head inside. I kick the door shut and lean against it. Stupid. Stupid. Stupid. I tap a fist against my forehead. Seriously, did I have to behave like an idiot?

"Oh my gosh! You like Austin?" Beck squeals, dancing up and down on her toes.

She and Macy stand just inside the living room. The way Macy leans against the wall suggests they've been there the whole time.

Heat singes my cheeks, and I hold a shaky palm to my forehead. "He thinks I'm an idiot."

Beck's glossy lips turn down in a playful pout. "I'm sure that's not true." A peek at her gleaming eyes suggests she's laughing at me.

"It wasn't that bad." Macy takes the tray from my limp hand. "You guys want one?"

We trail Macy to the open concept kitchen, bypassing her dad's office where his desk is drowning in paperwork. Coco trails us and meows at her empty food bowl.

"Aren't they for you and your parents?" Because there's no way Austin would just happen to know we were all here.

"Mom's off caffeine, and Dad won't drink anything reheated." Macy shuffles through the cups, peeking inside. She pulls back. "Sorry, Gwen. Looks like they're all coffee."

I shrug. "No big deal." I move to the pantry and get Coco a scoop of food. The feline purrs her thanks and digs in.

Macy takes one of the cups from the tray anyway and places it on the counter. "Well, you can take it to your mom."

"Thanks, she'll like that." It's been way too long since she's treated herself to a decent cup of coffee.

"So...Austin?" Beck takes a sip of the bitter smelling liquid and cocks one of her perfect eyebrows.

I press my lips together and turn my attention to Coco. "Nothing to tell."

"Oh, please. We're not blind." Beck elbows Macy who snickers.

I lean against the counter and push my lips into a smile. "Beck, where did you get that lip gloss?"

As predicted, she dives into a tale about finding the perfect shade of waxy goo. Who knew shopping for the best lip color could be filled with so many hurdles? Too bad I don't have my drums, or I'd definitely bang a few cymbals to punctuate the ending. As it is, I can't stop myself from tapping out a light beat on the counter.

Beck shoots me a side eye, and I stop, pulling my fingers into a knot in front of me.

We visit for a while more before Beck announces she has to pick up one of her little brothers from a sleepover. I excuse myself shortly after, take the cup for Mom, and head out.

A quick scan of the street reveals the creepy white car decided to move on. I loose an exhale and stuff the drumsticks from Luke into the back pocket of my jeans.

A cool breeze cuts through the neighborhood, and I tug my sweater tighter around myself to ward off the chill. Yeah, the sunshine was a liar today, and I was a fool not to wear my coat.

I turn the corner, and a rusted white car comes creeping around the bend. My stomach clenches. I shoot a look toward the windshield, but the tinted glass hides the driver's face. Crap. Crap. Crap. I increase my pace.

So does the driver.

The car's window rolls down, and a creep with a surprisingly young face leans toward me. "I need your help," he says in a British accent.

Yeah, right. Isn't that the line these guys use on little kids? There's no way I'm going to help him find a "lost puppy." I force one foot in front of the other.

"Gwen, it's about Macy." His dark hair rustles in the breeze, and the flap of his white coat shifts as he cranes his neck my way.

My steps falter. How does he know my name? Heck, how does he know Macy's? He's definitely not from school, and I don't recognize him from the coffee shop where Macy and Austin work. This has gone beyond creepy. My knees shake, but I bolt forward, boots slapping the sidewalk.

The car surges after me, and the driver continues his plea, "Macy's in trouble, I need your help to save her. Get in the car, Gwen."

With my heart ramming in my chest, I continue my sprint. Almost home. Almost home.

"Gwendolyn Isabella Gonzales, get in this car!"

I throw my head back and force my legs to go faster. The edges of my sweater flap in the wind.

The British stalker jolts the car to a halt and throws his door open.

My side aches, and my throat burns. Why is there no one out to help me? Footsteps pound the cement, pushing me onward.

My boot catches on an uneven lift in the sidewalk, and I tilt forward, arms flailing as I stumble sideways to keep my balance. The maniac grabs me from behind. I struggle, fighting to aim my mug of hot coffee in his face, screaming my head off the entire time. He's quicker. He wrenches the cup from my grasp. Hot liquid splashes my wrist. One strong arm locks around my waist, and the other smashes a scented cloth to my mouth and nose. The syrupy-sweet scent infiltrates my senses, slowing my thoughts, surrounding them with a thick fog. My eyelids sag.

No!

I thrash in the kidnapper's grip, kicking, elbowing, clawing. Whatever he's doused the rag in is too strong. My limbs spasm and flail, only to flop to my sides a moment later.

"I hoped it wouldn't come to this. But it's better if you're asleep anyway," the man says as control slips further from my body. And then my knees give out. His grip breaks, and I crash to the ground, the drumsticks tumble from my pocket and roll to the grass. I should have stabbed the things into the creep's eyes. But no matter how much I want to reach for them, I can't seem to make my fingers obey. My eyelids fall shut.

Chapter Three

My eyelids flutter as I fight to break free from the fog clogging my mind. I blink until the bleary world comes into focus. Blue and purple swirl together outside the car window. I blink again. Once. Twice. I shift, and pain flares through my temple. I squeeze my eyes shut until the pounding ebbs. When it does, I dare to take another peek. Yep, the colors are still there. Combine that with the overwhelming scent of coffee, and it's enough to make me nauseous.

A gentle hand taps my upper arm. I jump and swivel. The guy from before drives the vehicle. My heartrate surges into an unhealthy rhythm.

"Pretty, isn't it?" The driver offers me a brief glance.

I run my tongue over my dry lips. No, nothing is pretty about this situation.

"The sky." He gestures out the windshield before raking a hand through his dark hair.

I fumble for my buckle with a heavy hand and bump my other against the car door, searching for the handle. I've got to get out of here. Whatever it takes.

My kidnapper leans back in his chair and slides his hands into a more relaxed grip on the steering wheel. "I wouldn't do that if I were you. You get out, and you could fall forever."

I stop sliding the belt off my chest and cast a look around. The colorful sky traps the car on all sides. My stomach clenches. There has to be a way to get out of here. If not...I swallow and squirm in my chair. A hard lump presses against the back pocket of my jeans. I exhale a shaky breath while the hammering of my heart eases. The idiot forgot to take my phone.

"I'm calling the police." I punch in the emergency number.

He smirks, barely offering a look in my direction. "Go ahead."

"G-go ahead?" He knows they can track my phone, right? Sweat slides over my palm, and my jeweled case nearly slides from my grasp. I lift the phone to my ear. Nothing. My hand shakes, and I try again. Nothing. "Are you blocking the signal?" Is that even possible?

"Relax. It doesn't work here." He flips a long section of hair away from his eyes. He's young. Maybe twenty.

I suck in a series of rapid breaths. Every video I've ever seen on kidnapping suggests kicking out the taillights or fighting back when the creep tries to grab you. I obviously failed at that one, but none of them covered what happens when you've been thrown in the front seat. I need to stay calm. Just stay calm. I run my hand up and down the upholstery covering my chair until my fingers bump over something crusty caught in the aged fabric. I jerk my hand back to my lap.

The guy lifts a dented Styrofoam mug and takes a sip. He grimaces at the cup. "You couldn't have ordered a pour over?"

I stare at him. "You stole my coffee?"

He shrugs like kidnapping and coffee theft are an everyday occurrence. Maybe for him they are. "It's not like you were going to drink it. Besides, there's only a few drops left. *Someone* had to go and spill it."

I focus on the swirling colors outside my window. "Where are we?"

"We're in the Dream." He takes another gulp of coffee droplets.

"The Dream? Is it some kind of nightclub?"

The car dings an alarm, signaling the gas valve is heading toward empty.

"What?" He scrunches his face at me, ignoring the noise coming from his dashboard. "No. Dream. Like what you do at night in your sleep."

Great. I've been kidnapped by a lunatic. Once more, my heartbeat rockets into overdrive. Stay brave. I smooth my damp palms over my thighs. "Yeah, right." I focus out the window once more. "So, what do you want from me?"

"I told you. I need your help to save Macy."

"Save Macy?" I raise my eyebrows and bring my gaze back to his profile. "Save her from what?"

His dark stare meets mine. "From her dreams."

"Her dreams?"

"Are you going to repeat everything?" He shakes his head, banishing his hair from his eyes once more. "Yes, her dreams."

I stare at him for a long moment, looking for signs of a joke or at least some hint he knows what he's saying is off. My heart sinks when his expression doesn't change. "You're serious?"

He looks at me like I dented his car. "Dreams are no joking matter. I'm a Dream Guardian. Why would I joke about it?"

Not good. If nothing else, I need to try and stay on this lunatic's good side. I hold up a hand. "I'm just trying to understand why the heck you kidnapped me." You know, 'cause it's not typical human behavior.

He removes one hand from the steering wheel and rubs his forehead. "I've told you. To save Macy. And kidnapping is a strong word."

I raise an eyebrow.

He stares back.

Fine. "I need details." I shove the toe of my boot against the rumpled mat lining the floor.

"Details?" The psychopath stares at me.

My headache spikes, and I massage my temple. "Fine. We'll start small. What's your name?"

He bounces his knee. "Solomon."

I take a deep breath. I can do this. Maybe if I play along and get him to talk rationally, I can get him to let me go. "Okay, Solomon, what's going on with Macy?"

"Since her brother died, she's become...reckless in her dreams." He drums his thumbs against the steering wheel.

So much for rationality. Forget the fact he even knows about Luke. This is all insane. "So?"

He looks at me like I've suggested he shoot someone. "*So?* So!" The car swerves. Something rattles in the back-seat, and a renewed bout of coffee stench fills the air.

I brace my foot against the dashboard until the criss-crossed pattern of travel ebbs. "Settle down. What's wrong with that?"

"What's wrong with that?" He goes on to mutter to himself, and the car jerks again.

Not good. "Solomon."

He keeps mumbling, one hand flying about in emphatic gestures. "Ignorant...audacity...what does she think...Nightmares..."

I've got to get things under control. I slam against the door as the car swerves again. "Solomon."

"Of all the...I should..."

I snap my fingers. "Solomon."

He stops mid-sentence and glances at me like he forgot I'm here.

"You were saying?" Please say something that makes sense this time.

"Oh, right. She's become reckless in her dreams. If you die in the Dream, you could die in your sleep. The more times you die in your dreams, the greater the chance of you not waking up. A death in the Dream is traumatizing. Your heartrate accelerates. You can't breathe. Eventually, your body can't take it any longer, and your heart stops."

He stares at the steering wheel. "I've never known anyone to survive more than two deaths in the Dream."

I'm trapped in the car with a psycho. I press against my seat and stare at him. He's young…clean. Not someone you'd suspect of being absolutely crazy. What in the world am I supposed to do with this situation? I inhale and try to make my shoulders relax. For now, until I've found some landmark or something to figure out where I am, the only way through this seems to be playing along, so I do my best to choke out a reply, "So, we have to keep Macy from dying?" I scan the space outside my window again, but the swirling colors haven't changed.

The self-proclaimed Dream Guardian flashes a smile. "See? I knew you'd catch on."

Great, I'm glad I've impressed him. I try to keep my tone casual, "For how long? I mean, I can't stay forever." Head-lines of people being discovered months and even years after their disappearance flash through my mind.

"Just until Macy's settled into her new life."

I nod. I can do this. Just play along. "Got it. And my family? Won't they notice I'm gone?" How long will it take the police to track me down? Will I appear on one of those ads years from now with my picture aged up by a computer? That sends my heart racing, and I banish the thought. I. Will. Not. Panic.

"Not to worry, time works differently in the Dream."

Of course, it does. I should have seen that one coming. I hold back a snort. "So, I'll be home for dinner then?"

He pulls at the neckline of his t-shirt like the temperature has suddenly increased by ninety degrees.

I turn in my seat, fighting to catch his eye. "Solomon?"

"I had to take precautions." He shoots a look out his window.

Tension crawls up my spine. "What kind of precautions?" If he's hurt them…

He dares a quick look at me. "Your mum thinks you're taking a holiday with Beck and Macy."

I cross my arms. "Yeah, right. Like my mom bought that. Some guy with a British accent calls and says I'm spending the weekend with my friends? I don't think so."

"No, even better. I pretended to be Macy's mum." And he proceeds to lay on a thick southern accent that has even me picturing Mrs. Johnson.

I stare at him for a long moment before shaking my head. "Wow. Just wow."

"Your mum thinks it will be great for you girls to get away for a bit." Solomon props his elbow against his door. "She knows how you love Macy's grandparents' house."

I scowl. "How do you know about that?"

He goes still for a fraction of a second before he lifts a shoulder in a half-shrug. "Sometimes Macy dreams she's there. The countryside is one of her favorite places." He shifts the car into another gear. "Hold on, things are about to get bumpy." He takes one last sip of my coffee and throws the cup in the back. It smacks against something. Several objects rattle and shift.

I swivel to look in the back and find a few dozen disposable cups scattered around the backseat. Dark stains dot the carpeted floor and bench seats. "Have you heard of these brilliant new inventions? They're called trashcans." Maybe I should cut the sass, but he doesn't seem like he's going to kill me right at this moment, and that's just gross.

The cark jerks and slams downward. I'm flung against my door, sending a sharp pain through my side. That's going to leave a bruise. Maybe he does plan on killing me after all. The car rattles and several parts screech their protest as we take a sharp turn. The vehicle goes up on two wheels, pressing me tighter against my door. My teeth smack together.

"I told you to hold on." Sweat slides down his temple and glistens on his upper lip.

We bounce onto all four wheels once more, and sparks fly beside my window, illuminating the swirling colors still surrounding us. The ribbons of blue and purple tighten and contract, pressing closer to our vehicle with each spiking beat of my heart.

I plant one foot against the dashboard and grab hold of the handle above my door. "What's going on?" My head bobs from side to side. My temple smacks the window, and a pang ripples down my face.

"Just a little turbulence."

"Turbulence? There shouldn't be turbulence in a car!"

He slams on the gas and hurls us toward a black dot opening in the blue and purple atmosphere.

My heartrate flies off the charts. "Solomon?"

He doesn't look up. The hole begins to close. His eyes narrow.

My mouth goes dry. We're not going to make it. "Solomon!"

He jerks the wheel to the left, sending us skidding through the opening.

Everything goes dark with a spark of static.

Tires screech.

I scream.

Chapter Four

"We're alive." I hold a hand to my chest where my heart bashes against my sternum.

The psychopath beside me roars with laughter.

I shoot a glare in Solomon's direction, not that he can see it in this darkness. "Why are you laughing? We almost died."

"Sorry, sorry." He coughs and shifts.

Funny, he doesn't sound sorry.

I brush stray strands of hair out of my face with shaky fingers. There has to be a way to escape, but that would involve knowing where we are. I scan the area, but I can't see a thing in this blackness.

Solomon fumbles for something. Seconds later, a thin flashlight beam stings my eyes. He holds out his free hand, and I recoil, pressing against my door while I squint against the brightness.

"Gwen." He leans forward, dark eyes intense in the beam of the flashlight. "I'm not going to hurt you."

Tremors shake my limbs, and my breath catches somewhere inside of me. Now that we've stopped, what am I supposed to do? I fumble for my phone while maintaining eye contact with my kidnapper. When my hand closes over my case, I try to power it on. Nothing. I'd just charged it this morning. Ice cuts through my veins.

"Are you hurt?" Solomon presses closer, sweeping the flashlight over my hunched form.

I continue to cower while my hands turn clammy. We've stopped, and I have no way of contacting anyone now even if I could get a signal. And now I can't breathe right. I palm a hand against my chest, trying to get my lungs to expand.

Solomon's brow wrinkles, and he scoots toward me.

I scramble backward.

"Gwen?" He frowns.

I have to move. Respond. "Get that out of my face." I shove the flashlight aside, careful not to be overly aggressive. Last thing I need is for him to dump my body here where chances are slim I'll ever be found.

"Good, no apparent injuries. Let's go." He offers his hand.

I smash myself against the doorframe. If only it could swallow me whole. Suddenly, this car is the only safe thing left, because I have the feeling that as long as I'm sitting in this seat, he won't hurt me. "I'm not going anywhere with you." Maybe if I start screaming my head off, someone will hear me. The sinking sensation in my gut suggests it's not likely.

He leans back. "Haven't I proven myself trustworthy?" His brow wrinkles like my response actually baffles him.

Um, not so much. "Which part of kidnapping me and throwing me in your car was supposed to inspire trust?"

He slaps a hand against the dashboard. "You keep using that word."

I flinch away. Yep, totally should have cut the sass and kept my mouth shut.

Solomon sighs, pockets his keys, and flings his door open. The car shakes when he slams the door behind him. For some reason I'm sure makes perfect sense in his messed-up head, he extinguishes the flashlight, leaving me in blackness. Fine. Whatever. He'll go cool off or finish plotting my fate, and I'll sit here in the dark and figure out a plan. Or maybe not sit here. Maybe it's time to move. Plan as I go. I snatch my phone and ease my seatbelt off. I'll have to be quick. I'll only have one chance to run, and I'm betting he knows this area better than me. If I can just find somewhere to hide—

My door jerks open.

I jump.

Solomon turns on the flashlight so I can see the hand he offers me.

I stare at his palm, sweat sticking my shirt to my body.

He squats, angling the light so we can see each other, but it's not directly in my eyes. "Gwen, I promise I'm not going to hurt you."

I swallow and blink away the sudden burning in my eyes.

"For Macy?" His eyebrows slide closer together, and he holds my gaze, something like concern traveling across his face.

I dig my fingernails into my palms. I just need to bide my time. If I play along, I might get the opportunity to snatch the flashlight from him and make a run for it. "Okay."

He extends his hand once more.

I swing my phone at his temple like a bludgeon.

He snatches my wrist, twists the phone from my grasp, and tosses it in the backseat. "I wouldn't try that again."

I swallow. Hard.

He pulls me from the car. Pebbles scatter under my feet, giving way to something solid. Cement? Blacktop? Hard to say with only the weak beam of the flashlight to illuminate the area. A damp aroma clings to the air, and goosebumps flash over my arms.

Either not caring about me trying to get my bearings, or maybe trying to prevent that from happening, Solomon sets out a pace that has me racing to catch up. It's that or stand in the dark, and there's no way I'm doing that. I keep an eye out for any escape routes, but the flashlight only travels so far in the darkness, shrouding any potential exits in shadows.

"First order of business, we need to find Macy." Solomon turns to face me, the flashlight beam angled over my shoulder. "Oh, and I guess I should explain the rules."

You think? I cross my arms, bracing myself for whatever crazy he dreams up. "That would be helpful." Maybe he can also include a time limit for this little game.

"So, there's two rules." Solomon holds up two fingers. "Don't stand out, and whatever you do, don't die."

"That's it?" At least he's not crazy enough to come up with something overly complicated. The last thing I need is for him to kill me over some misunderstanding.

He rubs his chin for a moment before nodding. "Yep, that's it." He scratches at his earlobe. "Oh, I suppose I should mention that the Dream plays on your fears."

I study him from the tip of his shaggy head, down his thin, white...lab coat? All the way down to his polished dress shoes. How deeply does he believe this little charade?

Solomon starts forward once more but shoots a look over his shoulder after a few paces. "So, you know, don't think about things you're afraid of."

"Great, I'll keep that in mind." I scan the dimly lit area. There's lots of rubble, like the place went through an earthquake or something. Still no opportunities to slip away present themselves. My foot catches on a loose chunk of debris, and I plummet forward, arms flailing.

Solomon darts to my side and steadies me. "That's what I'm talking about. Rule number one. Don't stand out."

Yeah, 'cause I totally did that on purpose. I jerk away from his touch and rub at my elbow. "Sorry." I study the white stripe beside my boot. My scrutiny travels forward. More white stripes run across the ground. "Is this some kind of parking garage?"

"We Dream Guardians have to keep our vehicles somewhere." Solomon smirks and resumes walking.

I glance at him out of the corner of my eye. "Seriously?"

He chuckles. "I think you'll find there are a lot of strange things in the Dream."

Odd doesn't even cover what's going on here.

Solomon frowns. "Look, the mission is simple. All we have to do is follow the plan."

I take a deep breath. Pretend compliance. "Which is?"

"Rigorous Evaluation of Macy." He counts the words off on his fingers. "So, it's really quite straight forward." He shoots me a grin before squatting to examine something obscured by darkness.

"Mhmm." There has to be an exit around here somewhere.

"Repeat it back to me." Solomon snaps his fingers.

I start. "Huh?"

He angles the flashlight beam toward my face, though he's careful not to shine it directly in my eyes. "The mission."

"Relentless Evaluation of Macy?" I flounder.

He sighs and stands. "You have to pay attention. Rigorous Evaluation of Macy."

"Rigorous..." I duck under a pipe dangling too close to the ground.

"We'll shorten it to R.E.M. You can remember that at least, can't you?" His frown suggests he thinks otherwise.

"Of course." Last thing I need is to antagonize him, especially since I haven't exactly had a great track record so far. R.E.M. R.E.M...

"Good." My kidnapper turns his back and kicks a stone away, sending it rattling into the distance.

I have to get out of here. Soon. I quicken my pace.

"Wait, Gwen. There's a—"

My feet fly out from under me, and I skid down a dark slope into utter darkness. Chunks of gravel dig into my back, tearing up my clothes and skin. I cry out. My scream echoes around me, reverberating against the walls.

I crash against a flat surface and roll forward until I tumble to a stop. Debris digs into my ribs, and my palms sting. I groan and take a moment to assess my body. Nothing seems to be broken, though if the burning across my skin is any indication, I've probably got some nasty cuts. With a deep breath, I push myself to a sitting position and rub the forming knot beneath my messy bun. Pain spasms through my skull, and I quickly lower my hand.

"Look out below!" Solomon hollers.

I scramble to get out of the way, but his body slams into my side, sending me tumbling forward. I roll to a stop and ease into a sitting position halfway between lying and sitting.

"Watch it." I rub a freshly bruised elbow.

He flops his hair out of his eyes with one hand and holds up the flashlight with the other. "Terribly sorry. Didn't you hear my warning?"

An eyebrow quirks up before I can fight the reflex. "You might want to work on your timing."

He digs into the pocket of his lab coat and holds out a chocolate bar.

I eye the offering. "What's that for?" There's no way I'm letting him drug me again.

"I read somewhere that when a woman is angry, you should give her chocolate." He watches me with a chagrined expression.

"Are you serious?" The packaging doesn't appear to be tampered with, but I still eye him warily.

He draws his hand back like I'm a snarling dog ready to attack any second. "You don't want it?" A hint of hurt catches in his voice.

"Oh, no. I want it." I snatch the chocolate from his hand and make quick work of unwrapping the offering. A quick examination suggests the bar doesn't hide any needles or razors, and it smells like regular chocolate, so I shove the thing into my mouth. When the smooth, bittersweet flavor glides over my taste buds, I can't hold back the happy moan. It's nice to know the chocolate is a constant accessory to life even when everything else goes haywire.

"Better?" Solomon adjusts the lapels of his coat and eyes my face.

"Getting there." Now if I can figure out how to ditch this guy, life will be fabulous.

He stands and offers me a hand.

My chest tightens, but I accept. My fingers tremble against his palm. Hopefully, he doesn't notice. With my feet anchored, I pull away and dust some grime from the back of my jeans. "Where to now?"

"Now we find Macy." He tugs me forward, shining his flashlight as a guide.

"And how will we know where she is?" I crane my neck to look behind me. The wall rises high, so steep I couldn't climb back up if I tried. Which means I have to follow the crazy guy farther into the darkness. A shiver tickles my spine.

"*We* won't find her. *I* will." Solomon ducks under a low hanging cement beam. "I can sense when she's in the Dream."

"Well then, get to it." I make a little shooing motion with my hands. But really, how much longer am I going to have to play along? Too long, and I'm going to snap, I just know it.

He smirks and sets out at a jog, taking the light with him.

Follow or stagger around in the dark? Suppressing a groan, I take off after him. I do my best to pick a path through the hazardous parking garage. Not an easy task considering Solomon and his light are pulling farther and farther ahead, leaving my ankles vulnerable while I struggle to avoid chunks of cement and keep from twisting something. My boot rams into a pile of broken cement shards, sending painful reverberations through my big toe. Sucking back a cry, I scuttle around the thing and, despite the throbbing in my foot, trot to catch up to Solomon. He slows when I reach his side and turns his flashlight to the wall, peering into the thin beam. I crane my neck to see past him. The dusty light beam just illuminates a circular opening smashed through the wall. Whatever made that dent in the cement must have been pretty hefty. This place seriously should have been torn down a long time ago. Or maybe it's in the process of being torn down, and this "Dream Guardian" plans to leave me here to rot. In about six months to a year, they'll pull my body out of the rubble somewhere. The thought sends goosebumps poking across my skin, so I force it away.

Solomon glances over his shoulder. "Remember. Don't stand out and don't die."

"Yeah, I know. You already told me that." Which maybe means he isn't planning how to hide my remains. I cross my arms against the draft breezing through the opening. The structure groans ominously. Despite my best efforts at bravery, I shiver and move closer to my kidnapper. Maybe his body will shield me if this place crumbles in on us.

"Yes, but now you're going to put it into practice." He grabs my hand and pulls me through the circular shoot in the wall.

My feet fly out from under me, and my stomach flops as we descend. A blast of cool air slams my face and rocks bump my backside, jarring me with every passing millisecond. Solomon extinguishes the light, leaving us in darkness. A scream claws at the back of my throat, but he holds a hand over my mouth, stifling the cry. I keep my fingers knotted in the too big sleeve of his lab coat until we hit the ground. Pain scales my tailbone.

A coolness rules the air down here, and the growl of some kind of monster echoes through the cavern. The hair raises on my arms. The growl sounds again, reverberating through my eardrums. Something straight out of a horror movie. Ahead of us, a jagged opening in the wall showcases a flickering light in the distance. The light jumps and stutters as if cast by flames. The hairy outline of several beasts loom across the dusty ground, their shadows nearly stretching to my boots. Sweat slips down the back of my neck, and I can't help but curl in on myself, not even caring that I'm still sitting in my kidnapper's lap.

"What is that?" Nothing can hide the wobble in my voice.

"We have to go. Macy's in danger." Solomon dumps me on the ground and steps around me.

I dig my fingernails into the dust, every limb trembling.

"Gwen, come on." Solomon emphasizes his words with a sharp hand gesture.

I scramble to my feet and hurry after him if for no other reason than to not risk being left alone with those things to hunt me down. "There's something in there." I wave a hand at the crumbling opening where the unknown beasts reside.

"Yes, very observant of you." He shakes out his arms and bounces on his toes. And...is he doing that thing singers do with their lips when they're warming up?

I lean closer. "It's alive."

"Once again, something I'm already aware of." He casts me a cool look before tugging on his lapels and facing forward once more.

What do I do now? I can't climb that steep slope, and he's got the flashlight. If they kill him, they'll just come for me next, and there's no way I'll out run them while grappling around in the dark. I swallow hard and allow him to lead me inside the cavern. My pulse pounds in my temples. This is a terrible idea. My knees lock when we step through the opening.

A pack of large wolves circle a mound of crumbled roof on which a frazzled Macy seeks refuge. She scrambles backward, getting dangerously close to the edge of the rubble. My stomach sinks. Macy's here too? I dart a look Solomon's way. Did he also kidnap her? Or...has he been telling the truth this whole time? A shaky breath passes through my lips. That can't be possible...

Solomon extends an arm to hold me back. When did I start moving forward?

"You distract them; I'm going to get Macy."

"No, Solomon, I can't..." He's not listening. He's too busy searching his pockets for something. Several candy wrappers tumble to the ground. I make a grab for him, snagging his coat. Keeping him here.

Solomon's gaze finds mine. "Everything's going to be all right. Just buy me some time, and whatever you do, don't die." He pulls my fingers free from his sleeve.

I lick my dry lips. "Don't die. Got it." Macy. I have to do this for her.

"All right. Go." He charges, leaving me to scramble for some kind of plan.

I search the floor for anything remotely resembling a weapon. I find a chunk of cement and a dented iron bar. Blowing some hair out of my face, I take a few seconds to gather my courage before sliding half a step forward.

A wolf launches at Macy. She screeches as the beast's fangs lodge around her boot, and she goes down hard. The rest of the wolves descend on their fallen prey with growls and barks.

No. A sick sensation slashes through my chest. Macy! I can't lose her, too.

"Gwen, help!" Solomon dives into the pack and begins to fight his way to my friend's writhing body.

I launch the cement as hard as I can. It slams against the wolf's head, and with a whine, the animal falls into a hairy heap. Solomon continues pushing his way toward Macy, fighting off the other wolves. Blood stains his sleeve.

I charge forward, swinging my bar like a club. A second wolf collapses under my blow. More of the wolves have changed their attention from my best friend and the man pushing his way to her, and instead focus their beady eyes on me, I hoof it backward until I stumble against a second mound of rubble. I clamber on top, sending loose pebbles tumbling toward the wolves.

"Back off." I wave my bar at them.

The leader of the pack snaps at me, saliva dripping from his jowls. The others pace a circle behind him.

I inch backward, but I'm quickly running out of room. "Solomon?" My voice is an airy whisper.

A grunt and then a cry from one of the other wolves echoes through the room. I don't dare remove my gaze from the salivating wolf before me. My fearful face reflects in the creature's midnight pupils.

My pulse hammers, a thunderstorm within my veins.

Is it just me, or is the pack multiplying? Where there were once four or five wolves, there are now dozens circling beneath my refuge. Sweat slickens my palms, and my breathing accelerates.

The wolf in front of me swells in size, its body rumbling with toned muscles.

My mouth goes dry.

He snarls.

Leaps.

I whip up an arm to shield my throat from the monster's fangs. Fire burns through my arm as the wolf crunches down. I slam into the stone floor. My breath tumbles from my lungs as a hundred-something-pound wolf lands on my chest, crushing me with each passing second. My mouth opens and closes in breathless motions. A numbing buzz ripples through my body, paralyzing my senses.

I have to…do…something…

Fight.

I suck in a breath and scream out, "Solomon!" I'm wheezing now, lungs constricted beneath the weight pressing against my chest.

No help comes.

I thrash, flailing, kicking, slashing out with my nails. Anything to free my body from this oppressive weight. My fingernails catch the wolf in the face, raking across one eye and part of his nose. He stumbles and releases my arm. Our eyes meet. Hot breath beats against my face, warming my skin. I pant, waiting for razor sharp teeth to wrap around my throat.

The wolf snarls, breaking the spell. My throat runs dry. I have to move. Now. I fumble around the floor until my hand brushes the iron bar. My fingers close around the metal, and I swing with all my strength.

The iron connects against the side of the wolf's head with a crack, just as his teeth snap toward my exposed neck. With a yelp, the wolf crumples, joining the rest of his pack in a hairy heap on the ground.

"I've got her. I've got Macy," Solomon calls from somewhere in the room.

"Great," I pant.

Footsteps crunch toward me.

I labor to draw in a full breath while my heart drums in my chest. Maybe it wouldn't be a bad thing to just keep lying here. Here's good. Decently safe now that the pack's been dealt with. Yeah, maybe I'll lie here until the corpses start stinking.

Solomon bends over me and offers a hand. "Come on."

Ugh, fine. I allow him to pull me up on shaking legs. My eyes drift closed, and I fight to regulate my breathing.

"Gwen? Are you okay?" Macy touches my shoulder.

She's here. She's safe. I launch into my best friend's arms.

Macy staggers backward. "Gwen?"

"You're here. You're okay." She smells like dirt and sweat, but she's with me.

Macy pushes me back a step. "Gwen, what's wrong?" Her scrutiny sweeps my face, her eyebrows dipping lower by the second.

Solomon grabs my upper arm, and pulls me away from her. "What are you doing? Act natural," he hisses from the corner of his mouth.

I try to shake him off. "Enough already."

He tightens his hold. "Don't stand out, remember?"

Right. His rule number one. A shiver runs through me. An attack from a bunch of wolves has changed nothing. I'm still trapped in a game I don't understand. But it doesn't matter. I'm with Macy now. She'll help me figure out an escape. "I'm fine," I tell her. For the most part that is. I rub a hand over my tender head, and a lump meets my search, the leftover sign of my collision with the ground.

Macy reaches out a trembling hand. "Gwen, your arm."

I follow her gaze. Dark holes line my skin, and blood drains down my forearm. My stomach flips, and my breath quickens until static hammers in my ears.

Muttering to himself, Solomon shoves me into a sitting position, grabs the back of my neck, and pushes my head between my knees. Macy takes a gentler approach and rubs my back.

"Cover it," I say between attempts to hold back the bile clawing up my throat.

"With what?" Solomon searches his pockets, but only another round of crackling candy wrappers scatter to the ground.

I squeeze my eyes shut and force a quick inhale into my lungs. "I d-don't know. J-just use something."

"I'm not going to rip my shirt up if that's what you want." My kidnapper slaps frantic hands down the sides of his lab coat.

Macy gives him the "look." The one that always works when she helps me babysit the twins for Mom. Whatever they're doing, the pair always fall into line when Macy pulls out that particular trick.

Solomon blinks at her, but after a second, he tears a strip from the bottom of his black t-shirt. He proceeds to wrap the fabric around my arm with rough jerks. That's better. It still hurts like heck, but at least I can't see it anymore.

"Let's go." Solomon grabs my upper arm and pulls me to my feet. My head spins, and my knees sag beneath my weight. Solomon hefts me higher, and Macy takes my other arm in her tender grasp.

I can do this. I won't be sick.

Solomon leads the way out of the dark cave and into a dim, earthen passageway. Mr. Who-So-Should-Not-Be-A-Nurse turns on his flashlight, illuminating the new space. Roots poke out at odd angles, and dusty light shimmers through the air, brightening the space gradually. Weird.

Steadier on my feet now, I pull away from my companions and hobble along on my own. I have to duck repeatedly to avoid hitting my head on one of the knobby protrusions poking from the ceiling. Small chunks of dirt rain down from above. The small lumps pelt my hair and crumble over my shoulders. A shower will feel amazing after this.

Beside me, Macy jerks.

"Macy?" I give her a shake and scan her for any previously unnoticed injuries. Her hair hangs in matted tangles, but besides a few streaks of dirt and small scratches she seems normal. Her knees give out, and my grip on her arms is the only thing keeping her upright. "Solomon?"

Solomon's gaze darts between us. He eases forward, focus never leaving Macy. "Let her go, Gwendolyn."

"What?" Is he completely insane? "She'll fall."

Solomon's fingertips brush my shoulders. "Let her go."

Macy seizes. Her skin shimmers and fades, slowly turning translucent. I cry out, releasing my hold only to dive for her seconds later as she crashes toward the earth. Solomon catches me around the waist, halting my efforts. I kick against him and pound his arms with my fists, but he doesn't let go. Macy hits the ground, and her body slowly slips away, vanishing into the dirt floor.

I freeze. What? How? "Macy!" I lunge forward.

Solomon's strong arms hold me back. "Easy. It's all right."

I thrash, but his grip remains steady.

Solomon spins me around and clasps my face. "Gwen. It's all right. Macy just woke up. She's fine."

I search his dark eyes.

He gives a slow nod, hands lowering to my biceps. "She's fine."

She woke up? I brush my hair out of my eyes with a shaky hand. "This is real?" How can this be real? I clutch my stomach. Solomon must have laced that chocolate bar with something. This is a hallucination. Has to be. I drive my fist into my gut, trying to make myself vomit.

Solomon grabs my wrist, stopping me. "Are you all right?"

"No!" I try to pull away, but he tightens his grip.

"Talk to me, Gwen. What's going on?" His voice is far too soothing.

"Let me go, let me go!" I kick at his shins.

He springs away, hands raised. "Hey, now."

I stumble to the spot where Macy dissolved into the earth. The indention from her fall is still there. I drop to my knees and run my hands over the spot. I can feel it. If

I can feel it, then it can't be a hallucination, right? Which means… "It's real." How? How is this possible? I scramble to my feet and palm my chest, but the action does nothing to steady the quivering beat of my heart. This can't be possible. There's no way I can be stuck in Macy's dreams.

"What's wrong?" Solomon steps into my path and clears my tumbling hair from my eyes.

"Don't touch me!" I wrench away. "This is insane." With shaky steps, I back away from him.

"Gwen?" The frown on his face only grows, highlighting the brush of freckles speckling his nose.

"This place, Macy's dreams. You. Insane. All of it." I jerk my hand around, indicating each item listed, as if the harsh movements might actually help explain the emotions threatening to strangle me. By now, a hot sheen of liquid blurs my vision.

"Gwen." Solomon gently grasps my shoulders.

"I can't do this." I fight to suck in a full breath. "It can't be real."

"Gwen." Solomon leans down so he is at my eyelevel. "Everything's going to be all right."

I shake my head. "It's not possible."

He angles his body so his gaze stays locked on mine. "We just have to keep moving."

"I want to go home." I knot my trembling fingers in the lapels of his coat. Because, like it or not, right now he's the only thing I'm absolutely certain is real.

He's wearing his stupid lost puppy expression again.

My chin trembles, and I shake him a bit. "Take me home." And drat, that hot sheen spills over, and a tear slides down my cheek.

"I can't..."

I pull away and dig my hands into my hair. Pressure rises in my chest, urging me to scream, but I'm not brave enough to respond to the temptation. Instead, I whirl away from the boy who calls himself Macy's Dream Guardian and march down the dark passageway. Away from Solomon and his flashlight. Away from the crazy words spewing from his lips. If I'm stuck in Macy's dreams, how am I supposed to get myself out? Drums. I need my drums. I settle for drumming my palms against my thighs. I need my cymbals to truly capture the storm of thoughts clanging inside my head, but this will do for now. I drum until the raging thoughts settle, and one pops out amongst the rest, and I drift to a stop. How can I be stuck in a world that shouldn't exist?

Chapter Five

A damp aroma fills my nostrils with a scent akin to the one that appears after a heavy rain. Solomon's shoes crunch behind me while his flashlight illuminates the tunnel a few feet at a time.

"We should take care of your arm," Solomon mumbles.

Avoiding eye contact, I sweep a hand forward. "Lead the way." The words crack as they slip from my dry lips.

He shoots me a questioning look before easing to my side. Our steps fall into sync. I clench my jaw tight and knot my fingers into the sleeves of my sweater. My only option is to trust him to get us out of here. Without him, I have no chance of getting home.

Solomon leads me out of the creepy tunnel, and I find myself standing in front of a red door. Solomon fishes inside his pocket for a moment before he comes up with a set of keys. He inserts them into the lock and ushers me inside. I'm standing in a modern apartment. Black and white with hints of red gleam at me. I spin and find in the brief second before Solomon shuts the door, that all signs of the tunnel are gone. Only further proof Solomon's words are true. How can any of this be possible?

The Dream Guardian moves to the sparkling counter and flips on an espresso machine. The sleek appliance whirrs to life, greeting us with a soft hum. Solomon steps over to a white shelf, removes a large mug bearing a red shield logo with an intersecting 'D' and 'G', and sets it next to the machine. I tug my sleeve and linger near the door.

Solomon crosses to a drawer and withdraws a roll of bandages and rubbing alcohol. He gestures to one of the barstools lining his kitchen island. "Sit."

I perch on the edge of the stool and scan the rest of the apartment. A dark sofa sits in front of one of those electronic fireplaces, and a bonsai decorates a sleek coffee table. A red musical note hangs from the wall. Is he a fan of music, or is this one of those impersonal decorations added to bring a hint of color to the room?

"What is this place?" I ask.

"Home. Or at least the closest thing I have to one." He clears his throat. "What do you think?"

I lift a shoulder. "Not bad." Modern isn't my style, but he pulls it off tastefully.

He snags a remote from the counter and turns on a speaker. Soft classical music fills the apartment. Bach or maybe Beethoven. Classical has never really been my thing, so I don't know for sure.

Solomon moves to my side and peels the ragged strip of t-shirt from my arm. Red dots mar my skin, but at least the bleeding has stopped. Even still, my stomach churns. Yeah, there's no way I'll be following my mom's footsteps as a nurse. Time to distract myself.

I study Solomon as he bends over my arm and cleans the injury. The alcohol stings, but I clench my teeth and focus on the Dream Guardian. His hair is short on the back and sides, but the top hangs long over his eyes, reaching down to brush the thin freckles lining the bridge of his nose. A hint of wave teases his dark strands

"There, all done." Solomon gently secures the bandage on my arm. "The wound won't last long. It'll reset when a dream ends or begins. It takes a while the first time, but the longer you spend in the Dream, the quicker your wounds will heal."

Reset. Right, because this is real somehow.

I look away from him before I can be caught staring. My cheeks burn anyway. "Then why bother cleaning it?"

"We don't want any problems in the meantime." He shoves the bandages and cleaning supplies back into their drawer. "Last thing we need to deal with is an infection."

I study his wrapping job. Maybe he wouldn't totally suck as a nurse after all. "Thank you."

"It's the least I can do." He moves to his shiny espresso machine. "Coffee?"

"No, thanks." A reflexive grimace wrinkles my nose.

Solomon wags a finger. "Don't give me that look. I guarantee you've never tasted coffee like mine."

"And I can promise that it won't matter." I fold my hands in my lap.

His eyes sparkle as he accepts the challenge and busies himself with his precious machine, his one-size-too-big lab coat swishing around him.

"Solomon, how does this work?" I trace a finger along the counter.

He half turns and indicates a glowing orange button. "You see, this button here—"

"Not the machine. With the…" I force myself to choke out the word, "…Dream."

He sighs and stops fussing with the coffee maker. "Macy needs help. I'm her Guardian. You're her best friend."

"That doesn't answer anything." I lean forward. "How and when do I get to go home?"

The Dream Guardian snatches up a towel and swipes along the inside of a white mug. "When everything with Macy is resolved."

"And that will be?"

He doesn't look at me. "However long it takes."

"But how do I get home?"

He sighs. Lowers the coffee mug. "All I can say is I'll get you back." He holds my stare. "I promise."

Well, he's certainly being helpful. I huff. "You can't tell me how?"

He fiddles with his cup again. "It's complicated."

I dig my fingers into my hair. "Fine." We'll come back to the question later. Now for something easier. "What's with the lab coat?"

Solomon shoots me a smirk. "Like it? Very fashion forward, don't you think?"

Um… "That's not exactly the first thing that came to mind." Weird would be more accurate.

He smiles like I've paid him a compliment.

I blink at him and reach to rotate one of the studs near the top of my ear. "Doesn't it have any practical use? You know, for the Dream?"

He flaps the edges. "It's got deep pockets."

My mouth inches open, and I clamp my lips shut. Something has got to be off in that guy's brain.

Soon, the sound of Solomon creating an espresso fills the room even as the smell drifts to my nose. Sweet and bitter war with each other and somehow blend into a scent that is familiar. An ache forms in my chest while Solomon performs his latte art. For a moment, it isn't Solomon standing over the cup. Instead, the fuzzy outline of a caramel-haired figure fills my vision.

"Gwen?"

I blink away the half memory and find Solomon standing across from me, holding out his finished masterpiece. A frothy heart rests atop the dark liquid. My stomach twists. The foam image reeks of familiarity. A memory far beyond my reach. Hello, bizarre déjà vu.

Solomon crosses his arms and raises a brow. "Well?"

I shake the odd feeling away and bring the cup to my lips, almost inhaling a nose full of foamy milk. I cough and take a sip. No matter how I fight the twitch of my lips, I can't hold back the grimace. To rid myself of the bitter taste, I run my tongue over my teeth a few times.

The Dream Guardian deflates. "Seriously?"

I push the mug away and lick the foam off my lips. "I'm sorry. I'm just not a coffee girl." Not anymore.

He mutters something unintelligible under his breath and scoops the cup up, taking a sip of his own. A frown pulls his thick eyebrows down. "That's a perfectly good espresso."

I hold up my hands. "It is. I just don't like coffee."

He shakes his head and rests the mug on the counter. "We'll get back to the coffee debacle later. For now, we need to focus on you." He jabs a finger in my direction.

I lean away from him, and my barstool creaks beneath my shifting weight. "Me?"

"You need to control your fear during the dreams." Solomon takes one last gulp of coffee before turning to the sink and washing out his cup. "Fear only makes the Nightmares stronger."

The way the wolf swelled with muscle flickers through my mind, and I shudder. "How? It all seems so real."

He spins toward me. "This is real. Gwen, this is life and death."

I gulp and hold his gaze. "You said the Dream resets. How can the Nightmares actually harm me?"

"If you're lucky enough to escape with your life, you have to wait for the Dream to reset before your wounds vanish. That could be hours. Possibly days if, for some reason, the Dreamer doesn't wake up. During all of that time, the wounds are very real. You could bleed out. Lose a limb." He dries the cup with rough swipes of his towel.

The throbbing in my arm only serves to lend truth to his words. I trace a light finger over the bandage. This is real. I could die. Goosebumps spear my skin.

Solomon returns the cup to its spot on the shelf. "For the fear, concentrate on your breathing and making rational decisions. The moment you panic, the Nightmares feed and then it becomes harder to regain control."

I lick my lips. Even talking about it sends a tremor dancing down my spine. Get it together. I dig my fingernails into my palm. The last thing I need is for a monster to surge into the apartment.

"Do you understand?" The Dream Guardian braces his palms on the counter and raises an eyebrow.

"I think so." I squeeze my hands in my lap and think of Mom and Nana. Dad. Anything to keep disturbing thoughts from entering my head.

"Good." Solomon pushes away from the counter. "Wait here while I go change my shirt. It's time to go."

I dip my chin in acknowledgement and study the specks of white in the black countertop. I should be coming up with a plan, but my mind goes blank. Survive, I guess. Solomon no longer seems dangerous. Instead, he's probably my greatest asset right now. So then, I just need to help him help Macy. I swallow against the dryness clogging my throat.

After a couple minutes, Solomon reappears wearing a fresh t-shirt under his silly lab coat.

I swipe at the dirt covering my own clothes, a sudden heat warming my cheeks.

Solomon clears his throat. "It'll reset."

My head snaps up. "Then why did you change?"

"What? You expect me to wear a half-shredded t-shirt?"

"But you just said—"

He waves away my words. "True, I could wait, but I'd rather be fully clothed in the meantime. I'd extend you the same privilege, but I obviously..." his cheeks stain pink, and he waves a hand in my general direction. He clears his throat. "I don't have anything that would fit."

"Yeah, I get it." I rub my fingers against my temple where a headache is beginning to form, spurred on by information overload. My fingers come back streaked with dirt. Great.

"Um...you can at least...wash your face. If you want?" Solomon tucks his hands in his pockets and shifts from one foot to the other.

"Yeah, sure. Thanks." I slide off the stool.

He jerks his thumb at the hallway behind him. "The loo's back there."

I pass a room that must be Solomon's bedroom given the large black bed taking up most of the space, and then I come to a bathroom. I shut myself inside and turn the lock. For a moment, I press my back against the door and force myself to breathe. In and out. Until I feel like I can face this world again. I move to the sink and clench my trembling hands against the rim. With a deep breath, I turn on the water and splash the cool liquid against my face. Droplets run down my chin. I force another exhale from my lips and find my eyes in the mirror. Find Macy. Get home. I can do this.

I push out another breath and return to the kitchen.

"You ready?" The Dream Guardian practically bounces.

I can't conjure the enthusiasm to match his, so I lift a shoulder in a half-shrug. "Ready for what?"

"It's been a long day, I thought you could use some fun."

Fun? I can't stop my eyebrows from creeping up.

He narrows his eyes and makes a tsking noise. "You have such little faith."

"Listen, none of this has exactly been my idea of fun."

"You'll like this, I promise." He snags my hand and tugs me out the door.

The dark tunnel is long gone, replaced with a hallway that could belong in any apartment complex.

Solomon leads me to an elevator and jabs a button with the image of a beaker or maybe a cup stamped on its surface. I lean against the wall and grip the bar running across it. Solomon plants himself opposite me and grins as the elevator sweeps from one level to the next until the doors open with a gentle beep.

"This way." Solomon places a hand on my back and guides me into a dark hallway. Blue lights pulse on the ceiling and somewhere music roars with a steady emphasis on the bass.

"I'm not going clubbing with you." I dig in my feet.

He shoots me a look. "Relax, will you? I swear, this is nothing your mother wouldn't approve of."

That remains to be seen, but I'm not exactly eager to run around this unknown world on my own, so I tuck myself close to Solomon's side and let him lead the way. Elevators line every available space on the walls, and the farther we walk, the louder the music becomes.

I glance Solomon's way, and he grins before heading for a pair of wide doors at the end of the hall. He pushes them open, and we spill into what could be any bar or restaurant in my world.

Young people crowd every available table, booth, and stool at the counter.

A couple guitar players with blue-green hair, a drummer, and a guy on the keyboard play on a circular stage positioned in one corner of the room under flashing blue and purple lights.

"Hey, Solomon!" A guy in a green jacket, the kind with about a hundred pockets, raises a glass our way, and a blonde beside him rotates on her stool to grin her welcome.

Solomon waves and nudges me toward them.

I shove my hands in the back pockets of my jeans. "Um…I think maybe I'll just go back to your apartment." For some reason the thought of meeting these people who know Solomon makes this whole thing too real.

"I can't hear you," Solomon leans close to say and taps his ear. Which is such a lie because he winks before placing a hand on my back and forcing me toward the pair.

"Hey, who's your friend?" The guy in the jacket grins at me before performing one of those man handshakes with Solomon.

"Hunter, meet Gwen. Gwen, Hunter." Solomon pulls out a stool and motions for me to sit.

I ease onto the seat.

Hunter flashes me a grin, but when our eyes meet, his expression freezes. "You're—"

The blonde leans around him, her eyes wide. "Human."

"And this is Josie." Solomon takes a seat on my left.

"Solomon, mate..." Hunter gestures at me wordlessly before blowing out a breath and shoving a hand through his hair.

"Is this even allowed?" Josie drops her voice to a whisper and leans even farther over Hunter, tightening our circle.

"Well, yeah it's allowed, but you have to have special permission and high-level clearance..." Hunter trails off and fixes Solomon with a stare. "You do have permission, don't you?"

I shrink in on myself, but if Solomon's worried about the rules he doesn't show it, instead he laughs and reaches for a menu. "You know me better than that."

"And that's why—"

"Ah, enough work talk, make Gwen feel included." Solomon jerks his chin at me, and then both Hunter and Josie are staring again.

I squirm and pull my sleeve over my fist. "So...are you both—"

"Dream Guardians? Yeah." Hunter grabs a fry from his plate and then seems to forget to take a bite as he stares at me. "Sol—"

Josie slaps his arm. "No work talk, remember?"

Hunter clamps his mouth shut.

"What's the human world like?" Josie asks.

"Um...I don't know it's..." I tug on my sleeve, searching for a description. There's a reason I've never been able to write any songs of my own.

Solomon snaps the menu closed. "Come on, Josie, we've all been briefed."

"Well, briefed sure, but that's not the same as actually being in their world." She swirls her straw through her blue beverage only to send the liquid sloshing a second later. "Wait, Solomon, you must've…I mean Gwen had to get here somehow."

"If you're asking if I've been there, then yes. No, it's not as dull as the training made it seem, but they do have terrible taste in coffee, or maybe that's just Gwen." He slides a look my way.

"It was for my mom, and I didn't even order it."

"Why—"

Josie snaps her fingers. "Chill with the coffee chat, I've listened to enough of Solomon's sermons already."

"Yeah, tell us about you." Hunter nudges me with his elbow. "What does he need you for? Got any cool super powers or something we should know about?"

Josie hits his arm. "Don't be dumb." She rolls her eyes at me. "Don't mind him. His Dreamer's been on a superhero kick for months now."

"What's wrong with that?" Hunter demands.

"Nothing, it's just starting to rub off on you."

"His Dreamer…" I shift my gaze between the two of them. They look as real as I do. Like they could be anybody in my world, maybe even students at my school. No, actually a bit older. College students around Elijah's age, maybe.

"Sorry, this must all be so overwhelming for you," Josie says.

"Do you want a Blue Diamond?" Solomon nods to Josie's drink.

"Oh." I tug my sleeve over my knuckles. "I don't drink."

Josie snorts. "We don't either. It interferes with work."

Solomon bumps his shoulder against mine and leans in close. "See? Nothing your mum wouldn't approve of."

"Aw, leave her alone," Hunter says. "She's—"

"Solomon Custos!" A deep voice cuts through the entire room and everything falls silent.

Hunter, Josie, and Solomon all jump to attention, and a quick scan of the room shows every occupant has done the same. I follow their gazes and find a big man standing at a set of doors that have opened in the wall. He could be a Navy Seal with his buff figure and military style haircut.

The guy's eyes scan the room until he finds Solomon beside me. "Custos. In my office. Now." He swivels on his heel and storms back through the doorway.

"Busted." Josie stirs her drink.

"Are you in trouble?" I ask, making a point to sit on my hands to squash the sudden urge to grab hold of his lab coat and not let go. If this doesn't go well, if they don't let him come back, what am I going to do?

"Everything's going to be fine." He slides off the barstool. "That's just ol' Watcher. And this is one of his good moods." He winks, but I don't miss the look he shoots Hunter.

Hunter drapes an arm over my shoulders. "No worries, mate, we'll look out for her. This'll be just like Josie at six months."

At this, Solomon laughs and follows the path of his superior. The drummer on stage clangs his cymbal in a comedic beat. Solomon waves and steps through the door which closes up behind him, blending with the wall once more.

I bite my lip. There are no handles on this side. I couldn't follow even if I coughed up the courage to do so.

"Hey, he'll be fine." Hunter removes his arm from my shoulders and flags down the bartender. "We'll have another Blue Diamond over here."

The bartender shoots him a look as he swipes a rag through a glass. "You've maxed out your points for the month."

"Put it on Solomon's tab."

He gives a long sigh like they've had this conversation many times before and his voice drops to a monotone, "I can't do that, Mr. Peznic, without Mr. Custos here to give his permission."

"Come on now, Rick—"

The older man quirks an eyebrow. "Mr. Peznic—"

"Oh, just put it on my card." Josie swipes a blue card from her pocket and passes it over.

"Thank you, Ms. Warden." The bartender accepts the card, scans it, and then returns it to her.

"Thanks," I say.

Josie grins. "No problem."

"He likes you better." Hunter slumps in his chair.

"Yeah, because I pay up when it's due."

Hunter snorts and mutters something under his breath about favoritism.

Josie rolls her eyes.

I accept my drink and take a sip. It's sweet and tangy with a small hint of fruit and…mint? "Mmm."

"Good, right?" Josie asks.

I perform a bobblehead nod while sucking down another slurp. When I come up for air, I ask, "So, what happened at six months?"

They both stiffen.

I squirm, making my stool creak. "I mean, he said things with Solomon would be like—"

Josie slaps a hand on the counter. "We don't talk about six months."

I flinch. "Oh, I—"

"Let's tell her." Hunter brightens, and he bounces on his stool.

Josie's eyes narrow. "Hunter, I've been wrestling jack-in-the-boxes all day to save a two-year-old. I swear if you say another word, I will take you down."

His hands shoot toward the ceiling. "All right, all right, settle down. I won't breathe a word."

I slide my cup from one hand to the next. On to a safer topic. "How did you guys become Dream Guardians?"

They both give me blank looks.

"Did I say something wrong?" Again.

"No, not wrong exactly," Hunter says.

Josie clears her throat. "We're trained from a young age to protect you. It's all we ever know." Josie flicks her hair out of her eyes. "It's our life, our purpose, you know?"

"Oh." I rub my thumbnail and struggle to conjure up something else to say.

We sit in silence for a beat, but then Hunter and Josie both keep glancing at me like I'm a rarity, so I clear my throat. "So, tell me about your Dreamers...if that's allowed, I mean."

"Completely." Hunter crosses his arms. "I've been with my fellow a long time, and I swear if I have to wrestle his dentures out of the jaws of a dinosaur one more time, I'll quit."

"That's allowed? I mean, I guess I thought you guys would be assigned for life or something." Which I don't even know what led me to that conclusion, but it just seems...right.

Hunter sobers. "Yeah, something like that."

Josie pipes up, "My kid's two. We're finally past the dreams of bottles being taken away mid sip, so that's a plus."

This is crazy. Crazy weird, but also crazy cool. "Wait, so how old are you?" I ask Hunter.

He shrugs. "No way to calculate it in your terms, love."

"Mimicking me again, mate?" Solomon drops into the stool beside me.

Hunter raises a brow. "So, how did it go?"

"Oh, you know, the usual."

Josie smirks and takes a long drink. "He got red in the face, didn't he?"

"Started sweating, too."

"Are you in trouble?" I ask.

"Nothing I can't handle."

"Yeah, say that to that thing." Hunter stretches his leg past mine and nudges Solomon's ankle. "No way, dude! I can't believe you got a tracker." Hunter lets loose a low whistle.

I angle to the side and catch a glimpse of a small black box shackled to his ankle.

"Keep it down, will you?" Solomon hunches lower on the stool. "And buy me a drink while you're at it."

"You got swiped, too? Aw, man." Hunter swipes a hand down his face.

"Swiped?" I look to Josie for clarification.

She flashes her blue card again. "His points got frozen. And I'm afraid Hunter won't be any help with that. He's backed up by at least a month."

"Again?" Solomon drops his head into his hands and shoots his friend a look.

Hunter grins. "You expect anything less?"

Solomon snorts. "Of course not."

Josie flashes her card. "Want me to order you something?"

Solomon groans. "Nah. Come on, Gwen, we should get going."

I finish off the last sip of my Blue Diamond. "Thanks for this, and it was great meeting you both." I slide off my stool and wave at Hunter and Josie.

"Hey, bring her around again sometime, and it'll be our turn to ask the questions," Hunter hollers after us.

"Please, we won't be seeing him for a long time, Watcher's going to have him so busy he'll forget about us," Josie says.

Solomon places a guiding hand against my shoulder and ushers me back the way we came.

I rub my ear. "I'm sorry if I got you in trouble. Being here, I mean."

"Not your fault. As I recall, I didn't give you much of a choice."

I narrow my eyes at him. "That was totally against protocol, wasn't it?"

His lips twitch. "Maybe."

He leads me back to our elevator, though how he can tell which is which is beyond me. An idea strikes as he presses the up button.

"Wait, can I meet my Dream Guardian?"

Solomon stiffens. "No."

"Please?" I prop my hands under my chin and do my best impression of the twins when they beg Mom or Nana for candy.

"No." The elevator dings, and Solomon stomps inside.

"But why? I'm here. This is like a once in a lifetime opportunity." And yes, I do sound like a petulant child. I'm not even ashamed of the whining.

"I said no." Solomon jabs the button for what I assume is his apartment.

I slouch in the corner as the elevator glides into motion. "That's so not fair."

Solomon runs his fingers through his hair. "Please, can we just drop it?"

"Not until you tell me why." Cue crossed arms, and I'm almost annoying myself now.

"It's against protocol, and as you can see—" he motions toward the shackle around his ankle, "—I'm already in enough trouble as it is."

I purse my lips and stare up at the ceiling. "Fine."

"Listen, if I didn't have to follow the rules, I would let you—"

"I said fine."

"Yeah, but you don't sound like you mean it."

"Well, I don't, but it sounds like neither one of us has an option other than to be fine with it, so..." I shrug a shoulder. And now I'm acting like a brat. I massage the bridge of my nose with my thumb and forefinger. "Look, I'm sorry."

"No, I'm sorry." Solomon shifts and rubs the back of his neck. "I'm trained to be more patient than this."

"Trained?" I can't even hide the sarcasm dripping from my tone.

He winces.

Oh, right. I'm supposed to be stifling my inner child. "Sorry," I mumble.

"It's been a long day, let's just get you back to the apartment, okay?"

I nod and clamp my lips shut to keep back any other words I might regret.

Once the elevator springs open, Solomon makes quick work of ushering me inside his apartment and locking up behind him. And then we're both just standing there. Solomon rubs his palms down his jeans. I play with the edge of my sleeve.

He clears his throat. "You can take the bed. Sleep won't be quite the same as what you're used to, but you should still rest. Build your strength up."

"Right." I don't ask what sleep will be like. All I want is to fall into the bed and hide under the covers until this nightmare is over. I rub the grit from one eye.

"Right, well, goodnight." Then Solomon bobs an awkward half bow and heads for the couch. "Oh, Gwen." He turns back. "Thank you for being here."

I jam my hands into my back pockets. "Yeah, well I'd do anything for Macy, so..." I nod.

"Right, well, goodnight."

"Goodnight." I back toward the hall and turn into the bedroom.

Chapter Six

In the morning, I wake to the scent of peppermint. I shift in bed. The mattress is too hard, the comforter too silky. This isn't my bed. I jolt, only to relax a second later. I'm in the Dream. I angle my head toward the peppermint scent. A steaming mug sits on the nightstand, a teabag still bobbing in the lightly colored liquid. I sit up and rub my eyes. I should feel rested, but instead my eyes burn. Solomon was right. Sleeping in the Dream is way different than sleeping at home. It's like one of those naps when you're not fully asleep, and you can hear everything around you. I swear I could feel the beat of the Dream's pulse as I rested. Or maybe I'm just going crazy.

I tuck my wounded arm close to my side and reach for the tea with my good hand. Solomon didn't have to make it, but he did. Sweet. I cradle the mug close and lean back against the headboard. This is all insane, and as long as I stay tucked inside Solomon's little bedroom, I'm safe. Maybe. In any case, I refuse to move until I drink every last sip of this tea.

It's probably a good half hour before I slide out of bed. By then, there's nothing left in my mug besides the soggy teabag, and I have no excuses left to remain hidden. I tuck my feet into my boots and head for the kitchen where the espresso machine whirs into action.

"Hey," I say.

Solomon spins to face me. "Hey."

"Thanks...for this." I lift my empty mug.

His cheeks turn pink, and he nods before fussing with a knob on his machine.

"And look, I'm sorry. About last night I mean."

"Last night?" He peeks over his shoulder.

"My Dream Guardian." I prop my hip against the counter. And being a total brat, and well, pretty much everything, but the words settle awkwardly against my tongue, and I can't force myself to voice them.

"Ah, Gwen, about that—"

I wave off his words. "It's against protocol, and I don't want to get you in trouble. I get it. And I won't ask again."

He peeks at me through that long sweep of hair. "Thank you, Gwen."

Before this can get too sentimental, I eye the fridge. "You got anything to eat around here?"

He cringes. "Coffee?"

I narrow my eyes.

"There might be cereal in the cabinet?" He jerks his thumb toward one of the cabinets near the fridge.

I peek inside, and sure enough, there's a box of some kind of protein cereal mixture. Just so long as it's edible. "Bowl?"

He offers me a large mug.

It'll do. I open the fridge, but it's empty, except for a few cans of refrigerated coffee beverages. This guy has got a serious problem. "Milk?"

He jerks to a stop as he goes to throw away an empty carton. His eyes dart to the milk frother.

"Great." I push the fridge door shut. "I guess I'll just eat it dry."

"You could put—"

"Don't say coffee."

"Frothed milk?"

"Thanks for the offer, but I'll be fine." I take my mug of crunchy cereal and slide onto the barstool. "So, what do we do today?" Crunch. Crunch. Crunch.

"We wait for Macy to fall asleep. Then we evaluate her dreams and see how she's doing."

"And…?"

"And if she shows a great deal of improvement, then you get to go home." He takes a sip of his finished drink.

"Great, so we just wait then?"

"Until she enters the Dream, yes. We just have to—" He slams his drink down on the counter. "She's here."

My gut crunches tight.

Here we go.

"You ready?" The Dream Guardian bounces on his toes.

My hands are sweating, and I can't conjure the enthusiasm to match his, so I lift my shoulder in a half-shrug.

He leads the way to the red door blocking us from whatever crazy this world has to offer. A tremor travels through my fingers. What's going to happen when we step through to the other side?

Solomon flashes a smile. "Relax. Remember, the more scared you are, the worse things will be."

I tighten the band keeping my hair pulled back from my face and pray he doesn't see the way my hands shake. If only the golden spy hole could tell me what waits on the other side.

"I'm right here with you," Solomon murmurs as he steps past me.

I stiffen, but by then he's already at the door.

"You coming, Gweny?" His hand hovers over the handle.

I shoot him a glare. "Don't call me that."

"Really? I like it. Sorry, can't stop." He winks. "Gweny."

I brush past him and yank the door open. "Whatever you say, Solly."

When I step out of Solomon's apartment, the world shimmers and blurs for a split second, and there's a harsh scent like cleaning supplies and then I'm standing in a dark forest with wind howling all around me.

I shiver and shrink deeper into my sweater. I still. There's no pain in my arm. I jerk my sleeve up only to reveal perfect skin. The bite is gone. "Wow." This must be what Solomon meant by a dream reset. Totally cool.

"Stick close." Solomon creeps forward.

I trip over a thick root and stumble forward before catching my balance. "How 'bout a flashlight?"

"That would announce our presence."

Right. "Where's Macy?"

"She's here somewhere. I can feel her."

Feel her? What kind of crazy is that? "But—"

"Shh."

I bite my lip to keep any more questions silenced.

The wind thrashes harder, tearing at my hair, whistling past my ears so fast they ring.

A scream rises above the wind. Solomon breaks into a run, dragging me along with him. I stumble over the uneven ground and jerk free from Solomon's hold so I can balance better. A twig snaps into my cheek, leaving a stinging sensation. I clap a hand over the rising welt but keep going.

Another cry.

"This way." Solomon leaps over a brush of tangled foliage with the kind of agility I can only dream of. I wade through the tangle, thorns scraping against my jeans. They prick through the fabric, tearing into my skin. I grimace and push onward until I break free of the mess.

There, a flash of pink. Macy sprints through a patch of pines, her long hair whipping behind her. She cranes her neck to look at something over her shoulder. I follow the direction of her gaze. A long smear of shadow slithers along the ground, ducking behind trees only to spring forward a second later. Spindly fingers seem to stretch toward Macy from the darkness.

"Solomon!" He's so focused on reaching Macy he doesn't appear to have noticed what's chasing her. "Behind you, Solomon!" The wind steals my words, and I'm too late.

The shadow wraps around Solomon's leg, pulling him to the ground.

"Solomon!" Screaming isn't helping anything. I search the earth, for something, anything that could possibly help. My hand collides with a solid chunk of bark. I have no idea if this Shadow will even react, but I can't stand here and do nothing, so I pitch the thing like I used to throw baseballs around the yard with Luke. The bark hits the Shadow, and it recoils from Solomon, shaking out its airy fingers like maybe it feels pain.

Solomon is on his feet again, and he catches up to Macy, grabbing her by the elbow. He turns toward me. "Come on, Gwen."

I sprint for them, but I've drawn the Shadow's attention, and it veers for me. I gasp, and my heart slams in my chest as I skid to a stop and change directions. The Shadow mimics my movements. I backtrack. Trip over a stick. I hit the ground hard, sending a flash of pain up my tailbone. Sweat dampens my shirt against my back, and the Shadow swells closer. I scramble backward on my hands until I gain my feet once more and run. The Shadow leaps at me. I scream and veer to the side, narrowly missing a swipe of its spindly fingers.

I dart around a tree. My boots crash into something wet and sticky. They squelch into the ground as I struggle to free myself, but the more I struggle, the more I sink. I try to jerk free, but I lose my balance and fall. I catch myself with my hands, and they're immediately swallowed by cold, dark goop. Mud? Except it's alive and climbing up my waist. "Solomon!"

He's yelling something, but the wind is too loud. He tries to come for me, but the trees seem to close up like a wall between us. Macy screams as the Shadow reaches one hand through the barricade of trees, fingers clawing toward her.

"Macy!" I thrash against the muck, and it swallows my chest.

Solomon leaps between Macy and the Shadow.

"Get her out of here," I yell.

"I'm not leaving you here," he shouts back.

Is that a smile cracking through the Shadow that now turns its attention toward me? By now, all I can manage is a small wiggle of my torso. I can't even feel my legs.

No, no, no. I have to move.

But the Shadow is faster. Its dark hand curls around my throat, constricting my airway with a pressure that doesn't match the slippery vapor that is its hands.

I. Can't. Breathe.

Static pulses in my ears, and I can't even pull my fingers from the mud to claw at the fingers squeezing the life from my body. I can feel the veins bulging in my face.

And then Solomon is there, yanking me free from the mud and away from the Shadow. Air pulls into my lungs, and I'm choking. Coughing in the grass. To my left, Macy flickers and disappears.

"Breathe. Breathe, Gwen."

I'm trying.

Solomon rubs my back, and the world blurs. For a moment, I think I'm passing out, but then the ache frees my lungs, and I can breathe, and I'm on the floor in Solomon's apartment.

"Are you all right, Gwen?" He's kneeling over me, brow furrowed.

"Yeah. Yeah, I'm good." I palm my chest even though the air is now fresh and easy to breathe.

"Hey, you're all right now."

I snag his gaze, and he holds my stare for a long moment.

"Thank you." I mean every syllable.

He ducks his head and runs his fingers through his hair.

"Is that what you meant by Macy's dreams taking a turn for the worst?" I ask.

"They're not pretty," he says. "They just keep getting darker."

"Why me, Solomon? I almost died out there." I jerk a thumb toward his door. "Surely Hunter or Josie are more qualified to help you."

"They can't." He deflates and scooches so his back is pressed against the kitchen cabinets.

"Can't?"

"It's against the rules. Dream Guardians aren't allowed access to each other's Dreamers except on very rare occasions."

"That's a dumb rule."

He gives a breathy laugh. "I won't argue there, but a Dreamer must have absolute trust in their Guardian. If Guardians mix in a dream, it confuses the Dreamer and only makes things worse."

"I can't do this." I shiver at the thought of the Shadow and the phantom feel of its fingers pressed against my throat.

"Gwen..."

"I almost died!" I don't mean to shout, but I do.

"That was your first real time in a dream. It could have happened to anyone."

"I can't." I press a hand to my face and shake my head. "I want to go home."

"Gwen, please."

"You're not listening to me! I'm not going back in there."

He catches my hand and pulls it away from my face. "If it wasn't you, it could have easily been Macy. She's in such a fragile state right now...I would have lost her, Gwen. *You* would have lost her."

I swallow hard. He doesn't appear to be lying.

"Please stay." His voice drops to a whisper.

Beep.

A high-pitched blaring noise cuts through the apartment. I wince and snap my hands to my ears, but that does nothing to muffle the voice that crackles from unseen speakers.

"Solomon Custos, report to headquarters immediately."

A pause.

"Bring the girl."

The noise and voice go silent.

Solomon winces.

"What's going on?" I lower my hands to my lap.

"One way to find out." Solomon taps his knuckles against the band at his ankle and stands. He reaches for me, and I let him help me to my feet.

He guides me out the door and back to the elevator. This time, he pushes a different button, and when the doors spill open it's not to the Guardian hangout but a cold, sterile looking room. Screens cover almost every inch of the white walls. A man stands "at ease" with hands clasped behind his back, watching the video feed. I find my own face reflected on the screens. Watch myself flee the Shadow as Solomon pulls Macy to safety.

"Custos." The man doesn't even turn to face us.

Is it my imagination, or does Solomon angle ever so slightly in front of me?

"Watcher." Solomon snaps a salute.

The man with the buzzcut turns. His gaze sweeps Solomon before flicking to me. He only studies me for a moment before giving a dismissive grunt and turning his attention to Solomon once more. "What was that?" he demands, jerking his chin toward the footage playing out across the screens.

Solomon's Adam's apple bobs. "Sir?"

Watcher steps closer, and I take an instinctive step back. Solomon holds his ground between us.

"Your Dreamer almost died." Spittle sprays with Watcher's words.

"I reached her in time."

Watcher snorts. "Barely."

"What's the big deal?" I probably shouldn't butt in, but this guy needs to cool off. "He got Macy out okay."

Watcher's eyebrow hikes high, and he darts a look from me to Solomon. "What game are you playing, Custos?"

Solomon's gaze flickers and darts to the side.

I shrink in on myself. Great, I've only made things worse.

"Let's finish this in private," Watcher says. He taps a button on his watch and speaks into it. "Peznic, report to my office. Immediately."

A stiff silence falls over the room as we wait. Solomon stands "at ease," gaze fixed on a point over Watcher's shoulder. He may look relaxed, but I can see the pulse of his veins in his neck. Solomon is anything but calm.

And I don't know how I should stand. I don't think I'm technically in trouble. After all, I haven't really done anything except what Solomon's told me to do, and I'm not exactly under Watcher's command, so...I shift my stance, tucking my hands into the back pockets of my jeans only to bring them forward again to twist in front of me.

A door slides open, and Hunter strides in. "Peznic reporting for..." he trails off when he spots Solomon and me.

Watcher raises an eyebrow, and Hunter gives a belated salute. The commander stares at him for a good long time before releasing him. "Peznic. Take the girl down to the café. Custos will collect her when able."

"Yes, sir." Hunter snaps another salute before motioning for me to join him.

I cast a look over my shoulder at Solomon.

He offers a flicker of a smile.

"Come on." Hunter ushers me out the door.

It glides shut behind us.

"Is he going to be all right?" I linger outside, but the place must be sound proof, because not even a murmur passes through the walls.

Hunter places a hand on my back and directs me forward. "Solomon? Please. He'll be fine. This is far from the first tangle he's gotten himself into."

For some reason, that doesn't sit well. "He gets in trouble often?"

"Let's just say Watcher's a rule follower. Solomon's not. They butt heads. But then again, Watcher doesn't really get along with anybody, so..." he shrugs.

I wrap my arms around my middle. "Maybe we should stay."

"Nah, that could go on forever."

I stop walking.

He chuckles and nudges me forward. "Not that kind of forever. Come on, we'll go down to the café and get you something to eat while we wait." He checks his watch. "Nap time should be just about over for Josie. I'll tell her to meet us there."

"Oh, if she's tired then—"

"Not her naptime. Her Dreamer's. Two-year-old. Turns out they're very scheduled or supposed to be anyway."

"Supposed to be? What, your Dreamer wasn't?"

Hunter rubs the back of his neck. "I...I wasn't with him from the beginning. I was transferred later on."

I slide a glance at his face, not sure if I should keep asking, but he doesn't look away, so I do, "Transferred?"

"It doesn't happen often, mind you."

"But?"

Hunter leans closer, pushing against my back to keep me moving. "His Guardian was killed in action. I was a new recruit fresh out of training. They needed someone."

"Guardians can…" I don't finish. Don't want to know.

But Hunter must see the question on my face because he just nods.

That makes me shiver, and I pull my sweater tighter around my torso.

"Aw, come on, it happens. None of that." Hunter leads me into the café from last night.

Was it only last night? It feels like it's been a lifetime.

The space seems deserted with only a few Guardians sitting at tables and some soft instrumental music over the speakers instead of the band. Instead of heading to the counter, Hunter drops into a booth. I slide in across from him.

He flags down the waiter, and orders us both a couple of subs and some soda.

"I thought you couldn't—" I don't remember the exact term and wave my hand helplessly between him and the waiter. "You know."

"Ack, no worries. Josie will be here soon to pick up the tab."

I squirm in my seat. "Maybe I should—"

He snorts. "You don't have any points and besides, Josie won't mind."

I'm not so sure, and I hate to presume, but he's right about one thing. I don't have any points or whatever their currency is, to get a meal for myself, and a sub sounds way more appetizing than crunching down on more dry cereal in Solomon's apartment.

"So, you have questions, I presume?" Hunter folds his hands under his chin.

I do, but one stands out above the rest. "Is Solomon in trouble?"

"Not more than he can handle. Don't worry about him."

"It's just...I mean, I never meant to—"

"If Solomon's in trouble, he's brought it on himself. He'll be fine, okay?"

"Okay." I rub my hands down my jeans.

The waiter appears a moment later and slides our plates and drinks in front of us. Hunter digs in, devouring about half his sandwich before I even have a chance to take a bite of mine.

"So, lay them on me."

I pause in raising my sub to my mouth. "Lay...what on you?"

"All your questions. You can't possibly have none, and Solomon operates on more of a 'as you need to know' basis."

I take a bite and chew. He's right. Maybe he'll answer some of the stuff Solomon won't. I lower my sandwich. "Am I allowed to be here? Watcher doesn't seem to be happy, and—"

"Yes, and no."

I raise an eyebrow.

"Technically, no, you're not *supposed* to be here. But technically, you *can* be."

And now I might be getting a headache. "What?"

"Technically, Solomon's allowed to do anything that will benefit his Dreamer. But bringing you into the Dream...that's...well that's different." He waves a piece of tomato at me.

"Hey, what's going on?" Josie slides in next to Hunter and hip checks him further down the seat.

"Oh, I was just giving away Solomon's deepest, darkest secrets." Hunter winks at me.

Josie eyes him like she's not sure if she should believe him or not.

"I just had some questions, and Hunter offered to answer them, and—" And I'm rambling so I swallow back the rest of whatever nonsense I was going to blurt out.

"What's to know? He's obsessed with coffee, uses his pockets like trashcans, and his apartment is spotless, but he's a total slob when it comes to his car." Josie breaks the remainder of Hunter's sub in half and takes a bite.

Hunter almost chokes on his soda. "Hey!"

"Hey, yourself. I'm paying for it, right?"

"Well..." He just stares at her.

"So, what do you want to know?" Josie bounces in her seat as she leans across the table.

"Um, so tell me about how someone trains to become a Dream Guardian."

"Well, we're all Dream Guardians, so we're pretty much in training since...well, forever I guess."

"All right then, what's it like living in a Dream Guardian family? I mean mine is crazy, so I can only imagine what yours are like." I reach for my drink but stop when they both look at me with blank expressions. "What?"

"We don't…" Josie reaches for Hunter's napkin and dabs at her lips before lowering the paper to her lap. "We don't really have families."

Foot. In. My. Mouth. "I'm sorry." I tuck my hair behind my ear, praying it's too dark in here for them to see the heat burning my cheeks.

"Don't be. For every one of you, there's one of us." Josie shrugs. "To us, it's as simple as that."

Hunter slings an arm over her shoulders. "We make our own families."

I smile because I don't know what else to say or do.

"What else?" Josie drums her hands against the table.

All the questions I had seem dried up now as my brain struggles to catch up with this world I know next to nothing about.

"What are we talking about?"

I jump and find Solomon at my elbow.

"Just trying to fill Gwen in on everything you've been neglecting." Hunter pops a fallen banana pepper into his mouth.

"Hey, I know how to do my job, thank you."

"I think Watcher might disagree." Hunter says it like a joke, but Solomon's jaw tenses.

"Everything okay?" I whisper.

"Never better."

I push half my sub his way.

"I'll pay you back, Josie," he says before taking a bite.

"Josie? I'm the one who fed her." Hunter waves a hand at me. "You should be thanking *me*."

Josie elbows him. "Oh, please. We all know the plan was to mooch off of me."

And then all three of them are laughing. I look between this trio. The easiness between them. They could easily be siblings with their banter and the strings of history stretched between them. It's like a song written so every instrument has its moment to shine and yet also blend effortlessly together. Have Macy, Beck, and I ever had this kind of chemistry?

"Gwen, are you okay?" Solomon nudges me.

I jolt. "Yeah, fine."

He doesn't stop searching my face.

"Just tired. All this newness...it's a lot to take in."

"I get it. Want to head back now?"

"If you don't mind. I mean, is everything wrapped up with Watcher?"

"Oh, trust me, I've been reprimanded enough for one day, thank you." He slides out of the booth so I can climb out, too.

"Thanks for lunch, Josie," I say.

She smiles around a bite of sandwich.

"Josie?" Hunter protests. "What about me?"

"You too, Hunter." I wave, and Solomon and I exit the cafe.

"Is everything really okay?" I ask when we reach the elevator.

"It's fine. I promise. Come on, I have something I want to show you." When he steps inside, he presses a new button.

I eye him. "Where are we going?"

"You'll see."

"Oh, come on, not even a hint?"

"Now, where would be the fun in that?" He smirks.

I lean against the wall, crossing my arms and ankles, trying to look like I don't care. Amusement twinkles in his eyes. Yeah, I'm probably not pulling this off very well.

When the elevator dings, and the doors open, Solomon waves a hand out in front of us. "After you."

I stroll past him.

A set of cement steps wait for us. Seriously, he took me to a stairwell? "You're not planning to kill me and dump my body or something, are you?"

"Please, I would have done that in the parking garage if I was going to."

"I was thinking it would have been the perfect place." I trip on a broken step and catch myself against the wall.

Solomon snags my elbow. "You all right?"

"Fine." I straighten and continue up the cement blocks until we reach a thick door. "Is this going to lead somewhere good?"

"You tell me." He reaches around me and pushes the door open.

I step through the doorway and onto the roof of a sky-scraper. Soft pink clouds paint the sky, and dozens upon dozens of skyscrapers stretch across the skyline as far as I can see. "It's gorgeous."

"I told you it would be worth it." Solomon sits near the middle of the roof.

I join him, sidestepping a patch of ivy that has grown up the side of the building. "What is all this?"

"Every one of those skyscrapers belongs to a Dreamer."

"Woah." I take it all in again. Their windows gleam, and the line goes on for what must be forever. "They're incredible." I tilt my head and squint. "But none of them look like this one." None that I can see from here anyway. "Macy's is…"

"Run down."

I mean, I wasn't going to say it, but yeah. "Why?"

"It's all connected back to her dreams. With things so shattered in her waking world and her inability to cope…well, let's just say the nightmares aren't helping, and it all comes back around to a decaying tower."

I run my hand over the patch of roof where we sit. "So, that's why we need to help her."

Solomon nods.

"I'm in."

He blinks and gives a chuckle. "I thought you already were."

"I know, but this time I'm fully committed. I'm here to help. Whatever Macy needs." I spring to my feet.

Solomon catches my hand and gently tugs me back down. "Easy. There's plenty of time for all that. For now, breathe in the fresh air and relax." He angles his face toward the setting sun.

I shift beside him. "But—"

"Shh."

"Sol—"

He holds a finger to his lips.

I huff, but clamp my lips shut. Solomon sits and sits and sits. I follow his gaze to the red orb slipping away for the night. It really is breathtaking. All crimson and fire. If I were to play the drums for a soundtrack to capture this moment, it would be a soft, soothing beat. Or maybe even something with a safari vibe.

Solomon taps my arm. "I lost you."

I jolt. "Sorry."

"What were you thinking about?" He leans back on his elbows.

"Nothing." I shake my head.

"Aw, come on."

My cheeks warm. "It's stupid."

"Let me be the judge of that, Gonzales." He bumps my knee. "Come on, tell me."

I give him a long side-eye, but he just looks back like he's trying to read my mind. I fix my attention on the sunset. "I was trying to decide what kind of drumbeat would go with this moment."

He doesn't laugh. He just sits there, grinning.

"Stupid, right?" I tug at a loose thread on the cuff of my sweater.

"Not stupid. So, what did you decide?"

"About what?" I still in trying to capture the string and look back at him.

"About the beat." He gestures to the fiery orb suspended before us.

"Um…" I tuck my hair behind my ear.

"Don't leave me in suspense." He nudges my knee again. "Go on, tell me, Gonzales."

"Something soft and soothing. Like a lullaby or something. Or something a bit wild. Like you would hear on a safari." Heat creeps up my neck, and I finish with a lame, "I don't know."

"Lullaby. I like that."

"You do?" I dare a peek his way. He's staring at the sunset like he's actually considering what I've said. Funny, but Beck always pokes fun when I talk about the beats that pop into my head.

"Either one would fit. I—" Solomon snags my hand and pulls us both to our feet, body transforming from relaxed to alert in an instant.

"What is it?" I shoot a look around, but there's nothing off that I notice.

"Macy's dreaming. We need to go." He pulls me toward the door leading back to the stairwell.

I shoot one last look toward the sun and take a breath to commemorate this moment of peace.

Solomon pauses at the door, waiting for me. "Ready?"

"Let's do this."

Chapter Seven

We step through a burst of shimmering air and enter a new dream. It takes my eyes a moment to adjust, but my surroundings quickly solidify. I'm standing in the doorway of a practice room, watching a group of ballerinas stretch and chat.

Macy rises on her toes and spins into some move I should probably know the name of. Her ankle caves, and she stumbles sideways. Behind her, a group of leotard clad girls snicker, hands cupped over their mouths. Not that it helps muffle their cutting comments.

Macy flushes and stares at the mirrored wall, hands clasped in front of her stomach. Dark circles mar her pale skin, and she doesn't quite raise her head in the confident manner she used to. She inhales one breath. Two. Then turns her neck slightly, clearly drawn toward the gossip behind her.

My heart twists for my friend. How dare these girls mock her?

I move forward, but Solomon snags my sleeve, drawing me to a halt. "Don't."

"I should just let that continue?" I thrust a hand in the general direction of the busybodies.

He shakes his head, though the look in his eyes seems to question that action. "We can't go in. Not until things escalate."

"But is this real?"

"We're in the Dream, Gwen."

"I mean, do they bully her in real life?"

"Gwen..." He doesn't have to say anything else. I can see it in his eyes.

"She never told me." An ache forms deep inside. Did she tell Beck? Well, I'm going to do something about it. A look from Solomon commands me to wait. Fine. My chest burns, and I cross my arms, hip cocked. Every fiber of my being protests that this is wrong. And yet, I grind my teeth and hold my place.

"What's the matter, Macy?" A girl clothed in red moves to the mirror and checks her make-up. "Can't you dance anymore?"

Another ballerina arches her back in a stretch. "Guess she isn't the star after all."

The cackling herd of dancers chortle at the comments.

The girl in red smirks and turns on my friend. "I hope you won't miss the spotlight too much." She slides her sweat towel from her shoulders and tosses it against Macy's chest.

My friend doesn't say a word. She stares at the towel now clasped in her hands, her cheeks matching her pink leotard.

The fire in my chest explodes, and I push my way into the practice room, ignoring the strangled noises coming from Solomon.

"Enough." I bump against the red ballerina. Maybe hard enough to leave a bruise. She staggers back, red lips falling open in shock.

"Gwen?" Macy stares at me, blonde brows crinkled.

"Gwen," Solomon hisses.

Did he really expect me to stand by and do nothing?

"What are you doing here?" Macy cocks her head to the side.

The entire room stiffens with tension.

A shiver swirls through my stomach. Something is wrong.

The ballerinas circle, their eyes going cold, almost lifeless.

"Gwen?" The confusion on Macy's face grows.

My heartbeat speeds up, and a sinking sensation slips through my chest as the pack of ballerinas stare me down, heaving heavy breaths, hands fisted at their sides.

Solomon's cold fingers close around my fingers, squeezing. Hard.

Oh, snap.

I've broken the first rule of the Dream.

Don't stand out.

The ballerinas shuffle forward, their shoes scraping over the wooden floorboards, each small movement synchronized as they close in on Macy, Solomon, and me. I backpedal, but there's no room, and my back slams into Solomon's chest. His hands close around my upper arms.

Macy twitches, her shoulders slumping to join the posture of the other ballerinas. My knees sag. Will she turn against me, too?

"No." Solomon's breath blows against my hair.

The dancers charge. Several pass through a shimmering Macy. Macy dissolves in a sprinkle of pink glitter, but the others only deepen their snarls and come directly at me. My knees quiver, but my feet remain locked.

"Gwen." Solomon tugs my arm.

The ballerinas reach out, fingers bent like claws.

"We have to go." Solomon curls his arms around my middle and pulls me backward and through the wall behind us.

Our surroundings transform into a dark hallway lit by flickering florescent lights. Slick metal tiles line the ground and doorways trace the walls. The place smells of dust.

"Run." Solomon locks his fingers around mine and pulls. "We have to out run them. Get to my apartment. It's the only way to reset things now, unless you die."

But that in itself is breaking a rule of the Dream.

"I've never known anyone to survive more than two deaths in the Dream."

Yeah, that's not one I plan to break.

I puff alongside Solomon, unable to draw in a full breath around the thrumming of my pulse. A thousand feminine screams echo through the metal hallway, raising the hair on the back of my neck.

Solomon darts a look over his shoulder, his face growing paler in the dim light buzzing through the thin florescent strips.

Behind us, the breathing of our pursuers meshes together, blending into a beat matching the pounding of my heart. A hand reaches out and scrapes my bicep, fingernails snagging on my sweater. I scream. The hand tightens, pulling me backward.

"Gwen!" Solomon whips around, fingers sliding away from mine.

Our fingertips snag, and Solomon folds his hand around mine, squeezing as if my life depends on it. It does. A collection of hisses sweep against my ear, raising goosebumps on my arms.

They could kill me.

The thought is a weak pant in my body. A truth every fiber of my being attempts to deny. But the thought wells, churning through me with each dreadful moment. The sleeve of my sweater slides down my shoulder when more hands reach forward to join the first.

"Gwen." Solomon tugs on my hand, wrenching me forward a step.

The momentum allows me to pull free and stumble forward. Solomon wraps an arm around my shoulders, dragging me onward.

"Duck." He pulls my head against his chest and hurtles sideways, knocking us through one of the metal walls that only dissolves around our bodies.

Once more, the surroundings change, and I'm standing on the top of a tiered wooden platform, backed almost against a cliff. Teenagers swarm each level of the structure, swords in their grasps as they clash together in battle. My own sweaty fingers close around the sword I find in my hand. Solomon is at least five duels away from me, scrambling to keep his opponent at bay. Still, he keeps looking around. Scanning for me?

My lips part to shout his name, but a muscular girl with long blonde hair and a mustard colored tank top leaps in front of me, blade raised high. I hold up my own weapon, grateful for my younger years and stick battles in the backyard with Elijah. Only, this isn't the playful sparring my brother and I participated in back then. One wrong move, and I'll get worse than bruised knuckles.

The girl pushes me backward, accentuating each move with an eardrum wrecking war cry. I stumble under the assault until my heels teeter dangerously close to the edge of the platform.

A flash of victory sweeps through my opponent's eyes, and her lips tilt up. She leaps, black boots raising from the platform. The breath sweeps from my lungs, and things unfold in slow motion. I track every arc of the girl's fall, the downward plunge of her sword. I raise my blade, and the impact of her strike sends me to one knee. The girl screams and drives her foot down on my raised knee. A pang sizzles through my leg, and nausea tightens my stomach. I collapse against the wooden planks as agony streaks through my kneecap. A sneer flashes across my foe's lips as she advances.

"No." The word barely has time to slip from my lips before the girl drives her boot into my ribs, sending me tumbling over the edge of the platform.

I scream, clawing at the air. But there's nothing to catch me. I'm going to break the second rule of the Dream. I squeeze my eyes shut so I won't have to see. I slam into the ground. The air escapes from my lungs in one long puff. Around me, leaves kick up under my impact, swirling through the air. A river lays at my feet, gurgling toward who-knows-where. My fingers twitch in the leaves beneath me. Not dead then. But no matter how I try, it's the only movement I can manage.

A swarm of armed teenagers descend the platform, all headed toward...me.

I have to move. Get up. And yet, my eyelashes flicker, and my vision blurs.

I blink.

Once.

Twice.

The world snaps into focus, and air wheezes into my throbbing lungs. I have to get up. Now. I move my right foot, and a fiery spasm streaks through my knee. I grit my teeth against the waves of agony radiating through my knee cap and prop myself up on my elbows. There has to be a way out of this madness, but how?

The mass of teenagers out for my blood looms closer.

"Gwen!" The voice belongs to Solomon, but he's lost in the crowd, even with his ridiculous get-up.

I twist my fingers into the shriveled leaves around me and slide my leg up. Fire sparks within my knee. I hiss. There will be no running away from this.

"Gwen!" Solomon's call comes again. He's elbowing his way to the front of the pack until he breaks free, outpacing the fastest of my pursuers.

The Dream Guardian scrambles to my side, sending up a spray of leaves. He hefts me up in his arms, and I wrap mine around his neck and meet his panicked gaze.

"I'm sorry," I whisper into his shoulder.

The Guardian spins one direction, then another in a desperate search for safety. Finally, he turns and sloshes into the river, careful to keep me above the water. On the bank, the teenagers gather, weapons at the ready, but none dare to follow us.

The current tugs at Solomon, jerking him this way and that, but he wades deeper.

I cling to his neck and grimace while an ache courses through my knee with the uneven movements. The river water laps at my jeans, and then the frigid current sweeps up my waist, only to climb to my shoulders.

"Hold your breath." Solomon inhales, gives me only a second to do the same, then he sinks into the murky water, pulling me down with him.

I blink against the brownish liquid, but my vision remains fuzzy.

Solomon lowers me into the buoyant substance, careful to keep one hand wrapped around mine. He jerks my hand, pulling me down, down, down. My ears pop, and my lungs scream for air. How can the stream be this deep? We move toward a burst of white light at the bottom of the rocky river bed.

Is that...a hint of a red door? I kick hard with my good leg. Beside me, Solomon does the same, speeding up our progress. When the fingers of my free hand trail along the mud, we burst through the light and fall into the middle of Solomon's apartment, clothes as dry as the moment we left.

I heave in a ragged breath while Solomon pants beside me, lying flat on his back.

The pain in my knee has vanished, but somehow my adrenaline refuses to calm. I blink back a bout of moisture swirling across my vision. "I'm sorry, Solomon."

He rolls his head in my direction and holds my stare. "I know." He squeezes my hand.

Chapter Eight

I grip the sides of the bathroom sink, a wet hair dangling in front of my eyes, escaped from the towel holding up my strands. My jeans stick to my damp legs, and the humidity in the room is already drawing sweat from my pores. But I don't leave.

I took a shower as hot as my skin could bear, but I don't feel better. Instead, the images of the Dream flash through my mind. Macy. The ballerinas. Solomon's warnings. There. That's where it all went wrong. If I had just *listened*, none of that would have happened.

"*Ah, my Gweny, you must learn to listen.*" My dad's voice plays through my head, and the memory surfaces to go along with it. Him kneeling in front of me, tugging gently on one of my braids. I was seven, maybe eight, and had gotten in trouble at school for something. I can't even remember what I'd done, but Dad's words have always stuck. Unfortunately, I've yet to master the skill.

"Just listen," I growl at my reflection.

The girl scowls back.

A knock raps on the door. "Gwen? I've made you some tea."

Blast him, but he's too kind. Yelling I could take. A deep sigh of disappointment even. But instead of telling me all of the things I did wrong, Solomon seems intent on nursing me back to a stable state of mind.

And no matter how much I'd like to, I can't hide in here forever.

I yank the towel from my hair and take my time smoothing the wet cloth over the hanger. When the last wrinkle is erased, I unlock the door and pull it open.

Solomon stands there with his shoulder propped against the doorjamb, one hand cupping a steaming mug. "Here." He extends it toward me.

"Thanks." Our fingers bump as I accept the offering, and a spark zips up my arm.

He smiles, and I don't know what to say, so I squeeze past him and flee to the living room.

He doesn't follow. In fact, the shower is going again in a few minutes. I wince. There can't be much hot water left. Unless things work differently in the Dream, which is entirely possible.

I sit on Solomon's couch and take a sip of...chamomile tea. I let the soothing concoction slip down my throat and take a moment to inhale the sweet fumes. He must have put a little honey in it. Yes, this is exactly what I need.

Except I have to keep my hands cupped around the warm mug, otherwise I can't still the shaking. Thank goodness Solomon is in the bathroom and can't see. He tried to tell me it wasn't my fault. I don't believe him.

The sound of his shower running in the background mixes with the orchestra music spilling through the speakers.

Well, I can't undo what I did. I tighten my fingers around the cup. I'll just have to do better. No more breaking Dream rules.

I drum my fingers against the mug and wait.

Time creeps by.

Solomon comes out, dressed in fresh jeans and a t-shirt. His lab coat hangs near the front door. He rubs a towel over his dripping hair and plops onto the easy chair across from me. "Well, what should we do? We could head down to the café—"

"No." I shake my head. Somehow, I don't want to face the other Dream Guardians with my failure hanging over me.

Solomon leans forward. "Gwen, it wasn't your fault."

"Yeah, right." I don't even try to hold back my snort.

"Look, you're new to all of this. I should have kept better control of the situation."

"If I had just listened to you, none of that would have happened." I rub my knee even though it doesn't hurt anymore. I almost wish it did. Like a true reminder to not go rogue again.

"Nobody is perfect all the time."

"Yeah, well I wish I was."

"Gwen."

I duck my head and pick at my cuticles.

"Gwen." Solomon lowers himself so he's kneeling in front of me. "It wasn't your fault. You're fine. I'm fine."

I turn away so I don't have to see the earnest expression in his eyes. "What about Macy?"

"She's fine. Probably just woke with a bit of a shock, that's all."

Well, that's good. At least I haven't caused irreparable damage to my friend.

"Listen to me."

Dang it, there's that word. The dreaded *listen*. I force my gaze back to Solomon's.

"Listen." Solomon takes my hand and cups it in both of his. "It wasn't your fault, and you can't keep blaming yourself. No one was hurt. Now it's up to you what you do with this. Are you going to let it become a ghost that haunts your nightmares, or are you going to turn it into a learning experience and resolve not to make the same mistake again?"

He's talking to me like I'm five, but that doesn't change the truth of his words. I swallow. Hard. "I'm sorry."

"Oh, and you can stop saying that too." He releases my hand and moves back to his own seat.

"Okay." I straighten my posture and relax my hands.

"That's better. Now do you have the phrase "forgiven and forgotten" back in your world?"

"Something like that."

"Good. Watcher doesn't believe in the phrase, but Hunter, Josie, and I tend to favor it amongst ourselves. From now on, that's how we'll view this situation. Forgiven and forgotten."

I almost say I'm sorry again, but I swallow the words back. I switch them to, "Thank you," instead.

Solomon grins and drops back into his chair.

"So, now what?" I take another sip of tea.

"We wait."

I massage my forehead. "I've never been very good at that."

"I've noticed."

I toss a throw pillow at him.

"I have a surprise." Solomon waggles his eyebrows.

As if I need more of those in my life right now.

"No need to look so scared." He goes to the kitchen and pulls a bag from behind the counter.

I brace myself, for what I don't know, but if this world has taught me nothing else, it's taught me to be alert. Except no monster comes leaping out of the bag. Instead, Solomon pulls out baking supplies.

"I'm hoping you might know what to do with these, because if you're relying on me, then I'm afraid all is lost." It's almost cute how he ducks his head and peeks at me through his eyelashes.

Wait...cute? I shove the impression away and instead reach for a jar of cinnamon. "Yeah, I think I can find something to do with this."

"Good, because I don't know about you, but cereal only satisfies for so long."

"Scooch over." I bump him aside with my hip.

"As you say, my lady." He sweeps an arm out, giving me full command of the counter. He's not flirting, is he? No, no, that's impossible.

I clear my throat and focus on the ingredients. "You're in luck. This is everything I need to make my mom's cinnamon muffins. They're the best, especially if they're warm."

"You don't need to say anything else, I'm already drooling." He plants his hands on the counter. "What do you need me to do?"

"Find a bowl and a spatula. A muffin tin would be great, too."

"Uh…" He squirms and rubs the back of his neck.

Yeah, so the boy doesn't cook. "Coffee mugs will do." Forget the oven, we'll just pop these in his microwave.

That puts a confident bounce in his step, and he returns with his largest bowl, a spoon, and two wide rimmed coffee mugs.

"Perfect." Measuring spoons would be nice, but if he doesn't even have a spatula, I'm not going to bother asking for something as high-tech as proper measuring equipment. Instead, I snag his smallest mug from the shelf and eyeball the measurements. "Stir." I nudge the bowl and spoon to Solomon.

He stirs as I add the ingredients one by one. He sends a spray of flour puffing up. The white dust settles on my arm and cheek, and I'm afraid to check my hair.

"A little less enthusiastically, please." I grin and flick a few grains of cinnamon at him.

"Sorry, sorry." He coughs, and I swear he's trying to cover a laugh.

Cheeky.

I purse my lips and slide the bowl away from him. "Like this." I gently fold the batter together.

"Right. Got it." Solomon takes over.

I plant a hand on my hip and stare him down as he mimics my stirring.

"Better?"

"Better," I agree as I reach for the coffee mugs.

Solomon divides the batter between the two and we pop them in the microwave.

My stomach grumbles as the sweet, cinnamon aroma takes over the kitchen.

The second the microwave dings, Solomon snags the mugs and passes me the fluffier of the two creations.

"Thank you," I say.

"You know what would go great with these?" He raises his eyebrows.

I stifle a groan. "Don't say coffee."

"Party pooper." But he goes to the fridge and hefts a milk carton triumphantly.

Okay, yeah, that sounds good. I snag a second set of coffee mugs, and Solomon pours. With our meal set, we sit side-by-side on the barstools.

Solomon raises his spoon. "Cheers."

I clack mine against his. "Cheers."

The last mug is washed and dried when the world swirls, and a pungent waft of lemon cleaner leaves me nauseous. I blink hard to clear my vision and find myself standing on the roof of Macy's skyscraper. The sky is a brilliant blue and fluffy clouds surround us. The wind pulls strands of hair from my messy bun, and whips them across my face. Solomon gently moves me aside so he can join me.

"It's beautiful," I say as I take in the gorgeous skyline once more.

"It's dangerous." Solomon scans the rooftop. "This is a dream."

Yeah, I'm not even going to try to argue that one anymore. "I know."

He grabs my shoulders and gives me a shake. "Not just any dream. It's *Macy's* dream."

Macy's dream. My heartrate skyrockets as a thousand scenarios slam through my head. I spin around, searching the rooftop for my friend. What dangers await us on this tower? It isn't until I edge past a maintenance box that I find her. My gut performs a sickening twist. Macy stands on the ledge of the roof, her hair whipping in the wind.

"Macy?" My voice protests the volume it takes to be heard over the wind.

I swivel, searching for Solomon, but who knows where he's gotten himself to? I clench my fists and turn my attention back to Macy.

She's looking at me over her shoulder, lips lifted in a half smile. "Catch me, Gwen." She steps off the ledge.

Chapter Nine

"Macy!" I race to the rooftop's edge. The clouds hide Macy's form. My heart slams in my chest, and my knees tremble. "Macy."

"Catch me." Her voice drifts over the wind, carrying a tease of laughter.

Pulse thundering in my ears, I step onto the ledge and search once more for my friend. I spy her running down the side of the skyscraper. How can she stay suspended sideways? I shake my head. Why shouldn't she be able to? This is a dream after all.

"Gwen, what are you doing?" Solomon's accented voice comes from somewhere behind me.

Macy beckons with a playful wiggle of her hand. She looks happy. So free.

"Gwen?" Solomon again, his voice growing a bit more panicked.

"Come on." Macy throws her head back and laughs, the long strands of her blonde hair frolicking in the wind. "Gwen, come on."

I can't even see the ground from here. But this is just a dream. I won't fall. I won't let my fear turn this into a nightmare. Besides, Macy is happy. Is it so selfish to want some of that joy for myself, even momentarily? I suck in a breath and step off the ledge.

"Gwen!" Solomon's shout echoes through the air.

My stomach churns and slips to my toes as I plummet. I scream and flail, but there is nothing to do besides pray my family will be all right without me.

Macy runs at my side, keeping pace with my tumbling body. "Grab one of the clouds."

A green strip of ground reaches up to meet me. My heart stutters, and I plunge faster. Brutal wind attacks me from all sides, pushing and pulling, tearing and whipping until my skin aches.

I'm going to die.

"Gwen!" Macy hisses. "Grab a cloud."

The alternative of splattering into a thousand pieces pushes me to go for her crazy suggestion. I reach out with a shaking hand and snag a soft cloud. My body jerks to a sudden stop. My limbs throb from the aftereffects of adrenaline, but an airy chuckle slips from my lips. Because I'm still alive. Macy leaps from the side of the skyscraper to the cloud holding me in place.

"Come on." She waves me onward before leaping off the cloud and onto another.

"Macy, wait." I struggle to get my chest level with the top of the fluff and wiggle up until I'm lying on my stomach. The platform is like a sponge beneath my weight. I press a hand to my chest and labor to regulate my breathing. Man, I need to start working out.

"Hurry, they pop," Macy calls over her shoulder in a sing-song-voice.

As if hearing her words, the silky structure shudders beneath me.

I scramble to my feet. Tremors thrum through the structure, throwing me off balance. I crash sideways and tumble into the fluffy mound. Another quake thunders beneath me.

"Hurry." Macy's voice still carries a note of cheer.

I perform a push up Dad would be proud of and manage to scramble to my feet. My knees convulse along with the rocking cloud. A spray of white pops from the far end of my perch, and dissolves in a burst of shimmering color. A violent tremor sends me staggering sideways.

"Jump, Gwen!" Solomon yells.

I can't. I'll fall.

The cloud rumbles beneath me, sending my teeth smacking together.

"Jump!" Solomon roars.

I can't.

I have to.

The cloud begins to crumble beneath my feet, sealing my decision. I launch forward. My jump falls short. I reach out, fighting for a grip, and my hands brush the fluff of the next cloud for only a moment before I'm free falling through the sky.

I scream.

Solomon leans over the ledge of the skyscraper, yelling, face red.

The wind lashes at me, it's angry howl tearing through my ears. Strands of hair wrench from my bun.

Macy leaps down to fall beside me. "Poor, little Gweny. Need some help?"

The nickname grates my ears. Still, I reach out a hand.

She barks a laugh and kicks me in the side with her heeled boot. Pain streaks through my torso, and I fold into myself, huddled against the sensation as the impact sends me skittering. Only in the Dream would I be able to fall forever. If only pain would disappear the same way all sense of reason does. One thing is for sure. Something is terribly wrong with my best friend.

Solomon springs off the rooftop, sword drawn. Sword? When did he have time to find that? Macy whips a sword of her own out of nowhere. The two clash blades, and the impact sends them crashing onto a larger cloud. If Solomon is attacking the girl he's meant to protect, then something must have gone terribly, terribly wrong.

As they battle below me, I take matters into my own hands. If those two can control aspects of the Dream, maybe I can too. I flip onto my stomach skydiver style and angle my body so I slam into a cloud slightly above Solomon and Macy. My torso screams under the force of my landing. Who said clouds were allowed to become hard?

With a groan, I roll onto my back and wrap an arm around my waist. This dream stuff is crazy. I can fall but never make progress while others fall faster than me, and yet I can still batter my ribs. The cloud's surface softens beneath me, changing so that it cradles my bruised body.

"It's a little late for that," I mutter.

The clanging of swords rings out below me. I shift into a sitting position and peer over the edge. Macy and Solomon are still locked in battle.

Macy's lips tilt into a snarl, an expression I've never associated with her. She drives her boot into Solomon's gut, ramming him backward. He reels on the edge of the cloud, arms windmilling, back severely arched. My breath catches in my throat. Macy advances and cuts at him with her blade. Solomon blocks, but the force of the attack sends him tumbling off the cloud. My breath remains locked in my chest. If he dies...

Macy looks up. Her face darkens, and with agility only befitting a world such as this, she leaps up to join me on my perch. I scramble backward, still clutching my throbbing ribs.

Her lips tilt down in a pout. "Poor, little Gweny, what will you do without your Guardian?"

"He's not my Guardian. He's yours." I'm almost at the end of the cloud now. "What's going on, Macy?"

Her expression transforms into something dark and dangerous. "I'm going to enjoy this."

I scan the surrounding sky for Solomon, but he's nowhere to be found. He can't be gone. He can't be.

Her lip curls. "You always were clueless. You don't even know what's going on."

Can she blame me? All I know is my best friend in all the world has a murderous look in her eyes. Blame it on the loss of her brother or this crazy place, but whatever the case, I need to escape.

If Macy can pull a sword out of thin air, maybe I can find a way to defend myself. I dig my fingers into the cloud and rip off a chunk. I hurl it into her face.

While she claws at the fluff, I turn and jump for the next cloud. Macy's screech follows me, sending chills down my arms. I leap from one shaky platform to another. Macy follows behind me, her blade only ever one breath beyond reach.

"Gwen." Solomon crashes into my side. His arms wrap around me, and I cling to him. He sends us flying through the air.

We slam into another cloud and roll until I land on top of Solomon. The Guardian stares into the sky, motionless, eyes wide.

"Solomon?" I shake him.

He inhales sharply, blinks, and pushes me away. "We need to get out of here."

"What about Macy?" I scan the surrounding area for the mad woman. My hair has fallen free, and I use a hand to sweep it out of my face.

"Gwen, look out." For the second time, Solomon tackles me, only this time we don't go skittering into a freefall, we merely slam to the hard surface of the cloud.

Pain explodes through my back, and the air above me hisses when Macy's blade sweeps over my head. I kick out at her, catching her in the knee. She stumbles backward, and the cloud vibrates beneath us.

Solomon links his fingers through mine and pulls me to my feet. "Jump." He tugs me forward, and we leap from the cloud. It explodes in tiny fragments behind us.

Chapter Ten

We crash through one of the windows lining the sky-scraper. Glass shatters around me, landing in my hair, slicing my hand. The impact punches the air from my lungs, and I lay curled on the tile floor. Solomon eases to a sitting position and leans over me. Dust and glass coat his hair and a red line curves over his cheek. "Gwen?" His gaze snags on mine, concern darkening his eyes.

I don't move, joints locked tight. "What was that?"

He leans his head against the wall, panting. "It was a Nightmare." He runs a hand through his hair, sending slivers of glass to the floor.

I snort, swiping at my cheek. "Yeah, I got that." My fingers come away with a streak of red.

"No. *She* was a Nightmare." He searches my face. "It wasn't her. It wasn't Macy."

No, because she wouldn't act that way. Still… "It looked like her."

"They do that sometimes. They're a nasty bunch, Night-mares. Sometimes they wear masks into the dreams. That's why she looked like Macy."

Not Macy. I draw in a breath, and my heartrate slows. I sit up and scooch next to Solomon. Fire shoots through my ribs as I prop myself against the wall. "What did she want from me?"

He shrugs. "To make you afraid. The more afraid you are, the stronger they become. That's why there are Guardians. We save Dreamers from the beasts."

I press my sleeve to the cut on my cheek. "Is that why people usually wake up at the scariest parts of dreams?"

"You catch on quickly." He brushes a thumb down my cheek, sending a tingling sensation over my skin. "We should clean that."

"It's not that bad." Besides, what about the cuts lining his skin?

Solomon searches my face for several seconds before he holds out a hand. "Ready to find Macy?"

My heart bangs like drumsticks against a cymbal, and I shrink backward.

His lips twitch in a sympathetic smile. "The real Macy. The last one was just a distraction. She's here somewhere."

Right. Of course. I place my hand in his and allow him to pull me to my feet. Pain burns in my chest with each breath.

His brow wrinkles. "Are you all right?"

I rub a particularly achy bone. "Just a little sore."

"Let's hope the Dream resets soon." Solomon picks his way through the room which looks like it should belong in an apocalyptic movie. Pieces of furniture are strewn about, and random sheets of paper rustle over the carpet, pushed by the breeze drifting through the broken window. A musty smell clings to the area.

I limp after Solomon, struggling to breathe slowly to avoid causing my ribs to ache any more than they already do.

The Dream Guardian steps into the hall. The long passage is equally grimy, and the place is still. Too still. Broken glass crunches under my combat boots with each small step I take down the abandoned corridor. Yellowed wallpaper peels from the walls and is patterned with dark mold. Doors hang from loose hinges, and the ceiling appears to be on the verge of collapse. A shiver crawls down my spine, and I edge closer to Solomon. He leads the way to an aged elevator and pries the screeching doors open before he turns to me, waiting.

I eye the rust-spotted thing. "Yeah, I think I'll take the stairs."

"We don't have time." He motions for me to enter the deathtrap.

I cross my arms and raise an eyebrow. "Do you know how many dreams I've had about being stuck in an elevator? There's no way I'm getting in there."

All jovial remnants flee from his expression. "Macy could be in all kinds of trouble. Get in."

Further arguments swirl through my mind, but Solomon's jaw clenches so tight, it's not hard to imagine him tossing me over his shoulder. I enter the rickety elevator, and the thing groans. I lick my lips. Solomon steps inside, allowing the doors to snap shut. The floor dips beneath our feet at his added weight. Sweat pools on my palms.

"You're sure about this?" My stomach tightens at the thought of this metal tomb moving.

"You'll be fine." He flashes me a smile and punches his thumb into one of the many buttons dotting the walls that were probably shiny at some point in their lives. I hold my breath. Nothing happens.

Okay, we really should get out of here.

I take a step toward the doors, but Solomon stops me with an outheld arm. He kicks the control panel, and a faint glow pulses through the buttons.

"I really don't think—" My words cut off when the elevator gives one protesting screech and drops downward. My stomach flips. I grip Solomon's sleeve as we fly down. The pounding of my pulse doesn't settle until the elevator reaches the ground floor and gives a halfhearted ding. The doors rasp open, coughing us into the belly of an abandoned mall.

As so often happens in dreams, the setting shifts slightly, and I find myself standing on a rectangular platform with sides sloping down into pits of blackness. I'm still standing in the abandoned mall, but the elevator is gone and so is Solomon.

"Solomon?" My voice echoes through the empty building. I shiver, wishing with everything inside me for the presence of a boy in a silly white lab coat.

I spin in a circle, but everything is separated from me by the black trenches surrounding my perch. I suck in a few breaths and tuck some wayward strands of hair behind my ears. The rest of my hair is tied up in a bun that wasn't there before. All markings on my skin have faded as has the throbbing in my ribs. I have to stay calm. Find Solomon.

"Don't stand out, and whatever you do, don't die." His words play through my head.

Right. I can do this.

I eye the distance between me and the tiled floor of the mall. If I jump, will I make it? My stomach flops. If I miss, I'll fall into who knows what. I have to risk it. My pulse slams in my veins, but I brace my feet. Lick my lips. I've got one shot at this, or I might end up breaking Solomon's second rule for the Dream.

I race to the edge of the platform and spring forward, putting all I have into the jump. For one glorious moment, I sail forward and then I drop toward the dark abyss. My arms and legs flail. My hands slap against the yellowed tiles, and I scramble for a hold. I kick my legs against the air and dig my fingernails into the grout. The sweat on my palms leaves streaks on the floor as I slip toward the black trench below me. No, no, no! I grit my teeth and drag my fingernails. My sleeve snags on the chipped edge of a tile, slowing me enough that I can get one leg over the edge. From there, it only takes a bit of maneuvering until I'm lying on my stomach, safe from the darkness. Man, do my abs burn.

For a long moment, I suck in calming breaths, allowing my pulse to slow to its normal beat—or at least something resembling it. When some of the adrenaline eases from my body, I crawl to my feet and trudge past storefronts with broken windows and scattered merchandise. A hair-raising stillness clings to the building.

I shiver. "Solomon?"

How is it possible that we came down together, and now I can't find him anywhere?

I reach a pair of heavy doors leading out into bright sunshine and an empty parking lot. Yes! If I can get outside, maybe I can find help. Maybe Hunter or Josie is out there somewhere.

When I press against the doors, they refuse to budge. I search for a lock, but nothing reveals itself. This can't be right. I drive the heel of my boot into the door. The glass doesn't so much as shake beneath my kick. I ram it once. Twice. Three times, and not so much as a rattle. I slap my palm against the glass and turn away. What now?

Somewhere in the abandoned mall, a gunshot rings out.

I dive behind a decaying fern and cower there, ears ringing. I fight back a whimper and do my best to wrap myself into as small of a shape as I can manage. I have to stay calm. Maybe if I stay low, the danger will pass, and Solomon will find me.

Shouts ring out from somewhere above me, and then a man tumbles down from the level above. His body slams into the tiles mere feet from my hiding place. He hits with such force that the tiles cave from the impact, sending small shards flying. I throw my arms up to cover my face. Small tinkling sounds dance through the air while the pieces find new homes, along with a heavy layer of dust.

When the world settles, I glance up.

A girl with long blonde hair dashes down an out of order escalator, her pink sweater marred with grime and blood.

Macy.

Another shot rings out, and Macy ducks, arms covering her head. I start to call out, but the words lodge in my throat. How can I be sure this is the real Macy? She could be another trick of the Dream.

"Hurry, Macy." This shout comes from the level above me. The words are tinged with a British accent.

I lean forward. Solomon grapples with an armed man.

Macy's pace increases, sending her skidding onto her bottom on the out-of-order escalator.

A third henchman appears behind her. More voices ring through the mall. I lick my lips. I have to take a chance and believe this girl struggling to get back to her feet is the real deal.

I slip from my hiding spot. "Macy. Over here."

Her face lights with relief, and she races in my direction with a heavy-set creep on her heels.

I hold out my hand, and she snatches it, slipping her fingers around mine. Our shoes drum against the ground. Their rhythm melds with the huffing breath of the man behind us, and the noises hash out a beat that matches the adrenaline coursing through my body.

I veer toward a second set of doors leading out of the mall, but they only drift further and further from reach. Not good. I jerk Macy to the left and make a dash for the doorway of an abandoned store. If we can buy ourselves some time, maybe we can hide. Wait for Solomon to catch up. I slam into an invisible barrier and careen backward. No. I try again, and a pang shoots through my lip. Blood flavors my mouth. No good. I tug Macy away, the precious lead we had evaporating.

Time for a change of plans.

I yank Macy toward the platform in the center of the mall. With any luck, the henchman won't be able to make the jump. But if he can, we'll be trapped, and none of that will matter anyway if this guy's armed. I shake the thought away. With nowhere else to run, it's our best shot.

"Come on," I say, but Macy keeps stumbling, slowing down our escape.

I tighten my grip around her fingers and brace my feet when we approach the edge leading to the black slopes. I leap, taking her with me. My fingers come within a breath of the platform, but then Macy's weight pulls me down, and I'm falling. Cold sweat prickles my skin, and my stomach slips to my toes. My scream mixes with Macy's.

Chapter Eleven

I slam to the ground. Sharp bursts of pain fly through my tailbone and up my neck at the impact. Macy coughs beside me. More gunfire sounds above us.

Solomon.

My heart clenches.

How will I ever get home if he doesn't make it? Wait, no, I can't think that way. If I let fear take over, then this battle is over, and we don't stand a chance. I take a breath. First things first, assess for injuries and then plan. I don't have time to worry about Solomon. Macy has to be my first priority. I tighten my hold on her hand. She squeezes, letting me know she's all right, and we clamber to our feet.

"I think I see a light." Macy pulls me after her. Her steps are shaky, but she presses onward.

I stumble to keep up.

Grunts sound behind us when somebody or somebodies hit the ground. Feet pound after us. We've got to get out of here. Now.

"Faster." I push a hand against Macy's back. She trips, and I have to catch her elbow to keep her from falling. Is she hurt? It's impossible to tell in this darkness.

And then a light illuminates from behind us, and I run faster, practically dragging Macy behind me. She teeters sideways. I catch her, but it slows us down. The light pulls closer. Something brushes my back. I yelp and swing around, ready to fight, but instead I find myself looking into Solomon's face, illuminated by the stupid little flashlight he keeps in his pocket. Although I guess I can't call it stupid anymore since it's the only thing we have to guide us right now. Tears surge into my eyes at his presence, and I have to stifle the urge to hug him. He's all right, he's with us, and I'm not alone.

"Don't stop." He pulls me forward.

We charge toward the small splash of light in the distance, and I find myself skidding into a dimly lit parking garage. And there, sitting where we left it, is Solomon's car. He shoves me toward the driver's side.

"Get in."

Get in? "No, no, no." I shake my head. "I don't know how to drive."

He's not listening, but instead lifts a pale Macy into his arms. Blood dribbles down her temple. A chill cuts through me. She must have hit her head when we fell.

On shaky legs, I dash to the car and yank the door open. I slide behind the wheel and then just sit there. Now what? A whimper pulls at my throat. There's no way I can do this. Solomon shoves Macy into the backseat before leaping into the passenger side.

"What are you waiting for? Go!" He drums a fist against the dashboard.

"I don't know how to drive." I grip the steering wheel like I would Solomon's neck if I could afford to choke him.

He stares at me with wide eyes. "I'm on probation. It won't start for me."

And that's supposed to make me feel better? My palms turn sweaty against the leather wheel.

He takes my hand and makes me turn the key. The car revs to life. "See that pedal? Slam it against the floor." He cranes backward to see behind us.

I do as he instructs, and with screeching tires, we lunge forward.

Gunfire rips through the air. Bullets pelt the car. I hunch forward. The back window explodes, sending glass flying. Macy screams in the backseat, rolling so she is wedged between the two rows of seats. A spray of used Styrofoam cups springs up, sending drops of coffee flying.

I yank the steering wheel to the right, twisting the car into a sharp turn. My sweaty hands slip along the leather, and I tighten my fingers until my knuckles turn white. A wheel lifts off the ground, and the car accelerates as we rush down a ramp and deeper into the belly of the parking garage.

Heavy breathing on my right draws my attention to Solomon. He's got his head tilted back against his chair. He looks toward the ceiling, and sweat collects on his brow and upper lip. I scan lower. He has a hand clasped around his bicep. Blood seeps between his fingers. So. Much. Blood.

My mouth runs dry. "S-Solomon?"

He glances at me, and his face grows paler in the dim light offered by the glowing console. "Eyes on the road, Gonzales."

Right. I yank my gaze back to the windshield. A large cement column rises ahead in the darkness. A cry clambers up my throat and lodges there without time to escape. I slam my foot against the brake. The thing flops uselessly against the floorboards, and the car speeds on. I yank the steering wheel to the side. Too hard. The vehicle slams into a second support. Metal crunches against cement. My head strikes the steering wheel and bounces back against the headrest. Flames of sizzling pain streak through my neck while smoke wheezes from the hood.

Solomon fumbles with the door handle, leaving bloody smears behind. "Everyone out."

With sponge-like limbs, I manage to obey the order and spill out of the car. Macy crawls out of the back.

The Dream Guardian stares at his car, eyes wide. "No, no, no..." He runs his fingers through his hair.

I grip my arm and press my lips together for a moment before I dare to speak, "I told you I can't drive."

He whirls to face me. "You're seventeen."

"Yeah, and when Mom doesn't have the car at work, it's sitting in the shop. When exactly was I supposed to learn?" I cross my arms and raise my eyebrows, daring him to present a stronger argument.

"Stop it." Macy moves between us. "We don't have time for this. Those guys are still coming."

True to her words, tires screech above us.

I lock gazes with the guy whose car I just destroyed.

He glares like he wishes he could do anything but spend more time with me, but he sets his jaw. He grabs Macy's hand with his bloody one, and charges forward, leaving it up to me whether or not I want to follow.

I jog to catch up and take Macy's other hand. She leans into my support, and I can only imagine the headache she must have. Her cheek is coated with blood dripping from the wound at her temple. Head wounds bleed a lot. Everything's going to be fine. One time, Tommy smacked his head on the kitchen floor, and it felt like he'd bleed to death, but he'd been fine. This would turn out like that.

The rumble of tires screeches closer.

Thank goodness for the shelter of darkness. Our group isn't nearly fast enough to escape the gunmen on our own. Loose gravel churns under our boots, making our downhill descent hazardous. We're only aided by the small streams of light dancing through cracks in the crumbling structure of the parking garage. Time is marked by the huffing of breath coming from my two injured comrades, until Solomon falls to his haunches with a groan. Macy slips down beside him, touching a trembling hand to her forehead. I squat in front of them. They both look dreadfully pale in the dim light.

"We're done." I lick away the beads of sweat clinging to my upper lip and suck in a few breaths.

Solomon shakes his head. Tries to stand.

I place my hand on his knee, keeping him down. "We're done. You need to rest."

"No, I'm fine." His dark eyes hold pain, but he tries to rise once more and looks at anything but me.

Time to change tactics. I slide a glance in Macy's direction. "Macy needs rest."

His wandering attention fixes on her closed eyelids. "All right." He sags down once more.

Problem solved. I ease to the ground. "We should clean your wounds."

"No kidding." Solomon snorts and flings out a hand to gesture at our surroundings. "Do you see a hospital around here?"

I clench my hands. He's wounded, he's entitled to a little grumpiness.

He mirrors Macy's posture by leaning his head against the wall, eyes squeezed shut. I brush my hair behind my ears and study my companions. Solomon's left sleeve is dark in the weak light. Saturated with blood. Macy's cheek is streaked with more dark liquid than before.

Solomon's deep breathing fills the space between us. I risk edging forward and slip my hand into the pocket of his lab coat. My fingers brush against the handle of his flashlight, and I dig deeper. My skin collides with a pile of candy wrappers. I brush them away and bump into a small wooden handled object. A pocket knife? I wiggle the thing free, and a smile tugs at my lips. Nice. I pull the knife blade free, lean closer to Solomon, and lift the edge of his t-shirt. My fingers sweep against his hot torso. Should he be this warm?

His eyelashes flutter. "Hands off, Gonzales."

"Shush." I take the blade to the thin material of his t-shirt. The piece tears easily, and I wrap the fabric around the graze wound. What would I do if the bullet was lodged inside his flesh? I shudder. Thank goodness it isn't. The Dream Guardian groans when I tie off the bandage and move to Macy. After a brief inspection, it seems like the bleeding from her head has stopped, leaving a sticky mess in its place. That has to be good, right? If Mom were here, she'd probably insist on the wound being cleaned, but with no water to wash away the blood, I let Macy rest. I sit beside her and lean my head against the filthy wall.

The parking garage rumbles with the sound of our pursuers. I slip my fingers around Macy's and press them. She offers a squeeze of her own, and a lump settles in my throat. I move my head to her shoulder.

An image of the burly, mafia-style attackers flashes through my mind. What will they do if they find us? I have little hope we'll be able to outrun them at this point.

Squealing tires sound behind us. Everything in me jolts, and I glance over my shoulder.

A black van screeches to a halt, and several burly men clamber out, weapons drawn.

"Run." I nudge Macy forward. Solomon stares at the van, and I have to give him a shove to get him moving.

He stumbles forward, lurching like a dog with an injured hindleg. His entire sleeve is covered in blood now, despite my makeshift bandage. We don't have much time if the shade of his skin is anything to judge by.

"Faster." I push him deeper into the shadows. Gunfire cracks through the parking garage. Puffs of cement shatter when the bullets hit the ground, the walls. My ears ring, throwing me off balance.

Solomon stumbles and falls to his knees. He clutches his bad arm, and thick streams of red pool over his fingers. Not good. I push Macy onward and turn and grab fistfuls of the Dream Guardian's lab coat, yanking him to his feet.

"Come on." I hold his gaze. I can't do this without him.

His chin bobs, though there's no telling if the action is voluntary or a symptom of his blood loss. Doesn't matter. I'm taking the gesture as a yes.

Solomon sways in my grasp, but I steer him down a patch of sloped gravel which leads to the next level of darkness. Anything to escape the gunmen.

The gravel shifts and churns beneath my boots. My free arm spins as I fight to maintain my balance. Macy stumbles ahead of us, and her foot twists. With a small yelp, my friend crumples to the rocky floor. Solomon's knees give out, and I lose my grip. He tumbles the rest of the way down, eyes pulled shut.

"No!" Macy struggles to her feet and careens down after him, barely staying upright herself. She reaches him and rolls him onto his back. His eyelids flutter, and he blinks at her.

A bullet sprays the gravel beside me.

I duck. "Keep going." I yell to my friends who are taking their own little time getting themselves together.

Solomon looks up at me, face covered in sweat, eyes glassy in the small stream of light. His mouth hangs open like he can hear me but can't comprehend my words.

I slide to a stop beside him. "Go."

He crawls to his knees as if every movement hurts him.

Macy retches in a dark corner.

This isn't going to work.

I kneel in front of Solomon and clutch his clammy cheeks between my palms. "Get Macy out of here." I slide my gaze toward a dark passage.

He follows my stare.

"Can you do that?" I press gently on his face, drawing his focus once more.

His eyes search mine.

I force myself to smile. "I'll catch up."

"Gwen, no." His words are slurred.

"Don't worry, I know the rules." But my heartrate kicks up a tempo.

He grabs my wrist, but I pry his fingers loose.

"Take care of Macy." And with that, I get to my feet and dash up the slope and to the right, making sure light catches on me briefly.

"Over there!" Heavy footsteps sound behind me.

I keep low and to the shadows while I run, but this section of the parking garage hosts many slits and holes in its structure, allowing dusty light to float in, exposing me to the searching eyes of the Nightmares.

Shots ring out. I do my best to weave my way between pillars and behind abandoned cars, but they are sparse and only offer shelter for a moment. My breathing hitches. I have to get them farther from Macy and Solomon.

Be a little bit of a Guardian myself.

I take a moment with my back pressed to a pillar. Squeeze my eyes shut. It might mean breaking one of Solomon's rules, but if that's what it takes, that's what it takes. Inhale. Exhale. Open my eyes.

Let's go.

I dash toward a pair of steel doors, but my foot catches in a divot, and my knee twists. Fire spasms through my limb. I lurch forward, and manage to catch myself with my hands and avoid a faceplant. Boots pound behind me. I scramble to my feet and limp toward the doors. My injured knee quivers.

The cocking of a gun echoes through the empty space.

I swivel.

A bullet explodes from the barrel.

Fire pulsates in my chest, and blood blossoms through my sweater. My legs give out, and I collapse. I lay there, panting like a dog in summer. Who knew it was possible to feel this cold?

A large man with scars knotting his face approaches. Dust covers the toes of his combat boots. Boots that slam into my side, sending me rolling down a graveled slope. The little stones grind their way into the bullet hole, and agony flares through my chest.

I land on my stomach with my cheeks pressed to the ground. My eyelids grow heavy as if entranced by the sound of a thousand lullabies.

Chapter Twelve

I'm being swallowed by a dark abyss. It's like sinking in an ocean made by a black marker. I trail my hand through the dark waves beside me. Bright strokes of light cut through the shadows.

Beautiful.

I use my toes to leave similar lines behind me while I continue to sail through the empty space. The dark fades away, replaced by strokes of golden light. I laugh. Brilliant. Beautiful. I'm almost weightless. As if I'm no heavier than a drop of water. A silver dress clads my body, equally buoyant. The softness of the fabric rivals even the most comfortable pajamas in my closet.

An incessant beeping fills the smooth stillness, interrupting the peace of the moment,

And then the voices come.

"We're losing her."

"Doctor!"

Who needs a doctor? There's no one here but me.

Convulsions rock my body. Over and over, my torso contracts, folding in on itself and then springing apart. The beeping intensifies.

The hazy image of a middle-aged woman dances in front of me. *"Hold on, honey. Just hold on."*

An electronic buzzing blocks the beeping and the panicked voices.

"Clear."

A hot white light explodes in front of my eyes.

I'm tumbling, head first, flipping through a tunnel of darkness. There's no air to scream. My mouth works, but no oxygen enters or exits my lungs. I claw at the blackness, but there's no slowing my speed. I squeeze my eyes shut and dig my fingernails into my palms while my heart slams frantically in my chest. How long until the delicate organ shatters under the assault?

I slam into a stone floor. Pain spikes through my knees and elbows. Maybe I should have a broken something, but I don't, bless the Dream. A circular room with arches carved into the walls surrounds me. Crackling torches illuminate the dark, musty area, adding a hint of warmth to the place. Goosebumps rise along my arms. The entire room reeks of death.

"Ah, Gwendolyn Gonzales, so glad you could join me." A skeleton of a man walks toward me. His scraggly white hair hangs around his shoulders, and long, gray fingernails tap against his dark pants.

I ease to my feet and stumble back a pace. "What do you want?" My lungs constrict, limiting my air.

His cracked lips part, revealing yellow, crooked teeth. "Why, my dear, I'm here for you." He takes a step forward.

I retreat until my back hits a stone wall. A torch warms my cheek, its snapping flames matching the frantic rise and fall of my breathing. My knees shake.

The man laughs, but it sounds more like he's choking on his own spittle. His yellow eyes narrow. "Oh, darling, this is going to be quite fun."

My throat goes dry, and I press tighter against the wall. "I-I'm not afraid of you."

"No?" He pauses, head tilted to the side. "You should be." He coughs into his pale fist, and his entire body shakes under the effort it takes for him to clear his lungs.

What can this frail man do? I raise my chin. "I'm not."

His eyes narrow, and his posture takes on a threatening tilt. "Then fear these." He throws his hands up, and winged skeleton heads spill from his fingertips, all rushing at me, teeth chattering, spewing hateful words.

"Stupid."

"Worthless."

"Idiot."

"Lazy."

"I wish you'd never been born!"

I cower with my hands pressed to my ears in an effort to block out their cries. They only scream louder, filling my head with their poison. Skulls pelt me. Each time one hits my skin, searing pain engulfs me.

I scream along with the skulls, my voice blurring with theirs, "Solomon!"

Chapter Thirteen

C ool fingers brush my skin.

I lay unmoving, knees pulled to my chest, hands smashed to my ears. My breaths come in shallow gasps. I tremble, and tears burn my eyes. I want this to be over. I just want this to be over so I can go home.

"Gwen." Solomon brushes tendrils of hair off my damp forehead.

I fight to control the trembling of my chin. It doesn't work. A whimper creeps past the suppressed sobs forming an ache in my chest. Solomon slips his hands under my back and knees, and lifts me into his strong arms. My gaze finds the old man backing from the room, a hand pressed to his bleeding shoulder. I close my eyes, and memories of his fight with Solomon surface. The howl of pain when Solomon's sword dug into the fiend's flesh. With a soft hiccup, I turn my face into Solomon's collar.

"This isn't over," the old man hisses.

"You won't touch her again," Solomon retorts, arms tightening around me.

I dare a look at the skeletal creature across from us.

A hoarse cackle rasps from the man's decaying lips. "If you'd done your job right, I wouldn't have."

The Dream Guardian bristles and hefts me higher.

The man shimmers and fades, but his cackling echoes through the air. Before long, he vanishes completely.

Solomon cradles me close as the rest of the dream begins to crumble and disappear. I cling to him and breathe in his coffee scent. The aroma wraps around me, easing the tension in my body and replacing it with a deep nostalgia that whispers I am safe. Protected. A feeling I haven't associated with the smell in a long time.

The ceiling lightens and shifts to a welcoming white.

"You're trembling," Solomon says.

And I can't stop. Images of the skeleton heads flash through my mind. I squeeze my eyes shut and press my face tighter against Solomon's shoulder. His grip doesn't loosen, and I allow his rhythmic breathing to soothe my racing heart. Ever so slowly, the rigidness of my body relaxes, and my heartbeat steadies.

"You're safe, I promise." Solomon whispers into my ear.

I tighten my fingers around his lapel. "Where's Macy?"

He readjusts his grip. "Awake. For now."

I nod against his shoulder. Good. I'd rather not deal with her greatest fears right now.

The rest of the dream has shredded, and we stand in the center of Solomon's apartment. He eases me onto his couch, and I curl up like a small child. The cool leather sticks to my flushed cheek.

He paces back and forth, his shoes squeaking over the tiles. He shoves his fingers through his hair and spins to face me. "What happened?"

I shake my head.

He kneels beside me and takes my hand in his. "Please, Gwen. I need to know."

I whisper the story of the dark place with the gold streaks, and then, the moments before his arrival.

Solomon shoves a hand through his hair again. "This is all my fault. I should have been there."

I push myself to a sitting position, and my head throbs. "Sol—"

"I should have protected you."

I lick my lips. Force a smile. "You were wounded. Besides, your job is to protect Macy, not me."

His gaze slides away. "Macy. Right."

"I'm fine. He didn't hurt me."

Solomon's stare turns back to me, sorrow filling his eyes. "I'm sorry I wasn't there."

"Solomon, I'm all right, and you showed up when I needed you the most. I'd say that was a job well done, wouldn't you?"

He ducks his head.

This isn't over.

I shiver. "Did he mean it?"

"Mean what?" Now he looks me in the eye.

"The guy...look, I know he's just a figment of the Dream, and there's little to no overlap, but—"

Solomon snags my hand. "He's more than that Gwen. He's very, very dangerous."

"Who is he?"

"Coakley. Lord of the Nightmares."

The breath is stolen from my lungs, and my fingers go numb against Solomon's.

He rubs his thumb over my knuckles. "Listen to me. I'll never, never let him touch you again."

"But he could?" I choke out the question.

Solomon releases a heavy breath and slumps against the couch. "Nightmares exist in the Dream much the same way Dream Guardians do. Except where our calling is to protect, theirs is to destroy."

Goosebumps prickle my arms. "I want to go home."

"You can't." Solomon rubs his hands over his face.

"Solomon, please. I don't want some freaking Lord of the Nightmares stalking me!"

"I can't take you back!"

I jump at the volume of his voice.

But it isn't anger in his eyes when he looks at me. It's sorrow. Maybe guilt.

"What do you mean?" I force my voice to be calm.

"I can't take you back until my probation is lifted." He slams his fist against the little box at his ankle. "My vehicle is programmed not to start if I'm at the wheel with this thing on."

"Maybe Hunter or Josie—"

"No. It has to be me. I'm the one who brought you here."

"There has to be some way!"

"It's either the car, or if something happens to me..." He picks at a thread on his jeans.

"What do you mean?"

"If I die, well...then you get to go home."

I stiffen. "That's not the kind of solution I was looking for."

He lifts a shoulder in a shrug.

"Well, then how do we get your probation lifted?"

"We prove that we can help Macy, and if we can do it without any further incidents, then Watcher will have to remove his thumb."

"Okay, then that's what we'll do."

Our gazes hold.

Solomon ducks his head. "Gwen—"

"That's what we'll do," I repeat it like a mantra. Like if I say it enough times, it will soak into my bones, and nothing will be able to hold us back.

He opens his mouth to say something, but a harsh buzz cuts him off. His head snaps toward the door.

"Is something wrong?" I ask.

I can't be sure, but I think he mutters something under his breath as he scrambles off the floor.

"Solomon?" I half rise from the couch, but then he's pulling the door open, and a herd of people push inside, Watcher in the lead.

"Custos. You're being brought in for questioning. Resist, and I'll be forced to sedate you," Watcher snaps.

Two Guardians grab Solomon's arms roughly and shove him toward the threshold.

I spring off the couch. "Stop!"

Watcher eyes me. "Peznic, stay with the girl."

Hunter slinks around the others and enters the apartment. I want to yell at him for being part of this, but if my dad's time in the military has taught me anything, it's that a good soldier follows orders, so instead I focus on the man giving the commands

"You have to stop. Solomon hasn't done anything wrong."

Watcher steps up to meet me and jabs a beefy finger in my face. "You stay out of things you don't understand, girly."

Girly? Of all the condescending...

He jerks his chin at the Guardians manhandling Solomon, and they yank him out the door.

"Solomon!" I lunge for him.

Hunter catches me and pulls me back. "He'll be all right, just let him go."

I kick at Hunter's shins, but he tightens his hold and rotates me so I don't have enough space to strike him.

"Stay here, Gwen, I'll be all right," Solomon calls, but his voice is distant like they've already got him halfway down the hall.

"Miss Gonzales." Watcher nods and swivels on his heel, marching out the door.

One of his lackeys pulls the door shut with a soft click, leaving me with Hunter. He releases me.

Forget about following orders. "How could you just let them take him?"

"We don't have a choice, Gwen. It's protocol."

"So, they can just manhandle someone from their own house?"

"I'll admit, Watcher's tactics can be a bit...rough. Especially when it comes to Solomon."

"What's his problem?" I cross my arms and glare at the door like my stare will somehow penetrate through and stab Watcher in the back.

Hunter drops to the couch and massages a hand over his face. "He's just worried about Solomon defecting."

That stills me, and I drop onto the cushion beside him. "Defecting to what?"

Hunter grimaces and rubs his palms together.

"Defecting to what?" I add more demand to my tone.

His gaze flicks to mine and then away. "The Nightmares."

"That's ridiculous." I don't even have the words to follow up on that suggestion.

"The Nightmares have stolen some of our best Guardians over the years."

"Solomon would never."

"I know. But Watcher isn't convinced." Hunter shakes his head before he heaves a sigh that rumbles through his entire frame. "He's hard on all of us. But especially hard on Solomon."

"But why?"

Hunter clasps his hands between his knees. "Because he believes Solomon may someday be able to take over running...well, everything."

Chapter Fourteen

Time crawls by as we wait for Solomon's return.

"Are you sure this is just routine?" I gnaw on a hangnail as I pace the living room for what must be the hundredth time.

"Completely." Hunter sits sprawled out on the couch, ankles crossed and hands folded over his chest like an old guy dozing off while watching tv.

"But what are they doing to him?" It's the unknown that's killing me. How long? What are they doing? And Hunter's not being terribly helpful about any of it.

"Listen, they've probably got him hooked up to a lie detector and are going backwards and forwards through everything that's happened since he brought you in. And then everything with the gunmen, and then Coakley making an appearance..." Hunter shrugs.

"But it's not his fault!"

Hunter unfolds and leans forward, everything about him turning serious. "Listen."

Ugh, not that word again. Next time I pick a motivational learn-from-it-type word, it's going to be something like 'speak out'. Well, that's two words, but whatever.

"The moment Solomon brought you into the Dream, you became his responsibility. Anything you do that goes wrong reflects back on him. Watcher didn't like that he let you go off on your own, knowing the dangers, and obviously, it didn't end well."

"He was shot. I'd like to see how Watcher performs with a bullet in his arm."

Hunter chuckles.

"It's not funny," I snap.

"No, but it seems Solomon's found a Guardian of his own."

This doesn't sit well, so I shrug it off and conjure up a picture of Austin instead. Those dreamy caramel curls...

"Gwen." Hunter's voice pulls me back to the here and now.

Heat blasts across my face. I flop onto the couch. "Okay, so what do I do?"

"Keep your head down, and obey the rules."

"I didn't have a—"

"Choice. I know. You did the best you could have done in a difficult circumstance. Nobody is blaming you."

"But they're blaming Solomon."

Hunter sighs. "Look. It's not fair, I'll agree with you there, but if you want to help Solomon, do everything he tells you, and whatever you do, don't wander off on your own. Neither of you can afford another incident like the last one."

"And if this Nightmare Lord shows up again?" Even the thought sends shivers up and down my arms. I tug the ends of my sleeves over my hands.

"He won't." Hunter squeezes my knee. "Neither Watcher nor Solomon will let that happen. He's on your side, you know."

"Solomon?" I raise an eyebrow. I never would have believed it that first day, but now I know he would protect me.

"Watcher."

I prickle at the name but force myself to breathe evenly. "Forgive me if I doubt that."

Hunter just shakes his head. "You hungry?"

"I don't want to go out." I cross my arms and slump further into the couch cushions.

"I'm sure Solomon has something around here that's edible."

"Yeah, cereal and coffee." Shelves stocked with what must be every brand and flavor of coffee, but not a single apple in sight.

"Aw, come on, look on the bright side, there's water, too." He heads for the fridge.

I can't help but laugh.

"Where's the milk?" Hunter pokes his head into the fridge.

"I think we're out again. Solomon uses way too much on that thing." I wave a hand toward the espresso machine that sits too quiet with its owner dragged off to who-knows-where.

Hunter pokes his head out long enough to shoot me a raised eyebrow. "*We're?*"

Crap. Fire engulfs me from my neck to my ears. "Well, I mean, I am staying here."

"Yeah, yeah." He flaps a dismissive hand and makes a bunch of noise as he shuffles through the different compartments.

I reach for a throw pillow and squeeze it against my middle to keep in any more stupid comments.

"Well, this sucks." Hunter pushes the fridge door shut with a disgusted expression.

I hold up my hands. "Hey, don't look at me. You've been around the guy longer than I have. Surely, you could have taught him how to stock a fridge by now."

"That was supposed to be Josie's job." He winks. "Dry cereal it is then."

I don't even try to hold back my groan. "I can't wait until I can taste Nana's cooking again." Maybe I should offer to make muffins again, but it doesn't feel right with Solomon dragged off.

"Bring Solomon with you, maybe she'll teach the guy how to cook."

We share a smile, and then Hunter retrieves a box of cereal from the cabinet and brings it over without even bothering to get bowls.

"Here, make sure to get an extra handful of marshmallows, you deserve it." Hunter holds the box out to me.

"Marshmallows?" But even as I question his command, I obey.

Hunter fiddles with his hands.

I eye him, but don't press.

Finally, he looks at me. "Thank you."

"For what?" I ask before tossing back a handful of sugary junk food that my nana would never allow to be passed off as breakfast at my house.

"Saving Solomon."

I swallow my mouthful. "What do you mean?"

"A Guardian's mission is to always save his Dreamer or die trying. If you hadn't done what you did…" He swallows. "Anyway. Thank you."

"Yeah." I mean, what else can I say? No problem? That seems lame, so I just sit there squirming.

The door opens, and Solomon slides inside. Bags hang under his eyes, and the sleeve of his lab coat is pushed back to reveal a line of small bruises like he's been injected with something.

I wince. What did they do to him? I cross my arms to hold back the fire bubbling to life in my core. Watcher is way out of line here. Can't he take a moment and put himself in Solomon's shoes? I mean, if he has an alternative suggestion about how to handle what happened, I'd love to hear it.

"Thanks, mate." Solomon jerks his chin at Hunter.

They do another one of those man handshakes.

"No problem. You look awful, by the way," Hunter says.

"Eh, Watcher's getting soft in his old age." And yet Solomon rubs at his bruised arm.

"Yeah, like I believe that." Hunter claps him on the shoulder. "Let me know if you need anything." He gives me a chin lift. "Gwen."

"Thanks for staying," I say.

"I meant what I said," he says.

I don't know if he means about staying out of trouble, or thank you for protecting Solomon. Maybe he means all of it. I just smile.

He takes his leave, and Solomon slides the bolt into place behind him.

"You okay?" I ask.

"I'll be fine. Just want to lay down for a bit." He surveys the mess of cereal crumbs. "Unless you need anything?"

"No, I'm fine. You should take the bed this time."

"No, Gwen, that's not nec—"

"You need it more than I do."

"All right, but just for this time." He scratches his mussed hair.

I nod to make him feel better and watch as he shuffles off with one hand pressed against the wall. I squeeze my hands into fists. Whatever Watcher did, it's left Solomon a wreck.

Watcher doesn't want any more mistakes? Fine. I won't give him a single thing to complain about. I'll help Solomon erase any shadow of doubt from the man's mind about Solomon's future as a Guardian. Together we'll save Macy, and Watcher won't be able to say a single word except "well done."

Chapter Fifteen

W hen Solomon emerges from the bedroom, he looks ten times better. "Hey," he says.

"Hey." I push my disheveled hair out of my face and squirm into a sitting position. Ugh. Neck cramp. I massage the sore muscles.

Solomon chuckles.

"What?" I give him the stink-eye.

"You've—" He laughs and points to his cheek. "You've got something here."

I touch my cheek, and lines from having my skin pressed to the couch for so long meet my touch. Marvelous. I rub at my cheek, hoping to erase the marks. Somehow, I don't think I'm succeeding.

"Don't worry about it. You look cu—" He cuts himself off, red creeping up his neck.

I pretend I don't know what he was about to say and instead focus on straightening my sweater.

"So...breakfast at the café?"

"I could eat," I admit.

"After you." He bows and sweeps an arm toward the front door.

Dork. Except when he catches my eye as I pass him, the action suddenly doesn't feel so stupid after all. Something warm stirs to life inside my middle, recognizing the gesture.

Nuh-uh. I'm not doing this. I yank the door open and storm to the elevator. I take out my emotions by jabbing my thumb into the button that opens the doors. A pang sings through my thumbnail. Ouch. I suck on the nail until the pain eases.

Solomon jogs to catch up. "Are you always this grumpy in the morning?"

"Yes." The doors open, and I stomp inside.

Solomon's eyebrows shoot high, but he joins me. "I'll keep that in mind."

With a quiet thrum, the elevator dips into motion.

I lean against the wall and fold my arms over my chest as a barrier between my heart and the Dream Guardian across from me. I'm an idiot for even considering it. It would never work. Besides...I like Austin. Never mind that we haven't had a full conversation. We will. Someday.

"What are you thinking about?" Solomon asks.

Embarrassing. Heat shoots through my face. "Nothing," I snap.

He raises his hands, eyes wide.

Oops. I massage my forehead. "Really, it's nothing."

"Okay."

I bite my lip and stare at the floor.

The elevator creaks and shudders.

The hair on my neck rises. "What was that?"

"I'm sure it's nothing."

Jolt.

We jerk to a halt.

My breathing quakes, and I shake my head. "No, no, no. This can't be happening."

"It's not." Solomon jabs the button for the café again.

Metal screeches, but we don't move.

"We can't be stuck." I reach around him and jab the button for the doors.

Nothing.

Nope. I'm not doing this.

"Don't panic," Solomon says, fiddling with his watch.

"Don't panic? This is like my worst nightmare come to life." I plant my hands on my hips.

"Look, I'm messaging Hunter. He'll get things fixed in no time." Solomon's fingers tap across the surface of his watch.

"Right. Okay, that's good." I rub the back of my neck.

Solomon stills, and we wait.

Time crawls by.

"Well?" I ask.

Solomon shrugs. "Must be with his Dreamer."

Great. Fantastic. I swivel and pace the small, prison-like box.

"Gwen." Solomon snags my wrist and pulls me to a halt. "Hey. No big deal. As soon as his Dreamer wakes, he'll help us get this sorted in no time. The lift will be operational just like that." He snaps his fingers.

"Couldn't you message maintenance or something?"

"They're forever backed up unless you can corner one of them in person, but that's what I've asked Hunter to do." Solomon sits.

I stare down at him. "What are you doing?"

"Settling in to wait." He props his hands behind his head.

"Isn't there something else we can try?"

"Yes. Wait." His eyes sparkle.

Great, I'm entertaining him. With a huff, I drop to the corner opposite him.

"See, that's not so hard."

I cross my arms. "This is not funny."

"It's a little bit funny."

"No. It's. Not." Except my lips twitch.

Solomon nudges my foot with his, and my glare gives way to a grin.

"Fine. It's not that bad." My stomach grumbles.

He winces. "So much for breakfast."

"It's fine. I'm not that hungry." My stomach rumbles, announcing my lie.

"I think…" Solomon fishes through his pockets before coming up with a chocolate bar. He unwraps it, breaks it in half, and hands me the slightly bigger piece.

"Thanks."

We munch on the treat in silence, and when we've licked the last smears of chocolate from out fingertips, Solomon checks his watch.

"Anything?" I try not to sound too eager.

He shakes his head and drops his arm.

My instinct is to whine, but I've done enough of that already, so I scooch closer to Solomon. "Empty your pockets."

He raises an eyebrow.

"We've got to do *something* while we're stuck in here."

He still looks wary, but he turns out his pockets, sending a collection of candy wrappers to the floor.

I scoop up a handful and nod for him to do the same. "Have any reds?" Now I'm the one being a dork, but if the sparkle in his eyes is anything to go by, he doesn't mind.

"No. Go...trash picking?"

I laugh and snag a candy wrapper from the floor.

We play for as long as it takes to run out of wrappers, and Solomon wins with the most of one color.

I'm just about to mix them up again, but Solomon's watch beeps.

"Ah, perfect. I told you things would be fixed in no time. Hunter is on his way to track down maintenance as we speak." Solomon taps something out on his watch before looking at me. "See, not so bad."

"Yeah, okay, it wasn't that bad," I agree. "You were right."

"Oh, wait, I'm sorry, could you say that again?" He taps his ear. "I don't think I heard you right."

I shove his knee. "You'd better hope you heard right, because I am not saying it again."

He catches my hand. Doesn't let go.

My gaze jumps to his, my heart pounding in my chest. What is he doing?

"Gwen, I—"

Ding.

The elevator doors burst open, and then Hunter and a whole crew of people in coveralls are peering down at us.

I tug my hand free from Solomon's and scramble to my feet.

"You all right, mate?" Hunter peers down at Solomon.

He stands and straightens his lab coat. "Fine. Impeccable timing."

Hunter smirks. "Always."

"Bless you." I grab Hunter by his shoulders, plant a kiss on his cheek, and then squeeze past him and the huddle of maintenance workers. "Thank you, thank you all."

They all call out their well-wishes, and I veer for the café.

"You owe us breakfast," Solomon says to Hunter as the pair fall in on either side of me.

"Me? Didn't I save you two back there?" Hunter juts a thumb toward the elevator.

Solomon gives him some serious side-eye. "No, you owe me."

"Um, I'm pretty sure we owe him for life," I interject. "Honestly, I never want to get stuck in one of those things again. I mean who knows how long we would have been stuck in there if it wasn't for Hunter?" I shudder.

"Right. He's the hero," Solomon mutters.

"Show some gratitude." I shove his shoulder.

He laughs and holds up his hands. "All right, all right. Hunter has my eternal gratitude. Better?"

Hunter puffs out his chest. "It's a start."

I roll my eyes and duck inside the café. "Whatever. I'm starving."

$$\times$$

"Gwen." Solomon bends over me, shaking my shoulder.

I lift my head off my folded arm, wincing at the soreness of my neck. Yeesh, I must have taken a longer nap than I meant to. "What?"

"We have to go. Macy needs help."

I mop a hand over my face. Can't the girl go one sleep without dreaming?

He offers his palm, and I allow him to pull me up. He leads the way to the door, but I hesitate. What dangers await us on the other side? Cold seeps through my limbs, and a tremble travels down my fingers.

Solomon turns back, dark eyes searching mine. "Gwen?"

"I'm fine." Right. Totally unafraid. Except my feet are glued to the floor, and I'm okay with that.

"I've got you. I promise." He squeezes my hand.

"I've got you, Gwen. I promise." They're the same words my dad spoke when I jumped into a pool for the first time. He spoke them so many times after that, too. And he was always right.

Solomon tugs my hand. "Come on, you can do it."

I take a shaky breath and force my legs to move. When the door swings open, we step through a burst of light and sparkles and enter a new dream. I find myself standing on bright green grass that stretches to the horizon. Trees dutifully offer an abundance of shade on this sunny day. A cooling breeze whispers over the grass, and a pair of butterflies play tag.

A couple sits on an orange and white checkered blanket. Macy throws her head back, laughing, her blonde strands flitting in the breeze. The face of the boy beside her...I gasp. Macy is dreaming about Elijah? I dart Solomon a questioning look.

He presses a finger to his lips and pulls me behind a tree.

"What's going on?" I ask. "Why is Macy having a picnic with my brother?"

"Not all of Macy's dreams are nightmares." He glances back at the happy couple.

I fight a grimace.

He smirks and leans against the tree. "What's the matter? Don't like the idea of your brother and best friend getting together?"

I mimic his crossed arms. "I don't care if they date." Now that I've thought about it, they'd actually make a cute couple. "I just can't believe I didn't know Macy likes him." Did she tell Beck? I shift, not liking the squirmy feeling in my gut that reeks a little bit too much of jealousy.

He shrugs and takes a peek at the pair. "I'm glad she's finally having a good dream."

Warmth surges through my chest, and I straighten. "Does this mean I get to go home now?" Maybe we've done it. With this dream, Watcher can't possibly have anything to complain about.

Solomon winces. "Not quite yet."

"But—"

"Patience, Gonzales."

I roll my eyes and huff a breath. If all Macy is dreaming about is snuggling with my brother in a setting that could be straight from a fairytale, what is the point of even being here? "I want to go home, Solomon."

He leans toward Macy.

"Macy looks perfectly happy. I mean, how many days have I been here anyway? What if my mom tries calling me or runs across Macy at the coffee shop or something?" Surely by now, Mom and Nana are ready to have me back, and I can't imagine the twins haven't asked for me. Or heck, what about school? It can't still be the weekend back home, can it? It feels like I've been trapped here for a lifetime. And I never called Elijah back. By now, he'll think I'm mad at him or something, that or he'll be worried enough to get Mom digging for information, and that all leads back to me not being where I should be.

He still doesn't turn around.

I sigh and prop my hands on my hips. "Sol—"

He shakes his head and places a finger to his lips.

I raise an eyebrow.

"Listen."

I strain to hear something other than the murmurs from Macy and Elijah. For several long seconds, I don't hear anything, but then I pick up on it. My eyes widen, and I pull away, my gaze connecting with Solomon's. The same fear coursing through my body is mirrored in his pupils.

He knows what I do.

That buzzing means Macy's dream is about to turn into a nightmare.

Chapter Sixteen

"What do we do?" My pulse accelerates.

Macy is terrified of bees.

She's also deathly allergic.

"We have to get her out of here." Solomon braces his body like he's going to take off running.

Right. I replicate his posture.

Solomon shoots me a brief look. "Breathe, Gonzales."

I suck in an obedient gulp of air.

"We don't know the bees are going to attack."

I shake my head. "No, but we can make a pretty good guess."

He flashes a smirk. "Exactly. Which is why it's so important to be prepared for everything."

I turn my focus back to Macy and my brother. They're leaning forward. Macy's eyes are sliding closed as they angle their lips closer to each other. It feels too intrusive to watch, and just a smidge awkward. I turn away. Even if this is just a dream, they deserve some semblance of privacy.

Macy shrieks.

I swivel. She stands on the blanket, slapping her hands around. Hundreds of bees swarm around her. My brother has disappeared, no longer relevant to the dream.

I dart into the hoard of bees, cringing when the buzzing intensifies. Bees fly past my ears. Shivers dance up my spine.

"Gonzales!" Solomon calls after me.

But I don't stop. I plunge ahead.

"Macy." I grab her wrist and pull her forward. The bees change directions, following us. Don't let them sting her. Don't let them sting her. Please, don't let them sting her.

"I've never known anyone to survive more than two deaths in the Dream." Solomon's words play through my head.

I dart a look at my best friend. How many times has she died in her dreams? My mouth runs dry.

A bee releases its stinger into my skin, and a pang shoots through my neck. I slap a hand over the spot and race onward. Macy stumbles along beside me in her wedged sandals. Another quick stab pelts my arm. A third behind my ear. Itching, burning pain courses under my skin. Macy teeters off balance. Panicked tears stream down her face, but no signs of swelling dot her skin.

"Come on." Where can I take her? I half turn to ask Solomon, but he's lost in the swarm.

Macy jerks free from my hold and slaps at herself, screaming hysterically. I try to grab her, but she's moving too quickly.

"Macy, it's okay," I shout.

But she doesn't stop slapping at herself.

"Solomon?" Where is he? I crane my neck, but there are too many bees blocking my view.

"Wake her up." His voice is barely audible over the buzzing.

I dodge Macy's flailing limbs and grip her cheeks, forcing her to meet my eyes. "How?" I scream to the Guardian who should be the one handling this.

"Every Dreamer has a code phrase."

I swat at a bee. "Really helpful."

I tug Macy forward a few paces. The bees stay on track. Macy struggles to follow me, frantically waving off the swarm.

"Solomon." I grit my teeth and slap a bee that lands on my arm before it can release its stinger. What is he even doing? I whirl. A funnel of air circulates, sucking the bees down like a drain.

The funnel spins to my side and dissolves into the Guardian who takes his charge by the cheeks and locks eyes with her. Sweat slips down Solomon's temple, and an ashy-gray tinge colors his skin. Macy pants, staring at him like he's her lifeline. Solomon's features change and shift until his face matches Elijah's. "Lemon. Grandma. Country."

Macy's eyes roll up into her head, and she crashes backward, dissolving into the grass.

The bees freeze for a moment before dozens of small, yellow bodies pelt the ground. They pile on top of each other in thick heaps. For a long moment, they stay like this in a gruesome heap before they follow Macy and dissolve into nothingness. Half a second later, the dream follows suit, fading into tiny fragments until we're no longer stand-ing in a beautiful park. Instead, we're back in Solomon's apartment. I gasp and plant a hand on my chest as my heart rate settles.

I spin to face Solomon. "Code phrase? You couldn't have mentioned that a little bit earlier? Like maybe when those Nightmares were coming at us with guns!"

He bends over his knees, one hand clutching his chest. "I didn't think it mattered. They're only for emergencies when the Dreamer can't otherwise be safely removed."

"Didn't matter? Macy could have died, and neither one of us can afford to let that happen. Watcher would have been livid, and if something happened to you, or that stupid car of yours, I'd have no way of getting home." I'm shouting now, but I don't care.

Solomon's gaze drops to the floor. "I'm sorry." He sags forward and manages to catch himself with one hand.

"Solomon?" My voice comes out in a squeak.

A wet breath oozes from his lungs. "I'm fine."

Then why does he sound anything but?

He collapses.

I'm at his side in an instant, gripping his shoulders. "What's happening?" Cold prickles my limbs, and a shaky cadence takes over my breathing.

"The funnel. The disguise." He pants the words, face growing paler. "They're only supposed to be last minute efforts. A once in a lifetime get out of jail free card."

"I don't understand, the Dream reset. You should be fine." I palm his chest, searching for some wound.

He flicks his wrist up, revealing his slick watch. "This doesn't work like that. I have three minutes unless Macy falls back to sleep and dreams again." His arm drops against his stomach.

Three minutes? My hands tremble against the fabric of his t-shirt. "But you have to take me home."

His eyelids sweep down.

"Solomon, you will *not* leave me here." I give him a shake.

He doesn't open his eyes.

No. I tap a hand against his cheek. His skin is clammy against my touch. "Solomon!"

"Gwen…" He blinks at me, eyes murky. "You will go home."

"But I don't want to. Not like this. You're going to be fine, and then you're going to drive me home as soon as Watcher removes that stupid tracker."

His lips twitch in a shadow of a grin.

"Sol—"

Reflective panels appear in front of me, turning, showcasing every color until they collide into a whole.

Chapter Seventeen

I blink against the harsh burst of light until the Dream's setting comes into focus. I'm sitting in the school cafeteria with Macy, a half-eaten piece of meatloaf on my plate. She's laughing at something Mia, another girl at our table, said. Posters hang all around the cafeteria, welcoming us back to school.

I remember this. It was the first day of Junior year. The day we met Beck.

As if on cue, Beck steps into my line of vision, wearing her favorite beanie and leggings with cutoff shorts. She wears that signature new kid look. Eyes wide while she scans the tables for a place to sit.

Like I have no control over my body, I find myself nudging Macy with my elbow. She glances up and follows my gaze. A smile brightens her face, and she stands. Macy's always been the nicer one in our duo. When I'm not brave enough to step into a situation, I can always count on her. She approaches Beck, and the two exchange a few words before Macy leads the way back to our table.

"This is Gwen." Macy slides in beside me.

Beck shoots me a wobbly grin.

"Hi." I offer a small wave and shift in the cafeteria chair. The leg squeaks. A loud, awkward sound that fills the heavy silence.

Macy gestures to Mia. "And this is Mia."

Another tiny smile from Beck to acknowledge the introduction.

Macy beams at her. "And this is Beck. She just moved here."

"Where from?" Mia pushes her glasses farther up her nose.

"New York," Beck says.

And from there, we pepper Beck with questions until she's lost her uncertain look and is laughing along with us. Back before she started laughing *at* us.

I swallow hard as I watch the scene play out. If only this camaraderie had lasted. If Mia hadn't moved away, if Beck hadn't—

The Dream shifts, taking on the appearance of another day in the cafeteria. It's a few days after Mia's dad got a new job and moved the whole family to California. Beck has become a close friend in the last few months. But that doesn't keep her attention from wandering to the popular table every time we go to sit down. I clench my jaw. My friendship isn't enough for Beck. Ever since that first day, I can tell she's wanted more.

"Gwen?" Macy shoots me a worried look.

I shake off the feeling. Why are these emotions so poignant? I've already lived through this once.

I scan the cafeteria, but Solomon is nowhere to be found in the sea of blurred faces. Surely, if the dreams are continuing, then he is somewhere here with me. Unless he was wrong. What if his death doesn't send me home, and I'm stuck in a carousel of dreams forever? The thought makes my stomach churn, and I clutch the edge of the table to steady myself. I can't think about that now. For the moment, I have to remain calm and focus on surviving the here and now. I make my fingers relax, release the table, and drop them into my lap.

Beck sighs and turns away from the popular table, seeming to resign herself to our company. She brushes her espresso-colored hair off her face and offers Macy and me a tight smile. Macy, always the one to ignore any tension in the room, bursts into an excited documentary of her Christmas break.

One of the football players approaches and drapes an arm around Beck's shoulders. "Hey, Beck. You coming to the party Saturday?"

She laughs like him even having to ask is ridiculous. "Of course."

"Great, see you there." The guy saunters off with his hands in his pockets.

She offers a flirty wave before turning back to face me, eyes glinting with victory. But what exactly did she win? Even to this day, I can't pinpoint exactly when things became a competition between us.

"What was that about?" Macy squeezes a packet of ketchup on to her hamburger.

I pick up a French fry. "Yeah, what party?" They're the same words I said all those days ago, and they come out automatically now.

"Some of the football guys are throwing a big bash." She waves a dismissive hand like it's no big deal, but that light of victory still gleams in her eyes.

"Are we invited?" Macy squirms and wipes her hands on a napkin.

Beck actually snorts. "Don't be silly. Of course, you aren't invited. It's just for the popular kids."

I dig my fingernails into my palms. Don't stand out. Don't say anything that you'll regret. Keep your head down and get through it.

A pair of hands clasp my shoulders, gently massaging. "There you are."

Solomon.

That in itself is a relief, but it does nothing to undermine the heat smoldering in every cell of my body. The emotion is just as real now in the Dream as it was that day a little less than a year ago.

Solomon leans closer, tickling my skin with his breath. "Steady." His accent soothes the tension bunching my muscles.

Macy and Beck continue their conversation, oblivious to his presence.

A chill sweeps over me. Something is about to happen, and it's not going to be pretty. I can't explain why, but the feeling grows with every tick of the cafeteria clock.

Static pops in front of my vision. Bursts of white dots frizzle across my eyes until everything snaps into focus, and we're standing in a parking garage.

Solomon stands with his hands raised. A masked man holds a pistol to his head. I shiver beside Solomon, the hand of a second masked man digging into the space between my shoulder and collarbone. I hardly dare to breathe. My body shakes. Macy whimpers in the grasp of a third man who has a pistol pressed to her temple.

I. Hate. The. Dream.

The cool metal of a barrel presses into the tender skin below my jaw. "Where is it?"

Sweat trails down my back. "I don't know what you're talking about." I dart a glance around the parking garage. There has to be some kind of context.

A black van sits in a parking area two spaces away. An armored truck is parked to my left. Solomon, Macy, and I all wear gray coveralls. Were we transporting something? The truck isn't marked with a logo or any words that offer a clue to the situation, but that's my best guess. How am I supposed to know when the Dream dumped us into the middle of this?

"Where?" The man jabs the gun harder against my skin.

I wince and fail to hold back a whimper.

"Leave her alone." Solomon starts forward, but his captor wraps an arm around his neck, adding extra insurance to keep him from coming for me.

"Just give it to them." Macy sobs, her knees sagging so the man holding her at gunpoint has to support her weight.

I suck down a cry. What I wouldn't give to be able to acquiesce. I search Solomon's eyes for help, but he too wears a panicked expression. What does one do when even a Dream Guardian is helpless?

I look to Macy. Do I use the code on her? But then my gaze snags on Solomon. The way he almost died. I can't say them. Not until we can discuss the consequences. Then again, none of us may be getting out of this alive.

Solomon holds my stare. Nods.

A lump settles in my throat. I know exactly what he means to do and I can't stop him.

He looks to Macy. "Lemon—"

"No talking!" His captor clubs him in the head.

Solomon almost collapses. The man's hold is the only thing keeping him from hitting the pavement.

I cry out before I can stop myself.

Solomon heaves a breath and raises his head once more. "Grandma."

"You say one more word, and I'll shoot the girl." My captor digs the tip of his gun into my temple, and I whimper.

Solomon turns pale, and he snaps his mouth shut.

"That's better," his gunman says.

My assailant shoves me to my knees, and gravel presses against my kneecaps. "Give it to me."

I shake my head.

"No?" The man holding me pulls the gun away and gestures toward Solomon. "Perhaps you need some motivation?"

"I don't know what you're talking about!"

"We both know that's a lie."

"It's the truth." I scan the setting frantically, but there is nothing, *nothing* to provide context to the situation.

His fingers tighten against my collarbone, pinching skin and grinding against bone. "I'm running out of patience. Start talking, or I'll take out the boy."

"No, please." Tears flood my eyes. I search my memory for some fragment. Some hint of what they want, but I draw a blank. "Please." I whimper.

Solomon pants, and he runs his tongue over his upper lip where sweat collects. His attention darts around the room, as if searching for a way out of this disaster, but in the end, his shoulders slump.

"Very well." The man levels his gun at the kidnapper who is now my friend.

"No. Please, wait." There has to be some way out of this.

"Is there something you wish to give us?"

My pulse spikes. "We could make a deal."

"I don't think so." His aim doesn't waver from Solomon.

"Wait." I thrash, but I can't break his grip.

"I tire of these games. Either you tell me what I want to know, or I make you wish you had. What's it going to be?"

"I don't know!" I'm screaming the words frantically, over and over and over again.

A gunshot rings through the air. The sound echoes off the cement walls.

I scream.

A blossom of red opens on Macy's sweater, and she crumples to the ground

Chapter Eighteen

"No!" My captor dissolves, and I rush to Macy's side. Her warm blood soaks my hands. My fingers shake. How can I lose the one person who took the time to say "hi" that first day I was dropped off at Hibiscus Lane Elementary? The one who's been there for me every minute of every day. The girl who's only ever been one text message away. I plant my hands over the wound. "Stay with me." I can barely feel the movement of my lips. I can't do this. I need her. A sob catches in my throat. "Macy. Don't leave me. Please, don't leave me."

Solomon scrambles to my side in an instant, pressing two fingers to Macy's neck. He freezes.

"What is it?" What if Macy just stopped breathing in her sleep? She still hasn't disappeared. "Solomon?" Tension digs its nails into my shoulders.

He sits back on his heels and mops a hand over his face. "She's fine. Sometimes it takes them longer to fade away after dying." The words seem just as much for his benefit as mine.

Dying. "You mean…" I don't dare to voice the full question. I can't go there. I drop my bloody hands to my lap. Macy is fine. Right now, she's waking up back home, sitting bolt upright in bed, heart racing from the nightmare. But she's fine. Absolutely fine. I refuse to entertain thoughts of anything else.

But the dream Macy remains lifeless on the floor, blood draining from her body, swirling around her tangled mass of hair. Her eyes stare up at the ceiling, unblinking. Their sparkle has disappeared. Perhaps forever. I turn my face into Solomon's chest, fighting to blot the image from my mind. My shoulders heave as I weep. He cradles me close, and his lips press into my hair. The contact is so light and sweet that it makes me cry all the harder.

The Dream Guardian's body stiffens. "She's fading."

I turn back. True to his words, Macy dissolves into the cement floor.

I smile. Give a little, watery laugh. "She's all right."

Solomon remains rigid.

I pull back and look him in the eyes. "She's fine, right?"

Solomon's eyes fill, and he stares at the bloody puddle leftover from Macy's murder.

"Solomon?" I give him a shake.

His gaze drifts to meet mine.

"She's awake, right?" Please, please, say it's true.

His shoulders droop. "Only time will tell." He expels a shaky breath. "This is her third death in the Dream."

Third... "But that means..." I clasp a hand over my mouth, and I can't breathe. A pang cuts through my chest. Tightening. Squeezing. If his words are true, then I may never see my friend again. My mouth opens and closes, but I can't suck in any air. I wrap my fingers around Solomon's arm as an anchor to keep me from being carried off by the blackness creeping into the corners of my vision. If she's gone, then I won't have anyone to call on those late nights when Mom isn't home, and I just need to talk. There will be no one to laugh with or pretend that she's my personal chauffeur and drag me away from my drum kit and whisk me away on an adventure.

Solomon drops his forehead against mine. "It's all right. There's still a chance she woke up."

I force my chin up and down in a nod.

"Breathe, Gwen."

I do. In and out. In and out. In and out until I'm not just breathing, but now I'm sobbing. Not the cute movie kind, but big ugly cries, heaving breaths and snot. So much snot.

Solomon just holds me tighter.

Through my tears, I watch the empty spot where Macy was only minutes before. A waiting game. The torture already begins to wrap around my shoulders.

Chapter Nineteen

*T*ick.

Tock.

I clutch Solomon's watch in my fist. It works for him, but as I hold it, there's not a single number present on the object, and the hands don't move to acknowledge the time. They simply sit dormant while the dull ticking sound fills the air. I don't know why I hold it. It's not doing me any good, but it's tangible. Like if I sit here long enough, the thing will suddenly register numbers, and Macy will be here, or maybe even Solomon's probation will be lifted, and Watcher will let him take me home.

Watcher.

I snap up from the couch and race to where Solomon stands in front of his switched off espresso machine, staring through it like it's not even here. I snag his wrist. "We have to get out of here."

He startles, eyes wide. "What?"

"We have to go. Watcher probably saw all of that, and I know I don't really know him, but I've seen enough to know he's not going to be happy about any of that."

"I can't run, Gwen." His shoulders sag. "It's my fault."

"It's not. It's not your fault, and we can talk about this, but not here."

"If I was a better Guardian, then my Dreamer would never have been put in that situation. Or any of the ones before." A muscle ticks in his jaw.

"Solomon, you couldn't have controlled any of that. Not even Watcher can blame you for what happened." And why on earth is he talking about Macy in such a disassociated manner? Is this some symptom of shock, or does he truly not believe she's alive?

His eyebrows rise in a tired manner.

"It's. Not. Your. Fault." I slap a hand against the counter for emphasis.

He sighs and rubs the back of his neck. "It should have been me."

I step to his side. "Don't talk like that. Macy's fine." Because I refuse to believe otherwise.

"What if..." His hands fist, and he leaves the thought unfinished.

I place a hand on his shoulder and squeeze. "She's fine."

He shakes his head. "It should have been me."

"And what would have happened?"

"I would have died, and my Dreamer would have been assigned a new Guardian." He traces an invisible line on the counter. "You would have gone home."

"At that cost? I told you." I grip his arm. "We're going to help Macy, get your probation lifted, then you're going to take me home. It's going to be all right."

He ducks his head.

"But listen, we have to get out of here. I, for one, don't plan on sitting around until Watcher comes to chew you out."

"Gwen…" He heaves my name out like a sigh.

My attention catches on a brown object scuttling over the floor. I lean forward to get a better look. A spider.

"Give me your shoe." No need to get little guts smeared to the bottom of mine.

He stares at me, confusion clouding his expression. "Whatever for?"

I indicate the spider with my eyes.

Solomon's face pales. "Not good. Not good."

"It's just a spider." I roll my eyes. Maybe once upon a time, I was scared of them, but since everyone else in my family is terrified, someone had to step up as the designated spider smasher.

He rakes his fingers through his hair.

"Solomon?" The world around us darkens and shifts until we're standing in a forest. Thunder crashes in the distance, shaking the entire area. I grip Solomon's sleeve. "What's going on?"

He's too busy hyperventilating to answer.

But I don't need him to. My breath lodges in my throat, and my knees tremble when the main characters of this dream sequence appear. Four large, hairy spiders scramble toward us on long black legs. Solomon stands frozen, stare fixed on the beasts. I slide my hand down his arm until I find his hand. My fingers lock around his.

"The Dream plays on your fears." Solomon's previous words echo through my head.

I wet my lips and force my voice to work. "It's just a dream. Think about something else."

But he's not listening. He's too focused on the monsters coming toward us.

"Solomon." I squeeze his hand. Hard.

He doesn't move. Doesn't flinch.

"Come on." I tug on his hand and pull him toward the forest. With any luck, the spiders won't be able to squeeze between the trees.

Solomon stumbles along behind me, his boots dragging and catching on roots. Since when did this boy forget how to walk? He trips and goes sprawling. Our hands slip apart at the last minute, sparing me a similar fall.

He stares at the spiders, eyes wide. The creatures advance, forging a path through the foliage as they swell in size. Tree limbs crash to the leaf covered ground.

I kneel in front of the Guardian disabled by panic. I take Solomon's face between my hands and force him to look at me. If only he had a code phrase like Macy's. "Think about something else. Anything else."

Sweat shines on his face while he stares at me.

"Anything else." I hold his gaze.

A tree snaps in half when a giant spider shoulders past it.

"Please, Solomon."

He sucks in a deep breath and closes his eyes.

I pant. Waiting.

The spiders dissolve into the ground, and the trees fold into the grass. A stage framed by red curtains replaces the dark forest. Solomon stands at a pedestal, mouth poised in front of a microphone. An object covered in a blue sheet is set up behind him. I stand just beyond one of the curtains. From here, I have a view of the bright lights and the dark silhouettes of a crowd. So much better than the spiders.

Solomon glances at a white card and then back up. "I-I—" He swallows hard. "T-thank you for coming…uh…" Another deep gulp from the Dream Guardian. The mic picks up the sound, broadcasting it for all to hear.

I wince. Poor guy.

"Um…" He shoots me a pleading look.

Dang it.

Since when did I become this boy's Guardian?

A chuckle burbles from my throat as I ease onto the stage. "Hi." I offer the crowd a limp wave and take up position beside Solomon. "What's wrong?" I say through the side of my mouth. I force a smile for the sake of the audience.

"I can't—" He licks the sweat from his upper lip.

Great.

I nudge him aside with my hip and take up position in front of the microphone. "Good evening." Or at least I hope it's evening. "Thank you for joining my colleague and me for the…"

I dart a look Solomon's way.

"Unveiling," he says so low I can barely hear him, let alone the audience.

"For the unveiling." Of what I have no idea, but whatever. "It means a lot to us for you all to be here."

The crowd claps politely.

"And now, my colleague will unveil the…the thing."

He doesn't move.

"I'm talking about you." I kick his ankle.

He springs into action and darts to the covered object. He reaches for the cloth with shaking hands.

And freezes.

I roll my eyes playfully at the crowd and walk to the other side of the thing. "On three."

He nods.

"One," I say for all to hear.

"Two," the crowd joins in.

"Three."

With Solomon's help, I tear away the cloth, revealing some kind of robotic masterpiece. I flash a smile toward the onlookers, pretending like I have some idea of what the heck it is. Solomon beams proudly, reminding me of a new pet owner showing off their puppy's tricks.

The crowd shrieks their pleasure.

I grin at Solomon.

The stage swirls away in a blur of color, and we're standing back in his apartment.

"Thanks." He presses a hand to his chest.

"What are friends for?" I duck my head to hide my flushed cheeks.

He smiles, his gaze warming further.

Chapter Twenty

"**G**wen."

I jab at the round cereal floating in my milk. My eyelids drift down in heavy sweeps with each blink. How much longer will we be forced to wait? I rub at my eye with my index finger. At least Watcher hasn't shown up yet. Maybe he agrees with me that there was nothing else Solomon could've done. I don't quite believe it, but the fact he hasn't shown up to drag Solomon away seems to be a pretty good indicator.

"Gwen."

This time I look over my shoulder.

He grins like a kid on spring break.

My heart races. "Do you…"

"Yeah. She's here."

I drop my head into my hands and fight the sting of my nose. She's here. Finally.

Solomon jogs to the door and yanks it open. He turns expectantly to me. "You coming?"

I ease to a standing position.

Solomon leads the way out of his apartment, and we find ourselves peeking out from backstage while Macy dazzles an audience with her graceful ballet. Her purple tutu sparkles in the stage light. The music reels me in, pulling me deeper and deeper while the story of the ballet plays out in front of me. I smile while my friend dances. She weaves the audience deeper into the show with each movement of her body.

And then she stumbles.

The audience gasps.

Macy keeps going, fighting to maintain control of her routine.

She stumbles again, her foot bending sideways.

I clap a hand over my mouth, stifling a cry. If she isn't careful, she'll twist her ankle.

Macy leaps into the air, soaring up, up, up. Her knee buckles on the landing, and she crumples to the hard planks of the stage.

I start to rush to her, but Solomon grabs my elbow. "Stay here."

My lips part. When did he have time to change into attire appropriate for this setting? He leaps out onto the stage and to Macy's side. He offers my friend a hand up, and the two dance a beautiful duet. They are the king and queen of the stage, and I stand in the background like a third wheel. My chest pinches. At least Solomon doesn't need me anymore. Maybe he can finally take me home.

The curtain draws to a close, the dream fades away, and we're once again standing in Solomon's apartment.

"Well, what do you think?" Solomon grins at me.

I cross my arms. "That they should have given you the role of the princess."

He squints at my face and then his lips twitch. "You're jealous."

I snort. "And you're ridiculous."

"Careful now, you might give me a big head."

"Whatever." I huff and cross my arms. "Take me home, will you? You were able to save Macy just fine on your own." I try not to think of the dream before that. The one with the gunmen. Am I selfish for wanting to get out of here? It's not exactly like I'm abandoning my best friend...or am I? Ugh, this world is messing with reality, blurring the lines between what's real and what's not.

"Sorry, love. I can't." He shakes his foot, revealing that stupid tracker. An unspoken "not yet" hangs between us.

Right.

"I can treat you to dessert, though?"

How does he always know the right answer? I can't be mad at him for something that isn't his fault, so I lower my arms to my sides. "That would be nice. Thank you."

He shrugs and drops his hands into his pockets. "It's the least I can do."

We make our way down to the café where the band has a lively beat pulsing, and many Dream Guardians have gathered for an after-work break.

"There you two are." Hunter drapes an arm over each of our shoulders. "We've been waiting for you guys." He ushers us to a booth where Josie waits, an overflowing taco in front of her.

"It's dessert time, Josie." Solomon laughs and drops into the seat across from her.

"To me, this is dessert." Josie jabs a finger at the taco.

I perch on the bench beside Solomon. "My little sister would think the same thing."

"She's good people then." Josie winks and takes a bite. How she even fits her mouth around the thing is mindboggling.

"What do you want?" Solomon leans toward me.

"My treat," Hunter says. "Guess who finally paid off all his debts?"

"I'm shocked," Solomon deadpans.

"Flabbergasted." Josie licks sour cream off her fingers.

"That's great?" I add.

Josie snickers and picks up a piece of fallen tomato. "It's got to be a record."

Hunter stands and flourishes a blue card. "Mock all you want, but this is a momentous occasion."

"Huge." Solomon fights a smile.

"For that, I'm not buying you anything." He turns up his nose at Solomon before dipping close to me and whispering, "Besides, I don't have enough points left over anyway."

"Aw, mate, come on." Solomon straightens up.

"No, no, you lost your chance." Hunter smirks and looks to me. "What can I get you?"

"Cheesecake?" I look around for some kind of menu.

Hunter snaps his fingers. "Consider it done." He swivels on his heel and goes to flag down a waiter.

Josie rolls her eyes. "*So* dramatic."

Solomon laughs. "Would we have him any other way?"

"Nope."

I shift in my seat. "How was your day?" Night? Who even knows?

"Good. I got a break from Jack-in-the-boxes, so that's a plus, but I had to rescue my Dreamer from a pail of worms." Josie shudders. "I think I can still feel them crawling down my back."

Solomon grimaces.

A chill scuttles down my spine at the mere thought. "Ugh. I do not envy you."

"Yeah, I think I'd rather wrestle more Jack-in-the-boxes if this is going to be a thing." Josie stuffs another bite of taco into her mouth. Give the woman a taco, and anything dainty about her disappears.

"Your cheesecake." Hunter drops into the seat beside Josie and passes a beautiful slice of dairy-goodness my way. Strawberry sauce oozes down the sides of the cake.

I can't hold back a happy sequel. For a moment, I'm tempted to be like Josie and let manners fly, but then Hunter passes me a fork, and I rein myself in.

One bite is all it takes to pull a happy moan from deep within my soul. "Oh, this makes all of today worth it."

The others laugh.

"Are there any left in back?" Solomon asks.

Hunter shakes his head and folds his arms on the table. "Sorry, this was the last piece, and I had to use all of my charms to get it."

"What charms?" Josie shoves his shoulder.

Hunter gasps in mock-offense. "I can be very charming when I want to be, thanks."

The two go onto bicker, and I tune them out as I realize Solomon is staring down my cheesecake.

"Okay," I say, brandishing my fork. "You had to go through today, too, so I think you deserve a bite." I offer him a generous forkful.

"Hey!" Hunter protests as Solomon accepts the mouthful. "I don't buy cheesecake for just anybody."

"Think of it as payment for all the times I've covered for you," Solomon says.

"Please." Hunter bats the words away. "Friends don't keep track."

"You so do," Josie cuts in.

He squirms and adjusts the collar of his jacket. "All right, all right. Enough about me, you'll bore poor Gwen."

Solomon snorts. "Fine. How about a round of tea and coffee?"

Josie shoves aside her empty plate and passes Solomon her card. "Sounds good to me."

Solomon maneuvers past me and heads for the bar.

Hunter sobers the moment Solomon is out of earshot. "Any more problems with Watcher?"

I shake my head and cut off another bite of cake. "Not that I know of."

"Good." Josie tracks Solomon's movements. "He deserves a break."

Solomon returns with coffee for the three of them and a lavender black tea mix for me. I inhale the soothing scent. "Thank you."

He ducks his head and fiddles with the handle of his coffee mug. "It's no big deal."

We linger over our drinks, chatting about anything and everything.

$$\chi$$

After a semi-peaceful sleep with the help of the tea, I stand at the counter, eyeing the leftover baked goods, trying to decide if I remember the proper ratios for Nana's pancake recipe.

Solomon huddles over his espresso machine, nudging the thing to life.

"Do you have any eggs?" I ask. Man, I wish I had my phone to look up substitutes for some of the ingredients he's lacking.

"I don't think so." He shoots a doubtful look at the refrigerator.

I bite my lip. "Maybe if I just use milk?"

The whirr of his machine is the only reply, not that I exactly expect him to offer culinary advice. "I guess I'll just try it?" I look over my shoulder at Solomon.

He spins and grabs my hand.

I try to pull away. "Let go."

"She's back." He pulls me through the doorway.

This time we're standing in a hall lined with lockers.

"Gwen." Macy waves from her locker, the bangles on her arm clanking together.

I scan the familiar hallway. The banners welcoming us back to school, and the teenagers all decked out in their first day of school attire. Macy is dreaming about the first day of Senior year.

An elbow slams against my ribs. "Act natural."

Yeah, well, let's see how well he does when I smash *him* in the ribs. I refrain from glaring at Solomon and instead lift a hand in greeting. Beck walks up behind me and slips her elbow through mine. I tense my limbs. Anything to keep from flinching at her touch.

"Aren't you excited?" Beck gushes. "Seniors. Finally!"

She walks right past Solomon.

He smirks and leans close to my ear. "It's called blending in. You might want to try it sometime."

I roll my eyes. "Whatever."

"Gwen?" Beck frowns at me.

I stir myself before Solomon can admonish me not to break the first rule of the Dream. "Exciting." Right. Because I even care. To Beck, Senior year is just another opportunity to climb the social ladder.

Solomon shoots me a warning look.

I force myself to smile at Beck. How can she not tell it isn't real?

Because she's not paying attention to me. She sends a flirty wave toward a group of football players. Someone catcalls when she passes. I duck my head.

"Be right back." She slips away, off to talk to some girl in designer jeans rummaging through her locker.

Not that I care. Of course, I don't. I keep walking and slam into something. Err, someone. "S-sorry," I stutter when I pull away and stare into the face of Austin Taylor.

He flashes his unnaturally white teeth. "No problem."

My mouth goes dry.

"Are you going to ogle him like he's a piece of chocolate cake this whole dream, or are you going to help me watch out for Macy?" Solomon growls in my ear, breaking the spell.

I duck my head and skitter around Austin, cheeks burning.

Macy touches my shoulder. "Are you okay?"

I brush my hair behind my ear. "Yeah, just embarrassed."

"Give it five minutes, and no one will even remember." Her brow furrows in sympathy.

Yeah, like I could ever be that lucky.

Beck appears seconds later. "Oh, girl. Do I see a prom date in the future?"

I offer a shaky laugh. "Don't be silly. I doubt he even knows my name."

Solomon snorts and rolls his eyes from where he leans against a nearby locker, hoodie up, earbuds in. Hoodie? What happened to the lab coat?

I resist the urge to reach around Beck and kick his shins.

Macy spins around and closes her locker.

The sound vibrates through my bones. Macy disappears, and Solomon and I are back in his apartment. He pulls a face.

I cross my arms. "What?"

"What do you see in that guy?"

Other than the fact that he's drop dead gorgeous? "He's nice?" It comes out as a question. I straighten my spine in hopes of adding the missing authority to my words.

Solomon stuffs his hands in his pockets and props his back against the wall. "How would you know? You've barely talked to him. I'd wager you haven't exchanged more than ten words."

"We have so."

"Really? You know, just liking someone for their looks isn't really love, right? Try infatuation."

"You don't even have any idea what you're talking about." Still, I can't seem to maintain eye contact.

"His teeth are scarily white."

I pull a mug from his shelf and fill it at the sink. "You're judging him by his dental hygiene?"

"So are you."

I tighten my grip on the mug's handle. "Whatever." I drain my beverage in one gulp.

Solomon's eye twitches. "He can't even make good coffee."

Of all the... "How would you know?"

He rubs the back of his neck. "I just...know things."

I cock an eyebrow. Ready. Aim. Fire. "Well, if you ask me, you're the one who's starting to sound jealous."

His cheeks turn pink, and he stuffs his hands in his pockets. "It's not...it's not like that."

"Well, it's none of your business anyway." I brush past him and flop onto the couch. "That dream was fine. Can you talk Watcher into letting you take me home now?"

His throat bobs. "Not yet."

I grind my teeth and pull in a sharp breath. "When?"

"Soon." Solomon stares at the ground while drawing circles with his shoe.

"You keep saying that. When?" I ask. "What happens if my mom tries to contact me?"

"She won't."

I roll my eyes. "How could you possibly know that?"

"I just do, okay?" He looks away, fueling the heat boiling inside me.

"No, it's not okay." I grab a pillow and launch to my feet. "I want a real answer."

He has the audacity to mock me, "What are you going to do? Smother me?"

"Solomon." I throw the pillow back onto the couch. Hard enough that a few feathers go flying.

"Soon. You'll go home soon. That's all that I can say for now. I'm sorry." His dark eyes reflect the sentiment behind his words.

"Ugh." I spin away. Is home too much to ask for? A pain cuts through my middle. All I want is my mom. Maybe it's babyish, but I've never claimed to be mature.

"Gwen, I—"

Everything changes in a burst of yellow light and lemon cleaner. I'm stuck in a hallway of white walls. Smooth tiles form a path beneath my feet. There's something familiar about this place. I've been here before. I close my eyes and force myself to concentrate. Where have I seen this hallway? Mom. This is her hospital.

I'm back.

"Mom!" I surge forward only to slam against something solid and hard. I bounce off. Ouch! I clap a hand to my forehead and step forward with more care this time. Still, something solid blocks my way. That makes no sense. There's only air ahead. Except when I raise my hand, there's a wall. Glass? I spin, but it's the same on all sides. I'm trapped in an invisible box.

"Mom?" I drum on the wall. "Mom, it's me, I'm back."

A doctor walks up, scanning the chart in his hand.

"Hey, let me out. I need to find my mom."

He keeps walking.

"I have to let her know I'm okay."

He doesn't give any indication he's heard me.

A group of nurses come by next, chatting amongst themselves. I wave, trying to get their attention. Not even one of them looks my way.

"Please. Please, I'm right here." I pound the wall until my palms sting.

A clicking noise sounds, and the walls shrink in on me. What must have been a comfortable six feet of space shrinks to four.

No, no, no.

I'm hitting the glass with the side of my fist now. "Let me out!"

Not the janitor, nor the patient in a hospital gown strolling past, gives me any attention.

And then I see her, frizzy curls pulled up into a messy bun, tired wrinkles lining her forehead and the skin around her eyes.

"Mom." I jump up and down, but she doesn't look up from the collection of papers in her hands. "I'm right here. Please, Mom." My chin shakes, and a burst of hot moisture blinds me for a moment. "You have to hear me."

But she doesn't, and she starts to walk away.

"No, Mom." I fling myself at the glass. It doesn't so much as vibrate. I'm drumming my fists against the hard surface, and they turn raw and red.

The box gives another creak and shifts smaller again until I'm almost smeared against the glass.

Mom's almost down the hall now.

"I need you, Mom. Please. Please." But she isn't coming. I press a shaky hand against the glass and watch her walk away. "Mom."

Solomon is there then, pressing his hand against mine on the other side of the barrier. His lips are moving, but I don't hear him. I don't want to. Because if he's here, then I'm not home. I'm still trapped in this carousel of nightmares. I crane to see over his shoulder, watching for the last image of my mom. I so desperately want to be out of the Dream. To be with her.

Solomon moves, blocking my view. His lips are moving.

I force back the sob that wants to surface. Force myself to breathe and focus on where I am instead of where I want to be.

Solomon is still trying to communicate something.

I shake my head. "I can't hear you."

His brow puckers, and his gaze moves away from me and instead roves over the contraption holding me captive.

The thing gives another ominous creak. I lunge for Solomon, but of course, he can't do anything other than spread out his palm against the glass.

"Help me!" I scream as the walls tighten around me, pressing against my back, my sides, my chest. My hot breath bounces back off the wall in front of me. My lungs constrict, and it's so much work to draw in another breath.

Solomon drops his forehead against the glass. If not for the barrier, we'd be only inches apart. And then he says something very carefully, but I don't understand.

"I don't know, I don't know!" I'm shaking my head and crying.

The walls constrict. A giant, hard boa constrictor strangling its prey.

Solomon taps the glass.

I find his eyes. Stay focused there. His deep, chocolate eyes seem to be trying to convey something. I dart a look to his lips again.

He mouths something. I don't catch the first part, but the second looks like, "Anything else."

Of course. This is my fear strangling me, not Macy's. My fear of not getting home. My fear that my mom will start worrying about me.

I press my hand against the space where Solomon's should be and squeeze my eyes shut.

Anything else.

I don't open my eyes until a dry breeze rustles through my hair. Then I squint against a blistering, bright sun. Dry sand crunches beneath my boots. I'm standing in a ruined city of sunbaked buildings. A goat trots in front of me, bleating in a panicked manner.

"What's—" I don't get the rest of the question out before a spray of gunfire cuts through the stillness. I drop to the sand, arms pulled over my head.

There's a series of shouts in a language I don't understand.

Pounding feet.

I don't know what's going on, but I can't stay out here in the open. I peek through my arms. The coast is clear for now. Staying low, I scramble for what looks to be an overturned booth and fallen awning.

I dive behind the makeshift shelter just as a round of bullets cuts into the sand mere feet away. I press my back against the booth, chest pounding. What do I do, what do I do?

Solomon.

I latch onto his name and force myself to breathe. Focus.

If I can find him, then he can help me get out of here.

Ever so carefully, I crane my neck to see around the corner of the booth. Combat boots ease into my line of vision.

I don't breathe.

Instead, I stay very, very still.

The form of a soldier steps into my vision, an American flag on the shoulder of his uniform. He almost looks like...then I catch sight of the patch that says Gonzales.

"Dad!"

His gaze snaps to me, and he's lowering his gun.

This is just a dream. I remind myself over and over, but I still can't help but smile at him through a burst of tears. If a dream version of Dad is here, he'll help me. He'll help me find Solomon, and then...

"Gwen?"

"It's me, Dad." I'm not sure how to not break the first rule of the Dream, but Solomon is nowhere to be seen. Maybe if I handle this very, very carefully, I won't stand out too much.

"What are you doing here, Gweny?"

"I—"

Another round of gunfire. A blossom of red cuts through Dad's uniform, and he slams backward. And then I don't care about my safety. I'm scrambling forward an all fours as he hits the sand. Grabbing him by his vest.

"Dad."

"Baby." He reaches a trembling hand to my cheek.

"Stay with me, Daddy." The tip of my nose burns. "Please, you have to stay with me until Solomon comes."

His brow wrinkles, but his shaking hand covers one of mine. "I'm right here, baby girl."

Those foreign voices sound closer. Shouting. A command maybe. Maybe they see me.

"You've got to go, Gweny." Dad squeezes my hand.

"No." I shake my head. "No, please don't make me go."

"You have to, baby. They're coming."

Nightmares. I can see them emerging from the shadows.

"Dad." I cling to him.

He pushes at me. "Go."

"No." I look around for Solomon, but I can't see him. More shots ring out in the distance, and I pray it has nothing to do with him.

"Gwen. Go." Dad shoves me away, one hand reaching for his gun.

I scramble against the sand until I find my footing, and then I run, arms covering my head. Bullets spray the building beside me as I turn a corner.

I trip.

Scramble up again.

"Solomon!" I can't help screaming his name.

Dust is kicked up by another round of bullets, but this time an answering round fires. Dad. I push the back of my hand against my mouth and force myself to think. I need to calm down. Everything will get better if I calm down. I scramble behind a trash heap and force myself to breathe despite the stench wafting from the waste. In. Out.

Footsteps crunch toward me.

I wrap my arms around my knees. Close my eyes, and force myself to breathe. To ease the wild beating of my heart.

A hand touches my shoulder.

I jump and swing my fist wildly.

Solomon catches my arm, stilling my strike before it can land. "Gwen?"

"I want to get out of here." I blink at him through a sheen of tears.

He swipes an escaped drop from under my eye. "Okay." He darts a look over his shoulder. "Just think about something happier."

"That's what I tried last time, and I wound up here."

"What did you think about?"

"My dad." In uniform. My hero.

"Think of a place. Somewhere peaceful."

I exhale. Grip his hand so we won't be separated again. And then I close my eyes.

Chapter Twenty-One

When I open my eyes, we're standing in Solomon's kitchen, his espresso machine humming in the background.

"There." Solomon squeezes my hand.

I slide my fingers free and tuck them into the back pocket of my jeans. "Thanks."

He grins. "It was all you."

But I wasn't truly calm until he got there. I run a hand through my hair, shaking it loose around my shoulders. "So, what now?"

"Well, I think Macy's awake right now, so what do you say about catching dinner in the café?"

"No. Watcher—"

"If he was going to chew me out, he would have done it by now. I think we're safe." He leans against the counter and shrugs. "Your call though. I always have more cereal." There's a wicked gleam in his eyes.

I raise my chin and almost say cereal's fine, but my stomach turns, growling for some real food. "Fine. The café then. As long as you're sure Watcher's not going to be there."

Solomon ducks his head and digs his hands deep into the pockets of his lab coat. "I can look after myself, Gweny."

"That's not what Hunter said," I mutter before narrowing my eyes. "I thought I told you not to call me that."

"Right. Right." He nods, but there's no remorse in the twitch of his lips.

I spin on my heel and head for the door. "Come on Solly, you're buying me dinner."

His chuckle tells me he's following.

The café is pulsing with live music when we arrive. The band's back, but they're missing their drummer. A shame too, because their song could really use some support from the drums.

"You should play," Solomon says.

I shake my head. "Nah, I'm not that good."

He quirks a brow.

I bump him with my shoulder. "Besides, I'm starving, and you promised to buy me dinner."

"How's he going to do that?" Hunter appears and slings an arm around Solomon's neck. "He got swiped, remember?"

"Which—" Solomon extracts himself from the headlock, "—is why you're here. You owe me one."

"You know, I'd love to—"

"Oh, don't give me that. I know you must have accumulated points by now if they didn't get all wiped out after last night."

"All right, all right." Hunter holds up his hands. "Fine. I'll buy dinner, but I'm doing it for her, not you." He wags a finger.

Solomon grins. "Just so long as we're fed, mate."

The guys lead the way to a table near the stage, and I follow with an eye toward the drumkit. Sweet. It must have double the equipment I have at home. I slide into my chair and tap out a rhythm on the edge of the table that compliments the song.

Solomon stops midsentence in whatever he was saying to Hunter and raises an eyebrow at my hands.

I quickly tuck them under my legs. "Sorry." I should know better by now. Beck's scolded me for the habit more times than I can count.

"You should play." He tilts his head toward the stage.

"No."

"I didn't know you played," Hunter says.

Warmth engulfs me from head to toe, and I fiddle with my silverware. "It's just a hobby."

"Solomon's right, you should get up there, and show us what you can do." Hunter nods toward the stage.

"No, I'm just here for the food."

"Which," Solomon turns toward Hunter, "you've so gener-ously offered to provide."

"Right." Hunter heaves a sigh and flags down a waiter. "But you owe me."

Once we've ordered, and our food and drinks have been delivered, I dig in without hesitation. The warm fried rice is everything I've been dreaming of since my last binge of cereal. A-m-a-z-i-n-g.

"Where's Josie?" I ask when I finally pull my face away from my plate.

"Nap time," Hunter says.

"Aah."

"Seen Watcher lately?" Hunter asks Solomon.

He shakes his head. "Nah, I've been a good boy."

Hunter snorts. "Yeah, I believe that."

They go on to talk about other things, and my attention drifts to the empty drums once more.

Solomon nudges my foot under the table. "All right, you ate. There's nothing stopping you now."

"No." I pull my sleeve down over my hand. "I wouldn't want to intrude."

"Please." He scrambles from his chair and pulls me from mine before I can stop him.

I shoot a desperate look toward Hunter, but he just sits back and whistles.

"Hey, Liam, need a drummer?" Solomon shouts to the guy singing into the microphone.

The song cuts off, and the guy eyes me. "You any good?"

I reach up to fiddle with the studs lining my ear. "I mean, I'm not bad…"

Solomon nudges me toward the stairs leading onto the stage. "She'll do fine, besides, none of us care."

"I care," Liam says, but his smile suggests there's no hard feelings. Actually, he reaches out to help me on stage.

The lights are warm up here and a bit blinding. Silence falls over the café, and even though I can't see them through the glare of the lights, I can feel the eyes of the Dream Guardians on me.

"Have at it." Liam gestures to the drums.

My footsteps echo off the stage as I move to the beauties and slide onto the round seat. A pair of worn sticks rest at the ready. I lock eyes with Liam. He nods, and the band strikes up where they left off. I bring the beat that's been playing in my head to life.

I let the beat play tag with the other instruments, weaving in and out, one moment supporting and the next stealing the show in a delicate balance. The drumbeat soars and dips, an accumulation of the time I've spent in the Dream. The cymbals add a playful tinkle to the background. A sprinkle of hope. That we'll all get through this okay. We'll save Macy, and then I'll go home. A quiet, softer beat thrums through my heart and out through my drumsticks. Twisted with longing. But for what? I pull my gaze away from the drums, and my gaze connects with Solomon's. He's beaming.

Chapter Twenty-Two

I toss and turn in the bed until the sheets tangle about my legs. What I wouldn't give to be back home where sleep is real. Oblivion tangible.

I lay there for a good while before giving up. I snag my sweater from the end of the bed and slip it on before padding to the curtained off glass doors that lead out to a balcony. I sweep aside the curtain and take in the thousands of skyscrapers that stretch across the horizon. They're dazzling with their lights. It's almost like going to the zoo at Christmas time. I flick the lock and step out.

The chill of night meets me, and I breathe in the fresh air.

Then wind tears at my hair. My sweater. Pushing and pulling. What the—

I try to turn and go back inside, but the wind strengthens until I have to squeeze my eyes shut.

And then the wind is gone. I dare to peek out at my surroundings, squinting against the light where before there was darkness.

Beck stands at the edge of the ocean, her back to me. The breeze pulls at her shoulder length curls, and she clutches a scarf close to her neck. Her turquoise coat gives her a majestic appearance. A shiver runs down my spine, and my hair stands on end. Something's wrong. Then it hits me. Beck hates that shade. So then, this isn't the real Beck, and I am still in the Dream.

She looks over her shoulder. "He's lying to you, Gweny."

I shiver in the breeze and cross my arms over my chest. Ignore the grate of the nickname against my nerves. "What are you talking about?"

The sand squelches beneath my boots. I stop when I reach my friend's side. The aroma of dead sea life drifts on the wind. Waves threaten to invade my combat boots.

She purses her lips and glances at me from the corner of her eye. "Whose dream is this?"

"Macy's." I raise my chin when I say it.

"Is that what he told you? I bet he told you he's her Guardian, too, huh?"

"Stop it."

Her eyes twinkle.

I clench the sleeves of my sweater. "He wouldn't do that." I almost wish she would go all Nightmare on me so I'd have an excuse to kick her butt.

"Ask him." Beck's dark, perfectly shaped eyebrows lift in a dare.

I take a weighted step back. "What?" I shouldn't trust her.

"Ask him whose Dream it is." She turns away, but looks back over her shoulder, lips twisted in a smirk. "I dare you."

She may not be a Nightmare, but her words are no less sharp. Isn't this what she's always trying to do? Tear things apart with her words. Sow seeds of doubt. Well, we'll see about that.

"I don't believe you," I say.

"We'll see." She raises her hand overhead in a wave.

The ocean shifts and changes. It is now darker. Stormy. Frothing at a patch of rocks on which I stand. Freezing rain pelts my skin. Goosebumps flash across my flesh, and my teeth chatter.

A wave breaks over the rocks, soaking my jeans from the shin down. Water sloshes in my boots. I need to climb to higher ground before the tide can swallow me.

"Solomon?" My call is swallowed by a clap of thunder.

He'll show up. Somehow, he always does. I just need to bide my time. Get to safer ground.

My boot slips against one of the wet stones. I catch myself against a rock with one hand. My palm slips against a jagged edge, and a red line opens along my palm. I hiss a breath and cradle my injured hand close.

Another wave strikes the rocks, hitting hard enough that the water bounces up and sprays me. I'm soaked now. I swipe my hair from my eyes and continue across the rocks, careful of how I position my feet with each step.

My teeth chatter painfully against each other.

I squint against the rain streaming across my vision. There. It looks like a cave. I can't risk going inside in case it floods with the rising tide, but maybe I can climb on top of it. That would buy me some time. Or at least it's a high vantage point I can use to look for Solomon.

I slosh my way there, and I pull myself up the uneven surface. My injured hand burns with each movement, and I'm now even more exposed to the wind than I was before. I flatten myself against the cave top.

"Solomon?" His name rubs my throat dry, but I call again. And again. And again.

The only answer is the thunder that shakes my bones.

"He's not coming." A voice whispers behind me.

My skin prickles, and my hair stands high on the back of my neck. I shouldn't be able to hear anything above the storm. And yet that whisper was clear. Too clear. Too...familiar.

Carefully, I rotate on the cave roof.

The aged Nightmare Lord kneels behind me, a dark cape keeping the rain at bay.

My lungs cramp. I can't exhale.

"Where's your precious Dream Guardian now, hmm?" Coakley's voice rasps, at odds with the smile creasing his cracked, dry lips.

"He's coming." I tilt my chin high. "He'll be here any minute."

He rises and creeps closer.

I recoil, but there's nowhere to go. Any further back, and I'll tip into the frothing ocean below.

Coakley stops only when his lips are inches from my ear. "I don't believe you."

I strike out, but my fist meets air. He's fast for a man who looks like a dried-up brussels sprout. I kick at him, but he dodges that, too. Another strike. This time, my fists connects with flesh.

Coakley stumbles back, his hood falling back to reveal his stringy hair. "Ah, you've got a bit more fight in you this time." He prods his busted lip with the back of his hand.

I clamber to my feet and face off with him.

"You don't want to fight a Nightmare, girl." Coakley pulls his hand away from his mouth.

"Yeah, but I won't go down without a fight, so..." I lift a shoulder in a shrug even as I raise my hands in front of my face.

"Your mistake."

Coakley charges.

I dodge. My boots slip against the wet rocks, and I go down on one knee. Coakley kicks out, catching me in the shoulder. I hit the ground. Roll. Push back to my feet. He's at the edge. If I could shove him over...

I race forward as fast as my half-frozen legs can carry me. I collide with his chest, my fingers knotting in his coat. He's reeling, feet slipping along the wet surface. I grit my teeth, brace my own feet, and shove.

Coakley cries out, arms windmilling, grabbing at anything as his feet meet air. I step back, chest heaving as he goes over. I did it.

"Gwen?" Solomon's accented call comes before another clap of thunder shakes the sky.

I turn toward his voice.

Something snags my boot. Gives a sharp tug. I lose my balance. Fall to my stomach. My chin bounces against the cave top, sending my teeth clashing together with a painful snap. And then I'm being yanked back, back, back.

"Solomon!" I scramble for a grip, but my wet hands skid along stone, finding nothing to stop my descent.

I can just make out his form down on the beach. He's too far. "Solomon!"

I'm falling.

Splash.

Water engulfs my head. Pours down my throat. I kick against the hand pulling me down, down, down.

My mom can't swim to save her life, but I mentally thank her for all the times she made Dad take us to the community pool and learn. I flail my arms, striking for the surface. But the weight at my ankle is too strong. Too insistent on pulling me down.

I crane my neck, fighting to see through the murky water. Coakley's eyes glow yellow, and his mouth is twisted in a sneer, heedless of the bubbles pouring from his nose. I kick out, catching him in the face.

His grip breaks.

I kick, propelling myself up.

My head bursts free from the liquid, and I suck in a breath. A wave slaps my face, and I get a lungful of water. I sputter and cough. Shake my head. Rain pours down, blinding me. I blink, turning this way and that in the waves, but I'm disoriented, and fog shrouds the shore.

"Solomon?" I spin in the water, again and again, let the waves carry me, but he's nowhere to be seen. "Solomon!"

A hand latches on to my calf, tugging me down. I scream before my head goes under. I thrash. Coakley's hands lock around my neck. I claw at his fingers. Rake my nails down his skin, but he doesn't release me. He drives his thumbs against my throat until everything is fire and pain, and then there is a burst of black.

Chapter Twenty-Three

I wake with a moan. Everything hurts. My throat. My head. I force my eyes open and squint at the semi-darkness clinging to the space. Weak moonlight trickles through the window pane placed high in the grimy stone wall. A cold draft sweeps through the room, prickling my arms with painful goosebumps. I roll my head to the side to take in the rest of the space. Bars twist from floor to ceiling. This isn't a room.

It's a prison.

I snap to a sitting position, and my lungs protest. I cough into my fist and press my back against the filthy stones to catch my breath.

Think.

Where am I?

I survey the small space again, but I can't see beyond the bars locking me inside. All right, wait for morning. Perhaps then I'll be able to get a better read on my situation. The thought of the long hours ahead of me sends sweat trickling from my pores, but I straighten my spine. If I've learned nothing else from the Dream, I have learned that panic only makes a bad situation worse.

Okay, am I hurt?

I don't think so. The pain in my lungs has already eased, and I suspect it has something to do with swallowing too much seawater. But if this is a new dream, and the fact that my clothes are dry along with the change in setting makes me think it is, then why do I have any effects left over from the previous one?

I run a hand through my tangled, salty hair. What I wouldn't give for a long soak in a hot bath. My throat aches, and I rub my fingers against my neck. Pain meets my touch. I suspect if I were to look into a mirror, I would find some bruising.

Well, I'm not going to fall apart, so I might as well see if there's a way to escape. I slide over to the bars and tug at each one, but they are solidly fixed into place. Hey, at least I can say I tried. I stand and pace beneath the window. There's no way I'd ever be able to squeeze through it. Really, a peephole would be a better descriptor than window. But perhaps if I scaled the wall and broke the glass, I could stick an arm out and wave. It's a long shot that anyone would see me, but it's worth filing away as an option. Of course, there's always the risk that no one would see, and I'll be stuck in here with a broken window freezing to death.

Yeah, I'll shelve that idea for now.

I slide back to the floor and pull my sweater close. For now, it's a waiting game. Solomon's bound to turn up sometime, that or something in the Dream will change, and I'll be free.

X

Who knew waiting could be so boring?

I've already scratched a dozen games of tic-tac-toe into the dirt covering the stone floor by the time morning light spills through the grimy window. It does little to illuminate the space beyond my cell. Darkness and the beginnings of what looks to be a hallway are all I can make out.

Great.

I rub my dirty hands over my jeans, leaving streaks of grime.

Do I keep waiting for Solomon or try to act on my own? The idea makes my palms sweat, and I lick my dry lips. It doesn't sit well, but Solomon's already taken longer to show up than I would have liked, so I guess it's up to me.

I push to my feet and edge toward the door. A quick tug reveals it's no looser today than it was last night. I kick at the area where I estimate a lock to be. My boot clangs against the metal, and the sound echoes through the emptiness. No good. I take a step back and shake out my hands. Okay, now what? But I don't know. I don't know. I. Don't. Know.

Footsteps click in the darkness beyond my cell.

I press close to the bars. "Solomon?" I keep my voice just above a whisper.

"Afraid not, love." Coakley steps into the thin trickle of sunlight. Too bad it doesn't disintegrate him. Wait...that's vampires, isn't it?

I step away from the bars. "What do you want from me?"

His eyebrows rise. "From you? Absolutely nothing, other than your fear. It feeds us, you know."

The words make the skin behind my ears tingle, and I swallow hard.

Coakley inhales deeply and releases a low moan. "Yes, yes, precisely."

"I'm not afraid of you." My voice only shakes a tiny bit.

"You are a liar."

I clench my jaw.

His decaying lips stretch into a thin smile, and he rolls his head to the side. "Oh, don't look at me like that. I shan't keep you forever."

"Why not?" Not that I want him to.

"It is not my right, human."

"What then? You feed on me either until I stop fearing you, or you get full?" I cross my arms over my chest, both to ward off the chill that seeps through my core and because it makes me feel just a little bit tougher.

He laughs, that dry heaving laugh that sounds like the cough of a dying man. "A Nightmare is never filled, girl. No, I have another purpose in mind."

"I won't cooperate," I say.

His scrutiny flicks over me. "No, I don't suppose you will." But he doesn't seem bothered by this. Simply amused.

I cock my chin high.

Coakley runs his hand down the length of one of the bars. "No, my purpose is not with you. I'd much rather wait for that precious Dream Guardian of yours."

I stiffen. "What?"

His lips curl. "Yes, there's a bit of that tantalizing scent."

"Solomon will destroy you." I glower at him.

"We will see." He brushes at invisible lint on his sleeve. "We will see. Every Guardian has a price."

Price? One of my conversations with Hunter comes to mind, and I harden my jaw. "Solomon will never defect."

"Like I said, every Guardian has their price. We'll see if you are his."

I want to grab him by his scrawny little neck and throttle him, but I don't move. My boots are rooted to the stones at my feet.

Coakley inhales deeply before he chuckles and turns away, fading into the shadows beyond my cell.

"It won't work!" I yell at his back.

His laughter is his only reply.

Chapter Twenty-Four

I gnaw my thumbnail. Pace my cell. And watch the beam of sunlight shift across my floor. My best guess is that it's been a couple of hours since Coakley's visit, and Solomon still hasn't shown up. Good. Maybe if he just stays away, Coakley will get sick of this game and will let me go.

It doesn't seem likely, but maybe.

I try to ignore the sting settling in my chest. Because maybe Solomon doesn't care about what's happened to me. Has he even noticed I'm missing? Of course, he has. Right? But maybe he isn't coming.

And that hurts.

I cross my arms and lean against the wall. I don't care what Solomon thinks. For all I know, he's gallivanting across the Dream with Macy. Maybe he's abandoned me to my own Dream Guardian who may not even know I'm in this mess. I try not to picture Macy and Solomon dancing a duet, but the image flicks across my imagination all the same. And that's stupid. Since when am I the jealous type? And over my best friend, at that? Ugh.

I find a pebble and toss it against the wall. It clatters to the floor, and I repeat the action over and over and over again until a Nightmare comes with a plate for dinner.

"What is it?" I eye the hard lump next to a mug of water.

"Scone." The guy looks like a slightly younger version of Coakley. Pale skin. Pupils way dilated. Ashy blonde hair hanging in greasy strings to his shoulders.

"A scone?" I raise my eyebrows and poke a finger against the lump. It rattles against the metal plate.

"If you don't want it, princess, then give it back." He makes a lunge for it, but I pull the plate backward, out of his reach.

"I'll eat it."

"Good." He positions himself in the shadows across from me, eyes glowing in the semi-darkness.

I think I preferred being alone. I gnaw at the "scone," but eating it is easier said than done. It takes me a solid fifteen minutes to give up on nibbling sections off, and then I just dunk the thing in the water one section at a time and chew through soaked bites.

"You guys really need to hire a new cook," I say around a mouthful.

"Shut up," the Nightmare snarls.

I raise my hands to symbolize peace. I choke down the rest of the scone, drain the cup, which only leads to my throat burning for more, and sit back against the wall.

The guy materializes from the darkness. "Pass it back."

I lift the plate. I could bash his head with it, but I don't see any keys on him, so it wouldn't do much other than get me in trouble.

"Don't even think about it," Creepy-pants growls.

"I'm not thinking about anything." But I drop the plate and kick it to him. I don't even try to hide my smile when it clanks against the toe of his boot, and he grunts. Ha.

"That Dream Guardian better show up soon," the guy snarls as he retrieves the plate.

"Solomon hasn't shown up yet?" That's a relief. Except for the part where that means I'm still sitting in this cell. How long does Coakley have license to keep me?

The guy delivers a sharp glare and stomps away.

"Wait, do you play tic-tac-toe?" I call after him.

X

By the next evening, we're both tired of my attitude as he tries to shove dinner at me.

"I'm not hungry." I massage my forehead where a headache has grown all day.

"I told you. Coakley says you eat."

"Well, then I guess you get to be the guy to tell him I said no."

"He won't accept that as an answer."

"Lucky you."

"I'm trying to warn you."

I pull my hand away and eye him.

His eyes narrow. "I'm not the one who's going to be punished."

A shiver runs down my spine.

His nostrils flare like he's sucking in the scent.

These dudes are way creepy.

"Fine. Give me the stupid thing." I hold out my hand and beckon with my fingers.

He tosses the scone in my lap.

"So, what's your story?" I ask as I yank off a bite.

His scowl deepens. "Nothing you need to know."

"Oh, lighten up, Creepy-pants. You've got to give me something. I'm about to go crazy in this cell, and unfortunately for us, you're the only thing I have for company." I grimace as I swallow another bite. I may never eat another scone in my life. It's like choking down hard sand.

"Creepy-pants?" The guy eyes me.

"Unless you want to volunteer a better name?"

He looks away.

"Didn't think so." I dust some fallen crumbs from my jeans. "Listen, how long until Coakley releases me? I know there's an expiration date."

He snorts. "Yeah, and did he tell you what that looks like?"

"I think he's rather clinging to the idea Solomon's going to come in like a gallant knight in shining armor." And no way would Solomon be dumb enough. Surely by now, he's figured out this is all a big trap.

Creepy-pants snorts. "So, you are stupid."

It takes great restraint not to chuck the rest of the scone at him. I don't, only because I have the feeling I'm on the brink of gaining information. "Well?" I cock an eyebrow. "Are you going to explain, or are you just going to call names?"

The guy leans closer, his eyes sparking. "You want to know what's going to happen? You think Coakley's just going to turn you loose and wave goodbye? You're an idiot. He can do whatever he wants. Hurt you as much as he wants before he lets you go. He can turn you into a vegetable to rot in the Waking World. Not quite alive. Not quite asleep. So, if I were you, I'd pray your little Guardian shows up."

I'm pressed back against the wall now, heart thundering against my chest, palms slick with sweat. He's bluffing. He has to be.

Creepy-pants throws his head back and makes a big show of sucking in the scent of my fear. Sick. I force myself to breathe carefully. In. Out. Until my heartbeat regulates, and my lungs aren't quite so pinched.

"Sweet dreams, human girl." Creepy-pants blows me a kiss.

"Wait!"

He stops. Turns.

I lick my lips. "I meant what I said."

He cocks an eyebrow, hands shoved lazily into his jean pockets.

"Do you play tic-tac-toe?"

We play in the space just beyond my bars where I can easily slip my hand through. Circles and x's. Game after game after game. And still Solomon does not come. My stomach cramps, and it takes so much effort not to hope he'll show up. Because that is the selfish thing. Wanting him to come get me. If Coakley will punish me with a death of sorts, I should make it a heroic one. A martyr. Like I saved Solomon by keeping him out of the hands of the Nightmares or something.

But of course, I've done nothing.

Solomon has chosen not to come.

"You're getting weaker, you know," Creepy-pants says.

"Excuse me?" I snap my gaze up as I finish my third circle in a row.

"You can no longer hide your fear," Creepy-pants says, lips stretching into a smile.

I narrow my eyes. "I'm not afraid of you."

"No, but you are afraid." He rotates his head to the side. "Of what, I wonder? Does it have something to do with him?"

I rub my palm over the dirt, erasing our game. "You don't know what you're talking about."

His nostrils work as if he's inhaling double time like a scent hound. "You are afraid of what will happen if he does come. Worst of all, you are afraid of what will happen if he doesn't."

"That's ridiculous." I jab a series of quick lines through the dirt.

"I can smell it."

"You're sick, do you know that?" I grit my teeth tight.

He stares at the ground for a long moment before raising his eyes to meet mine. "No, I am strong."

"No, you're weak. What was your price? What did Coakley give you that made you fall at his feet?"

His bares his teeth. "I did not fall."

"Didn't you? You're his lap dog, right?" I sweep him with a dismissive gaze.

His nostrils flare, but this time it is not because he's feeding. "You know nothing. I am no one's dog."

I lean forward until my forehead is inches from the bars. "But you are not free."

"You know nothing!" He screams it this time and springs away from the ground. Away from my cell.

"You're so blind, you can't see it. You're his slave," I shout.

Creepy-pants swivels on his heel and marches away.

Chapter Twenty-Five

"Gwen?" The whisper wakes me.

I snap upright, chest heaving, squinting against the darkness. I imagined it. I must have. I'm just about to lay back down when the voice comes again,

"Gwen? Are you down here?"

It's Solomon. He's come.

I crawl to my door and peer through the darkness, but I still can't see him. "Solomon? Solomon, I'm here." I shouldn't be so glad to hear his voice. Shouldn't be trembling with relief. But I am. So, so glad.

His flashlight clicks on. He's still several cells away from me.

"Here." I stick my hand through the bars and wave like a madwoman.

"Gwen." He breaks into a jog and skids to a stop in front of my cell. Clasps my hand. So very tight and so very tangible. "Are you all right? Did he hurt you?"

I just stare at him through a sheen of tears. At last, I'm not alone.

"Gwen, did he hurt you?" He looks ready to storm back the way he came and take out some Nightmares, so I force myself to stutter out a blubbery "no."

"Good." He presses his forehead against the bars, inches from mine. "Good."

And then I remember. "You have to get out of here." I twist my hand free from his.

"We will. Let me just deal with the lock, then we'll—"

"No. No, listen to me, this is a trap. You have to go." I push at his shoulder.

Solomon catches my fingers, stilling me. "Hey. Shh."

But I won't. I pull away and push at him again. "You have to go. Get out of here, Solomon."

His face hardens in the shadows. "I won't leave without you."

I'd cling to him if I could. But I can't. It's far too dangerous. "You don't understand. Coakley's set a trap."

"I don't care." He shoves away from the bars and moves to the lock, rattling it around.

I follow him, fighting to make eye contact. "You're not listening to me."

"No, you're not listening. I will not leave you here." He locks eyes with me. "I won't do it, Gwen."

"But—"

He licks his lips and shoves a hand through his hair. "You don't have any idea what he could do to you."

Well, I do. Have an idea at least. But I press my lips tight and watch him.

"I won't do it, Gwen. Don't ask it of me." His eyes soften, and for one terrible moment, I think he might cry.

"All right." I shove my trembling hands into the back pockets of my jeans. Because I don't really want him to leave me here. Maybe it's the selfish thing to do, but I'll let him rescue me. Maybe if we're both smart about it, we'll get out here without Coakley even knowing. The churn of my stomach suggests the idea is ludicrous, but what is life without hope? So, I stand there chewing on my thumbnail while Solomon fusses with the lock.

"That's a bad habit, you know," he says.

I jerk my thumb away from my mouth. "I'm giving it up."

He cocks an eyebrow. "Yeah, that's going well."

"You're supposed to be encouraging. My emotional support—" My cheeks burn hot, and I cut myself off before I can finish that stupid comment.

Solomon chuckles and turns his attention back to the lock. "I think...I've...got it." The door swings open with a high-pitched groan.

I cover my ears and shoot a look down the hallway. As of now, there's still no flood of Nightmares coming at us, so that's something in our favor. But I don't trust it. Coakley has something up his sleeve, and I wouldn't put it past him if this is all part of his plan.

Solomon grabs my hand and drags me from the cell. "Follow me. Whatever happens, stick close."

I nod.

But that's not good enough. Solomon places his hands on either side of my face and holds my gaze. "Promise me,

Gwen. We can't afford for you to experience another death in the Dream."

What about him? But I don't voice the question. Instead, I lick my lips and promise, "All right."

He nods like he's sealing the promise into the fabric of time. "Let's go." He breaks into a run.

I stumble, legs aching from spending so long in the cell doing nothing. Solomon slows enough that I can keep up with his pace. He leads the way around a corner, through an archway, and then up a set of slick stone steps. I trip. Catch my balance against the wall.

Solomon looks back at me. "You okay?"

I nod, one hand against my chest. "Yeah." I really need to start working out when I get home. This is pathetic.

Footsteps sound in the distance.

Solomon grabs me and pulls me into the shadows.

I focus on steadying my breathing, my back almost pressed against his chest. We stand frozen, but what good is that when Nightmares feed on fear? Solomon rubs slow circles on my back much like Nana used to when I was little. I relax into his touch. Just breathe.

The footsteps clatter past.

"Okay," Solomon murmurs in my ear.

We step out of the shadows.

Solomon plasters himself to the wall and creeps forward, motioning for me to follow. I swallow hard and force myself to mirror his movements, all while keeping an eye on the shadows. The hair on the back of my neck prickles. This is too easy.

We turn through a corridor, and Solomon stops at a window. "We'll climb out here."

He's got to be joking. We're at least three stories high in a castle that overlooks the drop off of a cliff slick with snow and ice.

"Come on, Gwen." He jerks at the window latch.

I take a step back. "No, there has to be another way."

He shoots me a look. "Then I would have led you there instead."

"I'm not climbing out that window."

"You don't have a choice." He pries open the window. "Out you go."

Cool wind whips at me, and I dig in my heels. "No, I can't." I shake my head, sending tendrils of hair dancing across my eyes. "I can't do this."

"You have to."

"No."

He starts to pick me up.

I dig my fingers into his shoulders, bunching up his lab coat. "Solomon!"

He sets me down. Searches my eyes. "What is it?"

"I can't climb down that." I glance out the window and shudder at the drop off.

"Why not?" He sounds exasperated.

I lick my lips and meet his eyes. "Because I'm afraid." And I can't be. If we're going to get out of this all right, I can't be afraid.

He searches my eyes. Nods. "Okay." He steps away from the window.

We link hands, and he pulls me down the corridor. Our footsteps seem to thunder as they echo off the empty walls. I keep glancing over my shoulder, expecting a Nightmare to be right behind us, but none ever show.

"Something's not right," I whisper to Solomon.

He squeezes my hand. "Just stay calm."

Right. The more I worry about things going wrong, the more likely it is they will.

He leads me down a flight of stairs and stops only when we reach a pair of side doors leading out into a decayed, snow-dusted garden. Solomon flips the lock and pulls me outside. The wind nips at me, stinging my nose, my cheeks. Even my jeans are inconsequential under the battery.

We round a corner, trampling a line of twisted, dried out ferns. Maybe we're really doing this. Maybe—

Shadows swell and close in around us. I slam into Solomon's back and stay there, pressed against him as the shadows take on forms mirroring humans. We're surrounded by a pack of Nightmares.

Coakley steps to the front, clapping his hands in slow-motion. "Well done, Guardian, well done. Valiant rescue."

I swallow a whimper and tighten my hold on Solomon's lab coat.

But if Solomon is afraid, he doesn't show it. Instead, he stands taller. "We're leaving."

The amusement falls from Coakley's face. "I don't think so."

Solomon's back tenses. "Think again." He whips his sword from its invisible sheath.

Coakley's hand fills with a blade of his own. "You can't stop me, Guardian."

"Brave words, Coakley."

"You'll never win against *us*."

At the word "us," all the other Nightmares draw their swords. I find Creepy-pants in the crowd, try to catch his eye, but he refuses to look at me.

"Not exactly fair odds, eh Coakley?" Solomon backs up slowly.

I move with him, hands still fisted in his lab coat.

Coakley chuckles. "A Nightmare never plays by the rules. But neither do you, so what does it matter?" He takes a step forward for every one we take backward.

We're easing out of the garden now, toward a mountain road twisting above a high drop off. My knees wobble. The army of Nightmares seem to swell.

Solomon reaches behind him and takes my wrist. "Shh."

I force myself to breathe. I keep my gaze on Solomon's back and not the army ahead of us.

Coakley extends his free hand toward Solomon. "Join us, boy. Buck the rules Watcher so likes to restrain you with."

A muscle twitches in Solomon's jaw.

"He's jealous of your talent." Coakley's words ring out above the wind.

Solomon scoots back another step.

"That's why he never lets you do what you're so good at."

Solomon's steps falter.

"He's holding you back."

Solomon. Stops. Moving.

Coakley grins and advances, circling like a vulture. "His robbing you of your full potential. You could be so much more than what he allows, Solomon Custos."

I push up on my tiptoes so my lips are near Solomon's ear. "Don't listen to him."

His eyes jerk toward me like a desperate man who's been offered a lifeline.

"It's all lies," I say.

Coakley's lips twist into a sneer as he watches us, but then he's creeping forward once more. "I could give you what you want. You'll be second to no one, save me. I won't question your every move. I'll give you the respect you deserve."

"Watcher knows your talents. He's trying to prepare you." I tighten my hold on his coat as if that will somehow keep him anchored in the truth.

But Solomon's attention is once more stuck on the Nightmare Lord.

Coakley's grin stretches wide. "That's right. Just ask any of them." He waves his arm toward his pack of Nightmares. "I value their talents. Never once have I held them back from reaching their full potential."

"This isn't what you want, Solomon," my words overlap the Nightmare's.

Solomon's feet shuffle forward an inch, his eyes wild and unfocused. I grip his coat harder and yank him back.

Coakley laughs at us.

Oh, can't he just choke on his own spit? "Solomon!"

"Join me." Coakley holds out his hand once more.

As if in a trance, Solomon brushes me off and teeters forward.

I lunge into his path, plant both hands on his shoulders, and push him back. "No!"

"You'll get all the power you deserve," Coakley says.

I fight to bring my eyes level with Solomon's. "He doesn't share power." I grip his shoulders and push up on my toes. "Look at them."

He's fighting to step around me.

I grab both sides of his face and force him to look to the side at the pack of Nightmares. "Look at them. They're his dogs, forced to wait on their master's bidding. They have no power of their own, only what he allows."

"We're no one's dogs," Creepy-pants growls.

Other Nightmares murmur their agreement. But none of them step forward. They're a mass of shadow behind their lord.

I keep my back turned to Coakley and stay step for step with Solomon despite the fact he's pushing forward. I'm not strong enough to restrain him, so my words will have to do the trick, "Watcher trusts you. He wants you to succeed. That's the only reason he pushes you so hard."

"Let him go, Gwendolyn." Coakley's words are a whisper on my neck.

I stiffen and look behind me. We've crossed the gap. The Nightmare Lord is only inches away, hovering behind me but not touching me.

I drop my hands away from Solomon's shoulders, ice replacing the blood in my veins.

"Good." Coakley nods his approval. "Very good."

Hot liquid burns my eyes. "You can't do this, Solomon."

He moves past me, eyes unfocused.

I snag his hand. Entwine our fingers. "Please."

Coakley chuckles low and mocking.

I force myself to focus only on Solomon. "Please, don't leave me."

That brings him to a stop. His attention wobbles back to me. Somehow, I know deep inside that this is it. If I am to persuade him, it must be now, or I will lose him forever. "Don't leave me."

Is that a hint of clarity washing across his vision?

Coakley growls. "Enough! Release the Guardian, and I will send you back to the Waking World unharmed."

Now it's my gaze snapping to meet his.

He chuckles. "That's right. I can offer you what Watcher and his Guardians cannot. You wish to wake? Fine. Consider it done, but the boy stays with me."

No. This is not the way. I know it deep in my core. I tune out the Nightmare Lord and lock eyes with Solomon. "It's all lies. Please, I need you. Help me save Macy, and then help me get home."

He swallows hard. Nods.

Hands grab me. Nails pinch my skin. Fingers bruise. I kick and flail. "Solomon!" Hands knot in my hair, pulling my head back, back, back, until my roots scream, and pain shoots down my neck.

Coakley throws his head back and cackles along to the howling of the wind.

Clarity snaps into Solomon's eyes, and he springs forward with a roar, cutting at the Nightmares holding me. They throw me to the ground and block off Solomon's access to me, weapons drawn as a barrier.

Two can play this game.

I shuffle my hands across the snowy ground, packing the wetness into hard balls, and chuck them at the Nightmares, aiming at heads, shoulders, the back of their knees. Several curse and spin toward me.

I scramble backward, snagging more snowballs as I go, but as the space shrinks between us, my hands turn sweaty. Snow is no match for swords. My heel strikes against something. I teeter, lose my balance, and fall hard on a patch of ice, sending a streak of pain up my hip.

Creepy-pants is the first to reach me, his skin ashy-gray in the dim sunlight.

"Please." I shake my head. Pat the ground for a weapon of any kind. My fingers bump a rock, and I scoop it up.

Creepy-pants advances, face twisted in a sneer. Any notion of a friendship between us evaporates in the gleam of his silver blade. I chuck the rock, but my aim is off, and the projectile sails over his shoulder without so much as tapping him.

I scramble backward, but he is quicker, grabbing a fistful of my sweater and jerking me to my feet. I grab his arm with both hands and try to twist free of his grip, but his forearm is like iron. He hauls me toward the edge of the cliff. I dig my feet in, but it only slows him minimally as he yanks me hard. I kick at his shin, and he swings me to the side, avoiding my strike.

"I'll show you that I am no one's dog." His nostrils flare.

"You're right, you're right. I shouldn't have said it." I glance desperately around for Solomon, but he is lost in the pack.

"I obey no one's orders but my own." He hauls me forward another foot.

I try to send all of my weight to my rear.

He only hefts me higher like he has super-human strength. Maybe he does.

"I was wrong. All right? I was wrong. That's what you want to hear, isn't it?"

"Hear? We can hear many things. It's what we believe that matters." A vein pulses in his forehead, and his grip turns crushing.

"So, what are you going to do?" My fingers quake, but I pluck at his anyway.

"I'm going to teach you to believe."

We're at the ledge now.

The wind tears at my hair.

Creepy-pants shoves me out, so my heels teeter on the edge of nothing.

My stomach flips. "Please..."

He shakes me, and I scream as one foot slips off the ledge.

"Gwen!" Solomon calls for me.

My mouth works, struggling for words even as Creepy-pants tilts me farther back. Only the toes of one foot keep me rooted to the ground. And even that is a quickly slipping connection the farther back he pushes me.

His lips tilt higher and higher into a grin.

I wrap my fingers around his wrist. This time not in an effort to break his grip, but to keep it in place.

"Please."

He lets go.

Chapter Twenty-Six

My scream pierces my eardrums.

Open air embraces my body, and I'm falling. And then arms are wrapping around me, and Solomon is there, his head close to mine. I stare into his eyes. There're things I want to say. Even just "thank you," for being here with me in the last seconds, but his eyes aren't those of the dying. No, a fire of concentration burns in his pupils.

"Don't be afraid." He has to shout for me to hear him over the roar of the wind.

His eyes stay locked on mine.

I fight back a whimper.

"Do you trust me, Gwen?"

"Yes." He probably doesn't hear the murmur, but I'm hoping he can read my answer on my lips.

"Then don't be afraid." He holds my stare.

I stare right on back. Clinging to him. To his words. They are nearly ridiculous with the wind rushing around us, and the knowledge that sooner rather than later, we will hit the ground. But I embrace them all the same and squeeze my eyes shut.

Don't be afraid?

Okay.

The howling of the wind stops. The sensation of falling ends.

"You did it, Gwen." Solomon's voice is a murmur, no longer a scream above the wind.

I peel my eyes open. I have done it. We're not tumbling away from the cliffside with the ground rushing up to meet us. Instead, we stand in the living room of Solomon's apartment, the electronic fireplace glowing welcomingly.

I can't help but laugh, and then I am crying.

"Shh." Solomon gathers me close and holds me, rubbing my back and murmuring indecipherable words in my ear.

I shut my eyes and press my cheek against his shoulder and try to pretend he is speaking Spanish and that it is Nana holding me. But Solomon's form is too solid, his voice too rich. But not unwelcome.

"Thank you, Gwen."

I pull back, swiping at my eyes. "For what? Getting captured? Because that didn't exactly turn out well. We both could have died."

"For saving me. Back there." He ducks his head, and his jaw works for a long moment before he visibly swallows. "Without you...I-I don't know what would have happened."

I close the gap between us and touch his cheek. "Don't ever doubt your worth as a Guardian, Solomon. You're the best one I know."

His lips quirk. "I'm the only one you know."

"Hunter, Josie, Watcher." I count them off on my fingers.

"Okay, okay." He raises his hands in surrender.

"But honestly, Solomon…you're the best. And you have something Watcher never will."

"Yeah, and what's that?" Solomon crosses his arms and bounces slightly on his toes.

"Compassion."

He holds my gaze.

"Coakley could offer you the world, but promise me you'll never listen, because it's all lies. Creepy-pants and all the others are just his dogs, waiting for a command from their master so they can roll over and serve. You're worth more than that."

"Creepy-pants?" Solomon raises an eyebrow.

I shove his shoulder. "You know what I mean."

He sobers. "Thank you, Gwen."

Suddenly, it's too hot in here. I back up, putting some space between us, and keep my gaze rooted on the floor. It's easier than looking him in the eyes for a second longer.

Solomon's watch pings.

His moan is all it takes to tell me who it is. "Watcher?"

"I have to meet him in his office."

"Great."

Solomon motions toward the door. "Come on."

"Do I have to?" The last thing I want is to listen to Solomon get chewed out by his boss…again.

"I'm not leaving you here alone."

"So, what? I accidently get kidnapped by the Nightmare Lord, and suddenly I get a ball and chain?"

He doesn't even blink. "Yes."

"Fabulous." Except, I'm not really mad at all. Just the idea of being alone is enough to send goosebumps flaring along my skin. So, I trail Solomon to the elevator and let the metal contraption box us in. I lean against the wall and toy with a loose thread on my sweater.

"You okay?" Solomon asks.

"Are..." I peek at him. "Are you going to be in a lot of trouble?"

He shrugs. "Eh, I'll be fine."

And maybe I'd believe him if I didn't catch the slight jiggle of his knee. I bite my lip to keep back any words that may try to escape, because nothing I could say would be particularly helpful in this situation.

"Gwen."

I raise my chin and meet Solomon's stare.

"It's not your job to worry about me." His expression is kind. Gentle.

Someone has to. It's what I want to say, but that might make things weird. Like I think I have some possessional right over him or something. Or maybe I'm over thinking it all. Either way, I don't know, so I keep my mouth shut.

The elevator hums softly as it descends.

"Everything will be fine, you'll see." Solomon winks as the elevator gives a soft shudder, announcing just before the beep, that we have landed.

Solomon steps through the doors first, and I trail after him. Our footsteps echo unnaturally in the hallway. I wrap my arms around my middle and shudder. Is this how it feels to walk to your own execution? A little dramatic maybe, but the tension along my spine builds with every step, and I don't trust Watcher to handle this situation without yelling and maybe saying something we'll all regret later.

"Hey!" Hunter is seated at the bar and waves us down.

Solomon just nods as we pass, veering toward the doors hiding Watcher's surveillance room.

"Why do you two look like someone kicked a puppy?" Hunter lowers his drink.

"I think someone's about to get kicked," I murmur, lingering long enough to jerk my chin at Solomon's back.

"Ah…" Hunter ducks his head and fiddles with his glass.

Suddenly, I feel like I should explain. "Look, it's my fault—"

"No, I don't want to hear it." Hunter waves away my words. "It's Watcher's business. Besides, it's always a Guardian's responsibility. You're not supposed to be here, remember?" His lips quirk up.

"Right."

"Gwen?"

I turn.

Solomon has paused outside Watcher's doors, waiting for me.

"Good luck." Hunter lifts his glass in a salute.

I nod and join Solomon.

"Ready?" He shakes out his arms and rolls his shoulders.

"I don't think I'll ever be, but since we don't have much of a choice…" I shrug.

Solomon steps through the doors, and I follow.

Watcher is, of course, waiting for us. Though he doesn't acknowledge our entrance. He stands with his back facing us, arms crossed.

I ease behind Solomon and rub my fingers together. I don't know why, but this feels akin to being called out in class.

Solomon stands at attention, shoulders back, chin high. At least he is fearless.

"Did I, or did I not expressly instruct you to make sure something like this did not happen?" Watcher's question rings through the room.

I flinch.

Solomon remains steady, only the deep lift of his shoulder as he inhales before answering shows a reaction to Watcher's words. "You did, sir."

"So, I thought." Watcher's shoulders remain a rigid barrier.

Solomon's throat bobs.

He's just going to stand here and take this? I push past him. "None of this was Solomon's fault. I was the one who got taken. I—"

Watcher rotates to face me. "And tell me, Miss Gonzales, who was it that brought you into the Dream in the first place?"

I swallow hard, my fire diffusing. "I—" I can't help but dart a look at Solomon whose focus is fixed on the wall beyond both me and Watcher.

"Exactly, Miss Gonzales." He brushes past me, effectively dismissing me from the conversation.

I just stand there gaping like a baby who's seen a Christmas tree for the first time.

Watcher closes in on Solomon until the pair are inches apart. "You have twenty-four hours to resolve this situation, or I will have no choice but to demote you and have your Dreamer reassigned to a better suited Guardian."

Fire sparks in Solomon's eyes. "Seventy-two."

"Forty-eight."

They face off with a stare-down for a long moment before Solomon says, "Forty-eight."

For another heartbeat, they stare each other down before they both jerk their chins in sharp nods and step apart.

"Are you ready, Gwen?" Solomon asks.

It might sound casual, but tension lines his shoulders.

"Yeah." I tug my sleeves over my fists and skirt around Watcher.

"Forty-eight hours, Custos," Watcher says to our backs as we make our exit.

Chapter Twenty-Seven

We're quiet when we return to Solomon's apartment. He ducks into the bathroom to shower, and I drop onto a stool at the counter and gnaw my thumbnail. How we're going to resolve everything in forty-eight hours, I don't know.

I get up.

Pace.

Not that it helps.

Solomon's water runs for longer than usual. I wince. None of this is his fault, and yet I'm powerless to absolve him of guilt. I move to his shelf where he keeps his mugs. I reach for the largest and set it near the espresso machine. Next, I check the fridge and pull out a milk carton. It's light. Enough for either a bowl of cereal or foam for Solomon's coffee. The selfish part of me wants to guzzle it, but thinking about myself won't help anything. I set the carton beside the empty mug. Too bad I don't know how to actually work the machine. With my luck, I'd blow something up. Getting the ingredients out will have to be enough of a gesture.

I reach into a cabinet and retrieve the cereal box. The thing is all but crumbs now, but it will have to do. I shove a handful in my mouth and chew.

My gaze trails to the bathroom door, and one question looms with the growing pressure of a deadline. What if we fail? What happens to Solomon then?

But I don't have the answers to any of it, so I drop my head in my hands and wait.

"Gwen." Solomon taps my shoulder, startling me awake.

I jolt upright, cool air meeting the cheek that is warm from being pressed against the counter. His hair is dry, and he's wearing fresh clothes under his lab coat.

"How long was I asleep for?" I rub at my gritty eyes.

"Not long enough."

I shrug. "Who has time for that anyway? We're on a deadline."

He snaps his fingers. "Right you are. Which is why I woke you. Macy's here." He extends his hand. "Once more for old time's sake?"

"You think we can fix everything in one more go?" Someone needs to give me whatever optimist pill this boy took. Or maybe he's just hyped up on coffee.

"We can hope, can't we?" He grins and bows, wiggling his upturned fingers. "My lady?"

I roll my eyes, but place my hand in his.

Warm light envelopes us, and then there's a burst of lemon cleaner so pungent it makes me momentarily dizzy. I squeeze my eyes shut and focus on breathing through my mouth. In and out. And then the air settles around me, and I open my eyes.

Folk music gently strums through speakers, and the pungent aroma of coffee wafts through the building every time someone opens the door, sending a little bell jingling. I know this place. *Dashiell's*. Macy and Austin Taylor both work here part-time, and I've spent more hours after school here than I can count.

I scan the café for Solomon, but he's faded into the background. I can't explain it, but somehow, I know he is here. His presence is tangible though I have yet to find him in the crowd.

An espresso machine whirrs in the background, blending with the upbeat music, adding a lively atmosphere to the place. Friends and dates chatter at tables, and I scan each one as I make my way through the café. There has to be a reason for this dream, but what?

The overwhelming scent of coffee hits my nostrils as I pass a barista wiping up a spill. I grimace and hurry past.

"Gwen!" Macy waves a hand from where she and Beck sit at a circular table in the corner.

I paste on a smile and head their way. "Hey." I slide into the seat on Macy's left. The chair tilts off kilter, and I adjust my weight to compensate.

Macy beams her welcome before her brow wrinkles. "You haven't gotten anything to drink."

Beck's brows shoot up.

Heat burns my cheeks, and I tuck my hands under my legs. "I forgot to grab my purse."

Macy snatches up her clutch and pulls out a five-dollar-bill. "Go get something."

"Macy, I can't—"

"You can, and you will." She gives me a little nudge with her boot. "Go on."

I roll my eyes and sigh. "You're the best."

Her nose wrinkles as she laughs. "I know."

I slide off my chair, causing it to scrape against the tiled floor, only to freeze when I see the barista working the register. "I can't." I turn away and crawl back into the safety of my seat.

Macy exchanges a glance with Beck. "What's wrong?"

"I can't. *He's* here." As the words leave my mouth, the whole scene reeks of déjà vu. We've done this all before.

Another look between the two.

"Who?" Beck cranes her neck for a better view.

"Austin Taylor." My face burns as I say his name. I can't even keep my mouth shut. It's like I'm a puppet being directed by the whim of Macy's dream-memory.

"Girl, you have to man up sometime, and talk to him," Beck says.

I shake my head furiously, sending my hair slapping across my face. "I can't." I dart a look over my shoulder to be sure Austin hasn't overheard our conversation. He doesn't even glance our way. I release my breath and turn back to face my friends.

"Go talk to him," Macy urges.

"No way." My heart palpitates, and I run my sweaty palms down my jeans. Where in the Dream is Solomon when I need him?

"You can do it." Macy's bouncing in her chair now.

Beck gives me a shove. "Go!"

Like a robot, I start forward exactly like I did that day, but turn back, cheeks flaming. "What do I say?" Would it be wrong to pray Solomon isn't watching this right now?

"Order your drink, dummy," Beck says.

Right. Taking a deep breath for courage, I shuffle to the counter and step into line behind a tall, blonde woman who reeks of too much perfume which does nothing to cover the smell of cigarette smoke clinging to her jacket. I do my best to breathe through my mouth and mentally recite what I'll say to Austin.

"I'll have a small Chai Latte."

I should probably throw a "please" in there.

When I step up to the register, all thoughts of what I should say flit from my mind as I lock eyes with Austin Taylor.

Austin flashes a smile that makes my face flame once again. "What can I get you?"

"Uhh..." Words. Words...what are words? I flounder and scan the menu for something. Anything. I order the first thing on the board.

My stomach flutters as Austin holds out a hand. His head tilts to the side, and a slow smile eases over his face. "Uhh...Gwen, it's $3.50."

I stare at his extended palm. My heart surges and then stops as I imagine our fingers brushing. Warmth tingles through my fingertips, and my knees shake.

"Gwen?"

I blink, mesmerized by the variety of colors breaking up the green of his irises. "Yes?"

"For the macchiato. $3.50...please."

I lick my lips as I study the way his sandy hair touches his forehead, just enough to give him a boyish appearance without making him look scruffy. "Uh, huh."

His lips twitch, and I catch a hint of his dimples. "Gwen, you need to *give* me $3.50."

"Oh, right." I snap out of my trance and fish for Macy's money. Dumb, dumb, dumb. "Sorry."

Chuckling, Austin takes the bill and gets me change. His fingers brush my palm as he hands me the coins. Warmth gushes through me, and I quickly pull away, dropping a quarter in the process. It clinks against the counter like the nails that will slam into the coffin I plan to build for myself as soon as I can walk away and die of embarrassment in private. Austin is quick to retrieve the coin and hand it back to me, his smile never dimming.

"Thanks," I mutter without meeting his eyes. I wrap my sweater tighter around my waist and shuffle to the other side of the counter to wait for my drink.

"Honestly, do you even think it's healthy to like him when you can't even string a full sentence together?"

I jump at Solomon's voice. "What are you doing?"

"Surveillance." He tips a coffee mug toward where Macy and Beck sit, laughing at me behind their raised hands.

I moan and lean against the counter. "Great."

"Honestly though, why do you like him?" Solomon frowns at where Austin is chatting up the next teenage girl in line. Was that an eye twitch, or did he wink as he took her money?

I turn away from the pair and focus on Solomon. "He's nice."

"And how would you know? You've never had a conversation with him."

Are we really back to this? "I have so."

"A real conversation. You know, one where you both talk. Coherently."

"You don't have to make fun," I snap.

A barista slides my drink over to me, and I snatch it up.

"I'm not making fun," Solomon protests.

"Whatever." I stomp over to where my friends wait.

Macy waggles her eyebrows. "So?"

I hand her the change and groan. "He thinks I'm an idiot."

Beck's lips droop into a pout. "I'm sure that's not true."

I raise an eyebrow.

"Well, at least you talked to him," Macy says.

"Yeah, at this rate, maybe you can get him to ask you to prom," Beck adds.

I rub a hand over my forehead. "I'm not going."

"What?" Both girls shout.

"I'd have to get a dress, find a date...I just can't."

Beck tosses her tight curls. "What girl doesn't go to her senior prom?"

I squirm in my seat. If only Macy would wake up and spare me from having this conversation again. I shoot a look toward the table tucked into the corner where Solomon pretends to be scanning the cute signs with funny coffee sayings that hang all around the café.

Macy leans forward in her seat. "Come on, it'll be fun. And as for dates, you don't *have* to have one. We can all go together."

Beck snorts and rolls her eyes before taking a long sip of her iced coffee. "Whatever. Go together if you want. I'm going to get a proper date."

Now it's Macy's turn to roll her eyes. "Really? And who are you going to go with?"

Beck raises her chin. "Jake Anderson."

I can't hold back my laugh even though I know how this ends. "Yeah, and did you run that by his girlfriend?" I wince, but I can't take back the words this time any more than when this conversation took place in the waking world.

Just as I know they will, Beck's eyes flash fire. "Whatever." She slides off her chair and grabs her purse. "I have to go pick up my little brother."

I sober. "Oh, don't be mad, Beck."

Her lips stretch into a strained smile. "I'm not." She turns and strides away, her ankle boots clicking over the tiles. The bell jangles above the door as she leaves.

I shoot a worried look Macy's way.

She shrugs. "It's Beck. She'll go out, buy another pair of shoes for her collection, and then she'll be fine."

"Yeah, I guess you're right." I take a sip of my drink and gag. "Ugh." I push the offending substance away.

Macy frowns and tries to get a better view of my cup. "What did you order?"

"I have no idea. Something coffee. I was so panicked I just read something off the board."

Macy tosses her head back and laughs. An answering smile pulls at my own lips until I join her. We laugh until tears run down our cheeks. It's a good feeling. Even if this is only a memory, I haven't laughed like this since Luke's accident. For a moment, I want nothing more than to grab Macy and hug her tight, but I can't stand out, so I just smile at her and hope she at least gets a small idea of how much this moment means to me.

Macy grins back and picks up her clutch. "I really should be going, too."

"Yeah." I get up and take hold of my bumpy Styrofoam mug. "Me, too."

"Want a ride?" Macy asks, holding the door for me.

"Nah, the walk will be good for me." I salute with my coffee mug and watch as she crosses the parking lot, her frame slowly dissolving until the dream fades away, and I'm back in Solomon's apartment.

He frowns at me.

I hold up a warning finger. "Don't say a word. I'm not in the mood for a lecture."

"I'm just worried about you, Gwen. You could do so much better."

I shake my finger. "I don't want to hear it. It's not your business."

He ducks his head and nods. "You're right. Not my business." His shoulders slump, and he turns away.

"Solomon..." But I don't know what to say, so I let him walk away.

Chapter Twenty-Eight

I can't shake the niggling sensation that I should apologize. Which is dumb, of course, considering I didn't do anything. So, instead, I play the avoidance game. Creeping around quietly in the kitchen, snacking on cereal, and then making myself scarce when Solomon enters to fix a coffee for himself. I duck into the bathroom and only dare to emerge when the whirr of the machine dies away.

If I'm lucky, Solomon's feeling as awkward as I am and has retreated to his room. Which leaves the living room to me. I ease into the hallway and tiptoe to safety.

Except I'm not that lucky, after all.

Solomon waits for me in the kitchen, arms propped on the counter. "I think we should talk."

Hmm...conflict. Not really my favorite thing. My thumb twitches toward my mouth, but I stop myself just in time to keep from chewing my nail. Instead, I shove my hands into the back pockets of my jeans. "Yeah?" Lame start, but he's the one who came up with this idea in the first place, so it doesn't really matter.

He sighs and mops his hands over his face. "Look, I'm sorry."

I blink. "Okay...?" Not what I expected. At all.

He lowers his hands and meets my eyes. "I was out of line before. Your..." he swallows. "Your love life is not my business."

Love life? My cheeks burn hot. That's not exactly how I would describe it. Not yet anyway. But Solomon is looking at me, waiting for a response, and the last thing I want to do right now is get in another argument. "Thanks. I appreciate that." I tuck my hair behind my ear and try to keep from squirming in the stillness that follows.

"So, we're good?" He asks, gaze so desperately intense.

I can't help my grin as I sweep my boot against the floorboards. "Yeah, we're good."

"Good, cause we—"

A kaleidoscope of color bursts in front of my eyes. I cover them with my hand until the rotating splotches of color dim. When I dare a peek, my heart rate gallops. I'm home. Or at least stuck in a memory of it. The scene before me is steeped in a sense of déjà vu. I think it's from late summer when Mom was working overnight at the hospital and Elijah and I were assigned babysitting duty.

Solomon tucks himself into the shadows of the porch, blending seamlessly into the background like he does so well.

"Look what I found!" Maria hops up and down on the porch step, nearly teetering over in her too big rain boots. She holds up a leaf streaked in various shades of red and green. The thing is almost as large as her face. I reorient myself just in time to snag the back of her shirt, keeping her from tumbling headfirst onto the pavement below.

Macy looks up from where she sits on the driveway with Tommy, creating a chalk masterpiece, and bestows a beaming smile on my little sister. "Ooh, that's a good one."

Elijah slaps a tennis ball into his hockey net and wipes his forehead with the back of his arm. He bumps his backward hat, almost sending it tumbling to the pavement. "Nice job, squirt."

Beck picks at her cuticles from her position next to me on the porch. "It's a leaf."

"A cool one." Maria sticks her tongue out through the gap where she's missing two teeth.

I don't even bother reproaching her. Instead, I hide a grin behind my hand.

"Charming." Beck bounces her knee and checks her phone. "Ugh, where is my mom?"

"You should let Elijah take a look at the Bug," Macy says. "Maybe he could get it running again?"

"Thanks," Beck shoots Macy a sugary sweet smile, "but I want a professional."

Elijah hooks his hockey stick across his shoulders. "I don't mind."

"Thanks, but no." She springs up from the step. "There's my mom." She waves as a red minivan pulls up to the driveway.

Jeesh, does she have to be so eager to get out of here? I lock my jaw to keep my face from twitching into an expression that will look anything less than hospitable.

"You sure you don't want to stay and help us babysit?" Macy calls after her with a laugh.

Beck just waves over her head before diving into the passenger seat. Her mom honks before the two disappear down the road. Here one moment, and then poof...gone in an instant.

"So, pizza?" Elijah raises his eyebrows.

Nana would never allow it if she were here, always insisting on home cooked meals, but with her off on a trip to Florida with some friends...what she doesn't know won't hurt her.

"Yes!" Tommy pumps his fist.

"Only if we get ice cream after." Maria props her fists on her hips, looking way older than she should.

"Sure thing." Elijah swipes his cap off and plunks it down on her tangled mop of hair.

The scene fades away, leaving me back in Solomon's apartment, brow furrowed. Why is Macy dreaming about the past?

"You all right?" Solomon asks.

"Yeah, fine." I massage the side of my neck.

"You don't look it."

"Okay, fine," I huff. "Why is Macy so obsessed with the past lately?"

He shrugs. "Dreams are a way for a Dreamer to process their day. Could be an underlying emotion she's trying to process that we just aren't aware of."

Makes sense. If I were back home, I'd probably find a similar answer if I looked it up. "No fear though..."

"Sorry?" He leans back against the wall, eyebrows raised.

"She wasn't afraid," I repeat. "That's good, right?"

"Excellent."

We share a smile.

"Does that…" I lick my lips. Force myself to voice the question even as I erect an invisible wall to protect myself from the answer… "Does that mean I can go home soon?"

He pushes away from the wall, grin stretching extra wide. "We'll need Watcher's go ahead, but I can't imagine he'll withhold permission for too much longer, especially if Macy's dreams continue in this pattern."

I drop onto the couch, tuck my hands between my knees, and grin like an idiot.

Chapter Twenty-Nine

An alarm blares, jolting me into an upright position on the couch. Red lights flash, and I cover my ears as the alarm rises in pitch.

"Solomon? What's going on?" I call, hoping my voice is louder than the siren.

Solomon stumbles from his bedroom, jerking on his lab coat over his rumpled t-shirt and jeans. "We have to go. Now."

I'm mostly reading his lips and filling out the blanks in between the words I don't catch. I spring from the couch and meet him at the door. "Is it Macy?" I lean close so he might actually have a chance of hearing me.

He shakes his head and says something.

"What?" I watch his lips as he repeats himself, but I can't make it out and just end up shaking my head.

He bends down, positioning his lips close to my ear. "There's been an emergency."

"Macy?" I ask, carefully enunciating the word.

He shakes his head.

A dozen more questions swell up, but there's no way we'll actually be able to talk, so I swallow them back and let Solomon pull me from the apartment. He bypasses the elevator and instead, heads for the stairwell. I jog to keep up as Solomon descends, skipping multiple stairs at a time, practically flying around corners. I grip the metal banister and cradle my side with one hand as a growing pang cuts through me. But I don't slow. Instead, I focus on my feet so I don't miss a step and go careening down to break my neck.

Solomon waits for me at the bottom of the stairwell. When I reach him, he shoves the heavy door open, and we're in the hallway that leads to the café and Watcher's office. There's a sea of Guardians around us on all sides, all shoving toward the café. I snag a handful of Solomon's lab coat to avoid being separated in the press of bodies. Everyone is talking at once, the buzz of voices mixing with the wail of the alarm. It's enough to make my ears ache.

Solomon snags my hand and weaves his fingers through mine. He guides me through the crush, and we spill out of the hallway and into the café. Finally, the siren dies away, and we're left with the chatter of hundreds of voices.

"Come on," Solomon murmurs in my ear. He jerks his chin, directing my attention toward where Hunter paces in front of Watcher's office.

I let him lead me to the other Guardian.

"What's going on?" Solomon asks when we stop in front of Hunter.

Pain swells in the Guardian's eyes, and he has to try several times before words exit his lips, "Solomon...it's...it's Josie."

Solomon's fingers tense around mine, and I'm not even sure he realizes he takes a step backward. I touch my free hand to his back, just so he'll know I'm here.

"What—" Solomon has to swallow and try again, "what happened?"

"Things went bad, Sol. Really bad." Hunter squeezes his shoulder.

Solomon shakes his head like he can't quite digest the news. "That can't be…"

I should say something. But I don't know what. And I don't belong in this moment. Josie is part of their world, their family, not mine. All I can do is stand here, offering my presence as support.

Hunter starts to say something, but Watcher steps out of his office. My breath locks in my lungs. The man looks so different than the intimidating commander I've come to expect. His shoulders are slumped, a fresh growth of stubble spikes on his head, and bags hang beneath his eyes.

I swallow hard and ease closer to Solomon and Hunter.

"Guardians." Watcher's voice cracks. "One of our own has fallen to the Dream."

The crowd of gathered guardians murmur, heads hung low. Then, one by one, they start drumming their left foot against the floor. The beat reverberates through the room until my heart is drumming along.

Watcher lets the ceremony go on for a good minute before raising a hand, cutting off the stomping. "I need volunteers."

Both Solomon and Hunter straighten immediately, taking up a stance of war. Chins jutted, shoulders back. "We volunteer." Their voices ring out in unison, cutting through the thick silence.

Watcher winces, but nods his assent.

More voices rise, calling out their volunteer status.

"Prepare yourselves. We leave in ten." He jerks his chin in a final nod and turns on his heel. His office doors fall shut behind him.

Solomon turns on me. "Go back to the apartment and wait for me."

I shake my head. "Tell me what's going on first."

"We have to retrieve Josie's..." He chokes up.

I rub his arm. "Okay, but what do I do if Macy starts dreaming while you're gone?"

His eyes shift away, and he shakes his head, "I don't—"

Hunter comes over. "She's right, mate. If something happens while you're gone..." he eyes me in a way that is not reassuring. "Josie won't be the only one we'll be retrieving."

"A dream without a Guardian is no place for a human." Solomon's jaw goes tight, and his nostrils flare.

"And the alternative?" Hunter raises an eyebrow.

Solomon ducks his head.

"Whatever you think is best," I say, hugging my middle. I won't fight his decision or make this any harder than it needs to be.

Solomon meets my eyes. "Things will be chaotic. You'll be in danger."

I shrug. "Sounds like I'll be in danger either way."

"Whatever you decide, decide now," Watcher's voice behind me makes me jump.

I swivel and find him glowering behind us.

"Sir—" Hunter starts to babble some excuse.

Watcher holds up a fist, cutting him off. "She's your responsibility, Custos. You brought her here. You decide where you want her. Either way, it's on your shoulders."

Solomon eyes me, and I study him right back. He extends his hand, and I wrap my fingers through his.

"All right." Watcher's focus flickers to our joined hands, but he doesn't comment. "Guardians, follow me."

The volunteers fall into a stiff line behind him, and Solomon and I trail them.

"Whatever you do, stick with me," Solomon murmurs into my ear. "The dream will be glitchy."

"Glitchy?" I hope he doesn't notice how my hand is turning slick in his.

"Wild. Out of control. Unpredictable." Shadows fill his eyes. "This is dangerous, Gwen."

I squeeze his hand. "I'll be right next to you the entire time."

Solomon turns to face Hunter, and some message sweeps through their linked gaze. Both dip their chins in a solemn nod. Whatever pact they've made, I can only hope it goes well. No, not hope. We need something stronger. I *pray* this all goes well.

We file into a large elevator with Watcher facing the doors.

"You have to tell me exactly what to do," I whisper to Solomon.

His thumb twitches, rubbing against the back of my knuckles. A shiver jumps up my arm, and my breath catches. I study his tense jawline and press his hand tight.

The elevator dips down, down, down. I count the seconds, and it takes a good sixty before the elevator spills us into a dark parking garage.

Watcher murmurs a command into his watch, and a series of fluorescent lights flicker on in strips across the ceiling. The place smells of damp earth and stale gasoline.

The Guardians form a line near a screened off section of the garage and emerge decked out all in black, like a SWAT team. They even have the guns to match the getup. Solomon squeezes my hand and disappears only to return dressed in black. I'd be tempted to describe him as handsome if not for the very, very serious set of his face.

"What about me?" I ask when the last Guardian has gone through the screen, and I'm not waved through next.

"You're not a Guardian, so they're refusing to issue you protective materials."

"What? But I—"

He taps his finger against his lips. "Shh. You'll be fine. I swear, I won't let anything happen to you."

Haven't we both learned by now that a promise like that can't be kept? Not inside the Dream. But I doubt there is much Solomon can do about it, so I keep quiet.

Watcher leads the way to a series of black range rovers, and the Guardians pile inside. Solomon pulls me into the backseat of one, and Hunter squeezes in on my other side. The driver guns the gas, and the line of vehicles tear out of the garage and spill into the night. Dark streaks of purple swirl across the sky, and the car quakes. I grip Solomon's knee with one hand and grab the headrest of the seat in front of me to keep from being thrown across Hunter's lap.

Rain slashes across the windows and hammers the windshield. All is dark, save for the bob of the headlights illuminating the road, mere feet at a time.

The farther we go, the tenser both Hunter and Solomon become. If only there was something I could say to ease the tension, but really, what words can help in a situation like this? Instead, I keep my lips pressed tight.

Lighting zaps across the sky, followed by a crash of thunder.

The radio buzzes in the front with coded chatter I couldn't make out even if I tried, but both Solomon and Hunter lean in. The driver slams on the breaks as the message ends, and on every side, Dream Guardians shove their doors open, spilling into the night. I slide across the seat and duck after Solomon.

Rain pelts me. The droplets soak through my sweater and send shivers dancing across my limbs. My teeth chatter, and I shrink in on myself for warmth.

Our team huddles near the truck as the other range rovers jolt to a stop in a line beside ours. Watcher all but hurls himself from the passenger-side door of his vehicle and trudges forward. His boots squelch against the wet grass. When he's a few feet ahead of the rest of us, he turns.

"The mission is as follows: retrieve the Guardian's body, and return her Dreamer's surroundings to a state of stability. Jemima Armani, you will take over the duties of the Dreamer's Guardian."

A slim girl with two braids down her shoulders steps forward and dips her chin. I only see it because I'm standing behind her, and her hands are tucked behind her back, but her fingers tremble.

Hunter reaches forward and presses the girl's shoulder.

"What a way to get your first assignment," Solomon mutters under his breath.

My fingers twitch to offer his arm a sympathetic squeeze, but the hard line of his jaw suggests this is not the time. I plaster my hand to my wet jeans.

"Move out!" Watcher snaps, jolting his soldiers into action. "Stay in pairs."

The Guardians obey, stretching forward in a long line, the flashlights on their guns, combing the darkness.

Solomon raises his gun and motions for me to go left. I squint against the rain blurring everything not directly in front of me. Thunder crackles overhead, shaking me to the bone. I raise a hand to shield my eyes. Mud squelches underfoot and cakes my boots. We wade through a section of overgrown grass that slaps at my jeans.

Solomon scans the field with his flashlight, eyes flickering from one direction to the next. Hunter joins us, his visor pulled low over his face, but how he can see anything beyond the rain pouring down the face shield is beyond me.

"Report." The radios strapped to both Guardians' chests crackle with Watcher's command.

Solomon shakes his head, and Hunter pulls his radio free of its strap. "Nothing, sir."

"Keep looking. We don't leave until we've brought our Guardian home."

Hunter clears his throat and presses his eyes shut for a long moment. "Yes, sir."

The radio goes silent.

"Come on," Solomon says.

We move forward in sync. Both Solomon and Hunter with their guns raised, flashlight beams sweeping the field, and me sandwiched between the two, praying we'll find Josie's body soon and then be able to get out of here.

The earth vibrates beneath my feet. I careen into Solomon, almost knocking us both over. Hunter grabs my sleeve, keeping me upright. A terrible ripping sound vibrates through the atmosphere. Another mighty quake ripples through the ground. Solomon falls to his knees. I knot my fingers in Hunter's sleeve to keep from falling over. For one terrible moment, we stand frozen. Solomon glances over his shoulder.

He's on his feet in an instant. "Run!"

Hunter springs into action, dragging me after him.

I crane a look over my shoulder. The earth splits behind us, the cracks growing with every second, stretching closer and closer. Hunter no longer has to pull me. I pump my legs as fast as I can until my muscles burn and my lungs ache, but I don't stop. I just follow the dark outline of Hunter's back and trust Solomon is coming behind me.

Another earthquake shakes the world. I stumble. Fall to one knee. Solomon grabs me from behind and hauls me back to my feet. We're running, running, running. Sweat slips down my jawline and plasters my shirt to my skin. Pain splinters through my side. A crack runs along the length of grass to my left.

In the distance, a child wails. I stumble to a halt and strain to see through the pouring rain.

"Don't stop." Solomon catches my elbow.

"Do you hear that?" I swivel, searching for the source.

"Keep going, Gwen." He tries to wrestle me into motion.

I plant my feet. "There's a child," I have to scream it over another crack of thunder.

Solomon tugs me into motion. Hunter is farther ahead now, waving us onward.

"Solomon, there's a child!" I jerk my arm, trying to break his grip.

Another heartrending cry. This time Solomon's eyes go wide, and his steps falter, but he doesn't stop. Not fully.

He grabs his radio from his vest. "The Dreamer isn't awake."

Watcher swears on the other line. "Armani and I will find her. Get me my Guardian, Custos."

"Yes, sir." Solomon stashes the radio back on its loop and pulls me into a full run.

Another piercing wail.

My heart pinches. "Solomon, we have to help her."

"We obey orders, Gonzales."

"But—"

"A rogue dream is nothing to play around with. Let Jemima and Watcher do their job, and we'll do ours."

I swallow back another protest as the child's screams rise to join the thunder.

Hunter jumps up and down, waving for us to join him. "Come on!"

The ground rocks violently.

I stumble.

Solomon steadies me.

A giant quake grinds beneath our feet.

"Come—" Hunter's words break into a shout as the ground splinters beneath him. For one moment he's hovering in the air, and then he drops.

"Hunter!" Solomon roars.

Chapter Thirty

I scramble to the edge of the pit Hunter has fallen into.

"Gwen." Solomon grabs my waist, hauling me backward.

"We have to help him." I fight his grip.

"You can't fall in." He tugs me farther from the edge and drops me into the grass.

"But he..." My chin trembles, and I can't finish the sentence.

A sheen reflects off Solomon's eyes in the beam of his gun's flashlight. He squats beside me and pulls his radio from his vest. "Come in, Peznic."

Static clatters back at him.

"Blast it, Hunter, answer."

Nothing.

Solomon's face crumples, and he drops his head against the radio. His shoulders rise and fall in silent sobs. I scooch closer and wrap my arms around him. He doesn't collapse, but there is a subtle shift in his posture. Just a small bit of leaning my way. So, I hold him.

"I can't lose them both," Solomon's voice cracks.

"You won't." Please don't let my words be a lie. "We'll find Josie's...we'll find Josie, and then we'll come back for Hunter."

He nods. Eases away.

I let him go, but the moment I catch sight of his face, the way he's biting his lip like that will keep him from crying out, almost breaks my heart.

He clears his throat and raises his radio once more. "This is Custos. Peznic is down." He squeezes his eyes shut, and a tear slips down his cheek. "I repeat, Peznic is down."

Watcher responds with a round of words that would have the swear jar at home overflowing with cash. When he either runs out of words or breath, the line goes quiet.

"Sir?" Solomon's voice is tight.

"Keep going. The mission remains the same." A pause. "I'll send in a team to retrieve Peznic."

Solomon's face crumples, and he raises a hand to cover his eyes. He stands there nodding over and over again.

"Custos?" Watcher's tone tightens. "Do you copy?"

"Yes." It's a whisper, and Solomon has to repeat himself, "Yes, sir. I copy."

"Good." The connection goes dead.

I rub my hands down the sides of my jeans. I hate situations like this. I don't know whether I should say something or respect the tragedy and not say anything at all.

Solomon runs his sleeve across his eyes and stashes his radio. "Come on."

As we start forward, the ground no longer shakes beneath our feet. "Hey, it stopped."

"It got a victim. Now, it'll try another trick to see if more will fall."

I shiver and tuck myself a little closer to Solomon. "What makes a dream go rogue?"

"The Guardian fell. Nightmare poison won, and the dream has been contaminated. Now, it will take as many of us out with it as it can." Solomon veers toward a patch of dark trees stretching toward the sky.

I'm no expert on nightmares or even horror movies, but it doesn't seem like the safest of choices. Although that's not the point, is it?

Dried leaves crunch under foot, and the wind shakes naked tree branches. They rattle and sway, reaching knobby fingers toward us. Solomon sends his flashlight beam dancing back and forth, but the weak light does little to break up the shadows stretching all around.

"Maybe we should head back," I say.

Solomon shakes his head. "Josie's in here."

"How do you know?"

"What part of this nightmare could be more dangerous?" He turns sad eyes toward me.

I can't argue with that logic in a world like this, so I follow him deeper into the forest. Branches clack together in the wind, and I can only pray they don't fall and crush our skulls. Is that a hint of...peppermint...on the wind?

"Custos." I jump at the crackle of Solomon's radio. A twig snaps under my foot, and I startle a second time. Heat blasts through my cheeks.

"Custos, do you copy?" Watcher's tone warns of looming impatience.

Solomon braces his hand against a tree like any more bad news will send him toppling. "Sir?" His voice wobbles.

I ease a few steps closer so we're facing one another.

Solomon holds my gaze while we wait for Watcher's response.

"Status update," the boss demands.

"Gwen and I are in the woods heading..." Solomon's scrutiny flicks over the forest, "east."

"I've got another team headed your way. Keep looking."

"Yes, sir." A hesitation. "Sir, is there an update on Peznic?"

"Not yet. I've got a team headed in to make a retrieval. I'll update you when I know more, over." The radio goes dead.

Solomon pushes away from the tree and trudges onward.

A terrible screech rends the night, sending goosebumps flashing across my skin. I freeze mid-step. "What was that?"

Solomon stops and cocks his head. "It almost sounds like..." But he doesn't finish the sentence. He stands there with his brow furrowed.

But I know what he means. That sound is steeped in familiarity like lyrics to a song you can't quite remember.

The sound echoes through the forest once more. Almost like cackling with just a trickle of music in the background. I squint, trying to pull up the memory hovering on the edge of my conscious. I've heard this before. I'm certain of it.

It comes then, steeped in fog of a memory long ago and long forgotten, but it's there. The twins sit in a pile of wrapping paper, pacifiers tucked in their mouths, wide eyes gleaming in the light of the Christmas tree. They're one, maybe two. Dad sits on the floor in front of them, winding up a...

"Jack-in-the-box." I snag Solomon's hand and tug him forward. "We're close, I know it."

"Be careful," he whispers.

Right. This is still an out-of-control nightmare without the benefit of a Guardian keeping things under control.

"Stay with me, no matter what," Solomon says.

No need to remind me. "Right."

He sweeps back a branch, and we maneuver forward, slow and steady. The leaves still crunch under foot, but if I'm careful about it, I can keep the noise to a minimum. Solomon makes hardly any noise at all.

He speaks into his radio, "Custos reporting. I think we might have found something. Moving in. Over."

"Careful," comes the reply. "I want a report every five minutes, am I clear?"

"Yes, sir." Solomon stashes the radio and crouches low behind a length of shrubbery.

An echoing cackle sounds. Close. Much too close.

I duck low next to Solomon, chest going tight.

"Deep breaths, Gonzales." Solomon cranes his neck to see around the edge of the bushes.

I nod, even though he can't see me and rub my damp hands up and down the fabric covering my knees.

"I can't see," Solomon mutters.

I ease upward a few inches until my eyes are level with the top twigs.

A child's whimper draws my attention. A baby stands in the center of the clearing, tears gathered at the corners of her eyes, small hands wringing in front of her. A giant Jack-in-the-box looms in front of her, a Santa Claus with gleaming red eyes.

"Ho, ho, ho!" He bobs toward her.

She trots back. "Mama!" It's the kind of cry that makes snot and tears run down her face.

This is the part where her Dream Guardian is supposed to wake her up. Supposed to make everything all better. But, of course, Josie isn't here. Jemima and Watcher haven't arrived. There's no Guardian to save her.

Not if I have anything to say about it.

I move for her, but Solomon grabs my wrist, tugging me down, and then holding me in place. "No."

I twist my wrist, trying to break his grip. "We have to help her."

His fingers don't budge. "Stay here."

"I won't just—"

"I'll get her, but you've had too many incidents in the Dream. I won't lose you, too."

My mouth goes dry, and I stop fighting his grip.

"You'll stay?" He raises his eyebrows, gaze begging me to agree.

I nod.

"I'll get her," he whispers.

"No, wait. The gun." For some reason, I suddenly don't want to risk him leaving me.

Solomon shakes his head. "I can't. I might hit her."

A whimper pulls at my vocal cords, but I refuse to be that kind of girl. I swallow hard. "Go."

He creeps around the edge of the bush, and I slip into his abandoned space so I can see around the foliage. Solomon darts from tree to tree, working his way to the area behind the giant box creature.

"Ho! Ho! Ho!" The Santa roars at the baby.

She screams and tries to run to the left, chubby arms flailing, but he sways to block her path.

"Ho, ho, ho!"

The baby wails.

Solomon rushes for her, but the Santa rotates, back-handing him across the face. Solomon flies backward, striking a fallen tree.

He doesn't get up.

Chapter Thirty-One

I clamp a hand over my mouth to keep from screaming. I wait for three heartbeats, but Solomon doesn't so much as twitch. What do I do? What do I do? His radio. I should get it. Call Watcher.

I creep to the edge of the bush and brace my feet. When the Santa swivels to face the baby, I dart to one of the trees separating me from Solomon. I press my back to the tree and force myself to breathe. Two more trees. I can do this.

The baby's next scream tears at my heart, and I dig my fingers into the rough bark. But I can't protect her all on my own, and the Santa, at least, doesn't seem to be trying to hurt her. More like...play?

"Ho, ho, ho!"

Time to move. I sprint for the next tree and slide into place behind it.

Snap.

I bite my tongue and glance down at the splintered twig, half of which is still locked in place beneath my boot. Crap.

"What do you want for Christmas, little girl?" The Santa rotates toward my tree, beady eyes scanning the shadows.

I press the back of my head against the tree. Stupid, stupid, stupid. Now the Santa is between me and both Solomon and the girl.

"Custos?" Watcher's voice crackles distantly from Solomon's radio. "I thought I said reports every five minutes. What part of that was unclear?"

The Santa bobs his long, springy body toward Solomon.

"Custos? Do you copy?"

The baby squats now, hands holding her belly, eyes scrunched closed as she screams for her mama. I can't leave her like this, and there's no way I can get to Solomon at the moment.

"Blast it, Custos, answer me!"

If it weren't Watcher, I'd almost be tempted to think there was a note of concern in his tone. But whatever emotion Watcher's feeling isn't something I can afford to dwell on, not when Santa is distracted. I sprint for the child just as a shadow stretches across the ground and materializes into a Nightmare. No, not just any Nightmare, but the lord of them.

He slides toward the baby.

I move in first, scooping her into my arms. She clings to me, fingers pinching into my skin with one heck of a death grip. She buries her head into my shoulder and screams. I back step, putting space between us and Coakley even though it means moving closer to the evil Santa.

Coakley sneers at me. "Let me have her, girl."

I tighten my grip on the baby. "Never."

"You cannot save her." He takes one step forward for every one I take backward. "She has no Guardian."

I cup the back of the baby's head so she will not look and see him. "I won't let you touch her."

He laughs. "Measly human, don't you know that you have no power over me?"

The baby shrieks, tightening her grip on me. I don't dare turn to see what Santa is up to, but instead keep my gaze locked on Coakley's while I gently bounce and sway. "Leave."

He laughs and advances.

Ice shoots through my middle, and I trot backward.

"Ho, ho, ho!"

I hear the swish of air and duck low, pulling the baby tight against my chest. Santa's arm sweeps over my head. Coakley darts to the side to avoid being struck. I scramble behind Santa's box which plays a creepy version of "Jingle Bells," placing him between me and the Nightmare Lord. Santa may not be this kid's best friend, but right now, he's mine.

While Coakley and Santa are busy trying to ward each other off, I dart for Solomon.

His finger's twitch against the leaves on the ground, and he groans. He's alive. I hardly have time to be thankful before the crunch of footsteps over leaves warns of Coakley's approach. I put on more speed and slide to a stop beside Solomon.

"Solomon, wake up." I shake his shoulder and crane a look over my shoulder.

Coakley races toward us, ducking and weaving to avoid Santa's long arms.

"Solomon." I shake him hard and adjust my grip on the baby so she's positioned on my hip instead of against my chest. She peeks at the scene for one second before returning to screaming into my shoulder. My sleeve plasters to my skin, slick with tears and mucus.

Coakley snarls and leaps for us.

Santa backhands him. "Ho! Ho! Ho!"

The Nightmare Lord hits the ground hard and barely manages to roll onto his stomach.

Santa swivels our way and lunges on his springs. I duck behind the log. The air swishes above my head, but he's just short of being able to grab me. His cheeks burn red, and he roars at the sky.

I lick my lips and glance between him, the still winded Coakley, and Solomon who remains sprawled on the other side of the log. There's no way for this to end well, and I can't fight both Coakley and Santa on my own.

That leaves calling for backup. With one eye fixed on Santa because he's the closest at the moment, I press my back against the log and reach one hand over, fishing blindly for Solomon's radio.

Coakley snarls and pushes himself to all fours, shaking his head like he's trying to focus.

Santa tracks my movements with his beady eyes, and his mouth rounds. With a giant effort, he heaves his box forward. *Scooch. Scooch. Scooch.*

My fingers bump against Solomon's cheek. His neck. His vest. Where? Where? Where? My hand hits something solid. There. I fumble with the strap until I manage to detach the radio from his vest.

"Ho! Ho! Ho!" Santa leaps forward. The box hits the ground, and the earth trembles.

I fumble the radio, and it hits the leaves at my feet. No, no, no. I rake my hand through the leaves, searching in the darkness.

"Mama!" Wails the baby. By now, her voice is thick with mucus and raspy from overuse.

"Shh," I hush, but Santa's attention fixes on us.

Coakley is trying to edge around the Santa's box without being detected.

"Shh, shh." I bounce the baby and pat the ground. Leaves stick to my slick palms, and dried pine needles poke my skin. Then my fingers bump the hard lump of radio, and I snatch it up. I fumble to turn it around with one hand and press buttons until I get feedback. "Come in."

Static is my answer.

"Someone come in." I double check to be sure I'm pressing the right button.

Santa sweeps out an arm. I duck and his hand barely misses my scalp.

"Anyone," I yell into the radio.

Coakley has crept to the far left of Santa now, far out of the Jack-in-the-box's range. He slips a dagger from his waistband and circles toward us, a predatory gleam in his eyes.

My throat goes dry and my fingers tremble. I have to tighten them to keep from dropping the radio.

"Who is this?" The radio crackles to life in my hand.

"G-Gwen. Gonzales. I'm with Solomon, but he's—"

Coakley lunges.

I scream and scramble backward with one hand, dragging the baby with me.

Coakley towers over us. "Give me the child, Gwendolyn. I'll admit you've made a valiant effort. A brilliant little playact at being a Guardian, but the charade is up." Spindly shadows leach from his feet, stretching toward me.

On the radio, Watcher curses.

I shuffle backward until my spine hits a tree.

The shadows curl toward my boots.

I tighten my grip on the baby, holding her close even though there's nowhere else to go. I shake my head and pray Coakley can't see my chin tremble. "I won't let you take her."

He flicks his finger, and one of the shadows wraps around my ankle. "Hand her over, and there's no reason for you to be hurt."

As if I'd believe that. "No."

He snarls. "That child is my right. I have felled her Guardian, and I will stake my claim."

I bounce the child against my chest, keeping her head cupped against my shoulder. There's nothing left to say, so I simply glare at the Nightmare Lord.

He curls his finger into his palm, and the shadow constricts around my foot and pulls, inching me across the ground. I dig in my heels, but all that achieves is churning up a rut in the soft earth.

The shadow tugs until I am seated at the Nightmare Lord's feet. He kneels so we are at eyelevel and pinches my chin between two claw-like fingers. "You are very brave, I'll give you that."

I jerk my face free from his touch.

"The child." He extends a hand.

"You'll have to pry her from my dead body." I hold his stare in defiance.

He growls and straightens to his full height. "It will be my pleasure." He flicks his finger at another one of the shadows, and it slides along my arm and circles my throat.

I shiver, and a whimper escapes.

The shadow swells.

"Last chance." Coakley cocks one of his faded gray eyebrows.

I tighten my hold on the baby, tangling my fingers with the fabric of her shirt. Her cries fade to soft whimpers, and she's gone all but limp in my grasp.

Coakley cocks his finger, and the shadow tightens around my throat, cutting off my air. I resist the urge to claw at it. Instead, I dig in my heels, close my eyes, and grip the baby for all I'm worth.

And yet, my brain fogs. My lungs burn. My limbs grow fuzzy.

My grip on the child slips.

Chapter Thirty-Two

The moment the baby hits the leaves, the shadow tightens one last time against my throat before springing loose. I collapse onto my side, trying to remember how to breathe even as gray slithers into the corners of my vision.

Coakley steps forward, boots snapping the dried leaves, the sound echoing in my ear that is pressed to the earth.

"Ho! Ho! Ho!" Santa lunges forward, trying to stop the Nightmare Lord, but his long arms tangle in the tree branches, and he can do nothing more than thrash and rock his box back and forth.

Coakley curls one hand toward the babe.

I. Can't. Let. Him. Take. Her.

I muster all my strength, every last morsel of life that remains in my body, and kick out, catching the side of his knee.

Coakley releases a surprised cry and goes down hard.

The baby is on her feet now, waddling toward me.

She squats behind my back and pats my chest. She says something over and over again that sounds vaguely like "wake up."

But I don't have the strength to do anything more than lay here as a human barrier between her and the Nightmare Lord.

Coakley pushes to his feet, expression dark and twisted. "No more fun and games," he spits at me.

Santa roars at the sky.

I brace myself.

Beams of light flood the clearing.

"Stand back!" Watcher screams at Coakley.

The Nightmare Lord shies away from the light but snarls at the Guardian commander. "You have no right here."

Jemima steps from behind Watcher, chin cocked high. "On the contrary. I put myself forward and claim Guardianship of this Dreamer."

The babe stops patting me and turns toward Jemima, arms extended. A golden strand of light swirls from the child's chest and dissolves into the space where Jemima's heart is. Jemima scoops up the babe and a mask slips over her face that I can only assume is the child's mother. The baby stops crying.

"No!" Coakley howls.

Watcher levels his gun at the Nightmare Lord's chest. "I suggest you leave. You no longer have any authority here."

If Coakley were a toddler, this is where he'd stomp his foot and start screaming, but no. He is much more dangerous than that. He fixes his yellow stare on me. Unforgiving. Promising...something that makes a shiver tremble through my core. He rotates on his heel, and in a burst of shadow, he's gone.

Watcher eyes me. "You all right?"

I touch a hand to my throat where the phantom of Coakley's shadow still presses.

"Gonzales?" Watcher snaps.

"Fine. I'm fine." Except my fingers tremble when I press them into the leaves.

He jerks his chin in acknowledgement and turns toward where a group of Guardians kneel around Solomon. "Give me the man's status."

One of the Guardians pulls off his helmet, and I gasp. It's Hunter. He's got a scratch on his chin, and his hair is disheveled, but it's definitely him.

"He's alive, sir. Just unconscious. Has a nasty bump on the back of his head," Hunter says.

"Get him on a stretcher," Watcher orders two of the other Guardians.

They obey, pulling a device free from their packs that unfolds into a stretcher. It only takes them a moment to transfer Solomon on top. His only response is a low moan. I wince for him.

"At least he had the sense not to get himself killed." Watcher heaves a sigh and props his hands on his hips. "Peznic, stay with her."

"Yes, sir." Hunter straightens and steps away from Solomon.

I stand and brush debris from my jeans. It's not until Hunter is at my side that I realize Watcher wants him to stay with me.

"I don't need a babysitter," I murmur once Watcher's back is turned.

"Don't worry, I think you proved that." Hunter's lips twitch like he's holding back a smile. "This is just protocol to make sure you make it out safely."

"Ah." Yeah, I believe that. I tug on my sleeves, not sure what to do now.

Watcher is barking orders that have nothing to do with me, and they must be in some kind of code, or maybe I'm just too tired, because they don't make any sense to me.

"You did well, Gonzales." Hunter nods toward the baby who has snuggled into Jemima's arms.

"But she hasn't woken up."

"She will once this dream dissolves. Everything's gone a little too haywire for her to wake up now."

I'll never pretend to fully understand this place. "What about Santa?" I turn to look, but he's no longer tangled in the tree branches.

"Let's just say he's taken care of." Hunter grins.

I see them now, a group of Guardians sealing up the Jack-in-the-box.

"Peznic, get her out of here. Custos and the Dreamer too."

Hunter snaps to attention. "What about Josie?"

Watcher's eyes narrow, and he works his jaw, but in the end, he replies, "I'll stay."

Hunter's eyes widen. "But sir, the dream is unstable. With the Dreamer removed, it's only a matter of time before it..."

"Dissolves. I'm not stupid, Peznic, and I'll thank you to remember it. You have your orders, now shock us all, and follow them."

A muscle ticks in Hunter's jaw, but he swallows back whatever arguments must be playing through his head. "Yes, sir."

I don't know what exactly the pair are referencing, but if the way all the Guardians pause and salute is any indication, it can't be good.

Watcher clears his throat gruffly and pulls his gun from its holster. "Get out of here. All of you." He returns their salute, turns on his heel, and strides deeper into the forest.

My chest pinches tight. We're nowhere near the definition of close, but a note of mourning passes through me all the same. I press a hand to my chest, but the touch does little to ease the ache. So much has gone wrong already, and these Guardians need their leader to return.

Hunter touches my back. "Come on."

There's nothing for me to argue, so I fall into step beside him as he uses a series of hand signals to direct the Guardians who carry Solomon on a stretcher between them. Jemima encloses me on my other side, the baby tucked safely on one hip, eyelashes drooping heavily though she can't quite be described as asleep.

"Will she be all right?" I ask.

"Thanks to you." Jemima smiles over the child's fuzzy hair that is just starting to lengthen into toddler curls.

I brush a hand down the baby's arm and smile at her even though she tightens her grip on Jemima.

"This way." Hunter beckons us, and together we trudge out of the forest. The ground outside is still splintered and cracked. "Stay with your partner," Hunter barks.

The other Guardians nod.

Hunter cups my elbow. "You're with me."

I shoot a look toward Solomon, my arm feeling foreign in Hunter's grip.

"Don't worry, he'll be fine," Hunter says.

Trickles of heat creep into my face, and I don't know why. There's no reason to be embarrassed over worrying about Solomon. Besides, it's too dark out here for Hunter to even see my cheeks that must surely be turning pink.

We pick our path carefully across the field, stepping over the smaller cracks and working our way around the larger ones. The earth rolls under my feet. I teeter off balance.

Hunter catches my arm. "Careful."

"Why won't the dream reset?" I shoot a look to the baby who is happily snuggled in Jemima's arms.

"Too much damage has been done here. Once we get the Dreamer out, this dream will self-destruct."

I hesitate. Lick my lips. But I can't hold back the question, "Watcher?"

Hunter fixes his gaze straight ahead. "He'll make it out."

His tone is so final that I swallow back any other questions or doubts and follow him around a large gap in the ground.

When the range rovers come into view, we break into a jog.

Hunter yanks open the passenger door. "Get in."

I scramble into the seat and pull my seatbelt across my chest. Hunter races to the trunk and jerks it open. The Guardians load Solomon inside and squat in the back on either side of the stretcher. Jemima slides into the back seat and bounces the baby on her lap.

On either side of our vehicle, the other Guardians climb inside their cars, revving their engines to life. Hunter climbs into the driver's seat, turns the car on, and then just sits there, hands on the wheel, foot on the brake.

A voice comes through his radio, crackly and distant. "It's your call, Peznic."

Hunter's nostrils flare, and his jaw works for a long moment before he lifts his radio from his vest. "Are all teams accounted for?"

Nearly two dozen names and identification numbers come through the radio.

"We can't leave anyone behind," Jemima whispers from behind my seat. "Once the Dreamer is removed, this dream and all who are inside will dissolve."

I clench my hand around the door handle and wait until Hunter gives a final nod. "Good." Then he and all the conscious Guardians in our vehicle rattle off their last names and identification numbers.

"What do you want to do?" The first voice comes through again.

Hunter's gaze flicks to the final, empty vehicle left for Watcher.

"We follow orders. Move out." His voice breaks, and he drops the radio back against his chest. Then, he guns the engine and we're off.

The ground must be disturbed here as well. We jolt one way, then the next until I swear we're all going to develop whiplash. I grip the handle over my door and brace my feet against the floor, but my head still manages to bounce around like a bobblehead. Hunter weaves the car around the worst damage, and a snaking line of headlights follow behind us.

Solomon groans in the back.

Hunter's focus flicks to his rearview mirror. "Status report?"

I turn in my chair.

One of the Guardians presses his fingers into Solomon's neck. "His pulse is regulating. Should be gaining consciousness soon."

"Atta boy." Hunter's attention turns back to the road, but that doesn't stop his lips from quirking and him muttering under his breath, "You always had to be dramatic, didn't you?"

The baby begins to cry.

"What's going on, Jemima?" Hunter hunches forward over the wheel, squinting at the road in the ever-darkening light.

Jemima tries to hush the child, but she only cries harder. "I-I don't know."

Hunter slaps a hand against the steering wheel.

"Could be your driving?" One of the Guardians in the back volunteers.

Hunter only raises his eyes from the road long enough to shoot a glare into the mirror.

I gnaw my thumbnail and watch out my window. The last thing we need is another nasty monster jumping out at us. Worse, we don't need Coakley creeping out of the shadows.

"I'm sorry," Jemima says, voice sounding thick as if she's about to start crying.

"Not your fault. It takes time for a bond to fully develop." Hunter raises his radio to his mouth. "Keep your eyes peeled. Dreamer is agitated."

"She's a baby, Peznic. She might just need to wake up and get fed."

We all jump at the familiar voice.

"Sir?" Hunter's eyes flash wide, and he tightens his hold on the radio, driving with one hand.

We bounce over a section of particularly damaged ground. Ugh, I've never been one to get carsick, but if this doesn't smooth out soon, the baby won't be the only one crying. The car swerves, and I don't catch my balance in time. My head bounces off the window. Ouch. I rub the spot that might just bruise before we get out of here.

"Sir?" Hunter tries again, double checking to be sure his radio is still on.

All he gets is high-pitched feedback.

I wince and raise my shoulder to block my ear that is pointed toward him.

Hunter lets the radio fall back into place and mutters something under his breath. A torrent of rain douses our windshield, and a gust of wind pushes the car. The baby cries louder. Mud sprays up the side of the car, splattering my window.

I grip the edge of my seat. "Are we almost out?"

Hunter hunches further over the dashboard, squinting. "Should be. If we can just get—"

A large form steps into our path. Hunter slams on the breaks so hard that my seat belt locks, pressing into my chest. A large creature looms in front of us, yellow eyes narrowed at the windshield. I can't be sure, but it might be a cat with matted hair, only it's standing on its hindlegs. Behind us, the line of cars streaks to a stop.

"Ease up, will you? You're going to make me sick, mate." Solomon's groggy voice sounds from the back.

Oh, if it weren't for the row of seats between us, I'd hug him.

"You might want to see this before you judge." Hunter undoes his seatbelt.

"We're getting out?" I squeak.

"Nope. You and Jemima stay here." He pulls his gun from its holster.

There's a shuffling noise from the back, and then Solomon groans. "You've got to be kidding me."

"Stay here, man. We'll take care of this." In the rear mirror, he jerks his chin at the two Guardians squatting in the trunk. They nod back.

"Oh, not a chance, mate." Solomon pulls himself upright using the back of Jemima's seat.

"I don't think—" I start, but he waves me off.

Hunter catches my eye. "Stay." It's all he says before he flings the door open.

Chapter Thirty-Three

The Guardians approach the monster with weapons drawn, but the creature only blinks at them like it's not sure what the proper response is.

That's when the baby catches sight of it, and her screams pierce my ears.

The cat-monster's eyes turn to slits, and it steps forward, swatting at the Guardians with its claws extended. It catches one across the chest, sending him flying. I press my fingers to my lips, but that does little to stifle my cry. Where are Solomon and Hunter? With the rain, the dark, and the matching uniforms, I can't find Hunter. But there's Solomon without his helmet, creeping around to the back of the creature, weapon drawn.

Solomon's movements catch the baby's attention, and she whimpers.

The cat-monster stiffens and swivels.

"Jemima!" I yelp.

"I'm trying." She bounces the child and pats her back.

But the child won't be comforted. She cries harder, gaze locked on the cat.

Solomon doesn't have time to backtrack. He raises his gun.

The cat-monster lashes out.

Solomon fires.

The cat's claws catch him in the arm, sending him flying into the mud. Blood oozes down the monster's fur, but the bullet isn't enough to stop it. It knocks another Guardian into the air. I wince as the Guardian hits the ground. His neck is twisted at an odd angle. He will not be getting back up.

Hunter moves in front of the cat, gun leveled at it. He must have issued a command, because all at once, the other Guardians are easing backward.

"Give me the baby." I swivel in my seat.

Jemima hesitates. "I don't know."

"What's there to lose? Give her to me." I hold out my arms.

Jemima's gaze moves between the scene outside the windshield and the child on her lap.

"Jemima," I snap when Hunter has to dodge a swipe from the cat-monster.

She bites her lip and shoves the baby at me.

"Shh," I croon. I lay her in my arms and sway her back and forth. She's a bit too old for it, but nothing else comforted the twins like this. In a husky voice, I sing her a Spanish lullaby Nana sang to each of us when we were little.

She stops crying.

Tears remain at the corner of her oh-so-blue eyes, but her shrieks have stopped, and she lays still in my arms. Her weight is stiff and unyielding, but the crying has stopped.

"Tell Hunter to take the shot," I tell Jemima without breaking eye-contact with the baby.

"I—"

The baby's lip quivers.

I sing another verse before I dare to speak again, "Tell him. This may be his only chance."

Jemima snags her radio. "Take the shot, Peznic. The Dreamer is stable, but I don't know how much longer we can maintain the calm. Over."

"Copy that." Except its Solomon's voice that comes through.

My gaze jumps to the scene outside the windshield. Hunter is on the ground, face shield cracked and smeared with mud. Or is it blood? Solomon stands hunched over him, gun raised. The cat-monster looms toward them, lips pulled back, long fangs revealed.

I can't breathe.

The baby squirms in my grip, her heartbeat quickening against my arm. I bounce her and return to singing, messing up half the words, but I can't break my gaze away from the scene outside.

"Take the shot," Jemima says.

Solomon straightens. Takes aim.

I swear the cat-monster must hiss.

"Take the shot." I don't know if I say it out loud, or simply mouth it, but my soul takes up the cry. Take the shot. Take the shot.

The cat-monster leaps like a feline pouncing on its prey. I squeeze my eyes shut. The crack of the gun sounds and rattles through my bones. The baby screams.

Chapter Thirty-Four

"He's all right. They're all fine," Jemima says.

I peel my eyes open just to be sure. The cat-monster lays in a heap, unmoving. Solomon's pulling Hunter to his feet. They're all up and moving except the one Guardian who landed on his neck wrong. Two other Guardians hoist his body up and carry him off to one of the other vehicles.

Solomon helps Hunter to the driver's side before hopping into the back with Jemima. He pauses, halfway to sitting when he sees me.

Warmth warms me from my toes up. "What?"

"You've calmed her."

I peek down. Sure enough, she's got her thumb tucked in her mouth. Tears have left streaks down her cheeks, but no fresh ones move to take their place. She watches me, eyes moving back and forth like she's studying my face. I whisper another round of the song and gently sway her.

"Too bad you're human, you'd make a swell Guardian," Jemima says.

My cheeks hurt from how wide I smile, but I don't dare stop singing.

Solomon claps Hunter on the shoulder. "Get us out of here, mate."

Hunter tosses his cracked helmet to the floorboards, revealing a deep cut on his forehead, oozing blood. "All units move," he says into his radio as he peels around the monster's carcass. He smashes the gas pedal to the floor, and we zip toward a swirl of blue and purple forming in the distance.

"Watcher?" Solomon asks.

Hunter's jaw goes tight, and he shakes his head.

Solomon sighs and falls back against his seat.

When we're mere feet from the opening, Hunter pulls to the side and sticks his hand out the window, commanding the line of vehicles behind us to go through first.

"Shouldn't we go?" I ask, eyeing the baby in my arms. Yes, she's snuggled up to me and is content, but we've all seen how that can change in an instant.

"If she goes, that's it, dream over," Hunter says.

Solomon combs his fingers through his hair and winces when he comes to the spot where I'm sure there's got to be a serious bump from his collision with the fallen tree.

The last of the range rovers rockets past us, diving into the swirling formation. In a flash of light, it's gone.

Hunter revs the engine, but he doesn't go.

"What are you waiting for?" I ask.

His focus goes to the rearview mirror. Solomon turns in his seat.

It hits me. Watcher. They're waiting for Watcher.

I look out my window, hoping, hoping, hoping that last range rover will come into view. It doesn't. But that doesn't mean the view is empty. No, a length of giant vines ripples across the ground, shooting toward us.

"Go." I press my foot against the ground. What I wouldn't give for a gas pedal. "Hunter, go!"

He obeys, throwing the car forward.

A vine creeps toward the swirling opening. That can't be good.

Solomon mutters something under his breath. "Hunter—"

"I see it, man." Hunter slams the pedal to the floor, and we lurch forward.

Solomon rolls his window down and fires off a round at the vine. It shrivels beneath the assault, but another one curls forward to take its place.

"We can't let them block our exit." Jemima stands as best she can in the cramped vehicle.

Hunter removes one hand from the wheel and opens the sky roof for her.

The other two Guardians level their guns out Jemima's vacated window.

A horn honks.

I jump in my seat.

Solomon whoops.

"Get going, kids, and don't you dare stop for anything. I'll be right behind you," the words come through the radios loud and clear.

I can barely keep a cheer from releasing at the familiar voice. But I don't dare startle the baby. She whimpers every time one of the guns goes off, but she still hasn't managed to sit up enough to look out the window.

Hunter grins as he lifts his radio. "Copy that, sir."

We zoom forward.

The tires leave the ground, and then the purple and blue converge around us. With a flash of light, we're swallowed. I have to close my eyes against the harshness and lift my sweater to cover the baby's eyes.

In the next instant, the car is still.

I dare a peek through my lashes. The light has vanished, replaced by the dim interior of the parking garage. My arms are empty.

I gasp, and look around, like the babe has somehow sprung from my arms in the second it took for us to arrive.

Jemima leans between the front seats. "It's all right, Gwen. She woke up. Her dream can't harm her any longer."

I nod like this makes perfect sense, but no matter how much time I spend in the Dream world, I'll never get used to the jarring transitions. "What about Watcher?"

"Behind us," Solomon says.

I drop my head back against the headrest. Thank goodness.

"Everyone good?" Hunter asks as he shuts the car off.

Jemima pushes a flyaway strand of hair behind her ear. "Good."

The Guardians are dirty, and Solomon and Hunter both host patches of blood, but neither appear to be on his deathbed.

"Then let's go." They pile out of the car.

I ease out my door.

Watcher climbs from his range rover. Streaks of dirt line his cheeks, and a deep scratch runs from his temple to his chin.

"Sir?" Solomon steps forward, Hunter just behind him.

Watcher swallows hard before he jerks his chin at the trunk of his vehicle. "I found her."

The other Guardians have gathered around us now too. Each dirty from the mission, shoulders stiff. Tears run down Jemima's cheeks and more than one of the other faces.

Watcher sniffs. "Well done. Well done, all of you. Thank you for your service." His gaze flicks over them, lips moving silently as if counting. His expression goes hard. "Where's McCormack?"

A petite Guardian shoves forward, dabbing the back of her hand against her nose. "He fell, sir."

Watcher's gaze goes to the ceiling, but not before I catch sight of the red that rims his eyes. I press a hand to my throat. No matter what I've previously thought, or maybe even what Solomon and Hunter think, Watcher is a commander who cares for his soldiers. My dad would like him.

"Well," Watcher says when he's collected himself, "they'll be missed. We know what needs to be done."

Each of the Guardians snap a salute, and I ease out of the circle. I don't belong in this moment. This is their time to mourn their fallen friends.

Watcher returns the salute.

Solomon turns and comes to me. "You were great back there, you know. Jemima's right. If you weren't so...human, then you'd make a great Guardian."

"Thanks." I fold my arms over my chest and lean against the nearest car.

He frowns. "What's wrong?"

"Nothing."

"Ah, come on, I know you better than that by now."

I lick my lips, tasting salt. When did I start crying? "I'm just so sorry for all of you. And there's nothing I can do to make it better."

Solomon's throat visibly constricts.

I shouldn't have said anything. He said Josie was like his family, and here I am making everything about me. "Listen, I shouldn't have—"

"Gwen." He snags my hand, stilling my words. "Thank you."

"For what?"

"For being here. For caring. There's nothing any of us can do now except celebrate the lives our friends lived. To rejoice with them, knowing they've gone to dwell with the greatest Guardian of all."

I swipe at another tear. "Okay."

"Okay." He squeezes my hand before letting go.

Chapter Thirty-Five

I'm not allowed at the funeral. It's strictly a Guardian-only event. Which leaves me pacing the apartment, gnawing on my thumbnail while Solomon is holed up in his bedroom, watching a livestream of the events. But whatever happens at a Guardian's funeral, he can't share it with me.

And I won't intrude.

I drop onto the couch and grip my head in my hands. I just want to go home. If everything else already hasn't, this has solidified how real these dreams are. If it's not necessarily immediate life and death for Macy and me, it is for Solomon.

Surely, it must end soon.

Someway.

Somehow.

I try to sleep, but the couch offers little comfort. After what feels like hours, the hood light over Solomon's stove flicks on, and the soft hum of his espresso machine whirs to life.

He must be struggling to rest, too. Because why not turn to caffeine when sleep doesn't do the trick?

I push myself up and pad over to the kitchen.

The floor creaks under my foot.

Solomon looks up. "Hey." He rubs the back of his neck. "Did I wake you?"

"No." I push my hair behind my ear. "I couldn't sleep."

"Me neither, hence...well, this," he indicates the espresso machine with a sweep of his hand.

I take a step closer. "You know, maybe it's time you show me how to work this thing."

He grins. "Please, be my guest."

I step up to the machine, and Solomon hovers behind me, naming the different knobs and poking at buttons. I nod along even though I don't really get it. Solomon must know this, because he lifts my hands and walks me through the steps, his hands on mine, his breath warming my neck until goosebumps spring across my skin.

He's so close.

We're close.

Too close.

I duck under his arm. "Well, I don't think my calling in life is to be a barista, but thanks for showing me."

He just nods, a twinkle in his eye suggesting he knows exactly what has made my face go warm.

Solomon extends a hand. "Come on, I want to show you something."

"What?" I should refuse, put space between us, and remind us both of the impossible. But I don't.

He searches my gaze, looking for what, I don't know. "On the roof."

"All right."

Solomon disappears into his bedroom and returns with a throw blanket. He leads me through the corridor and up the stairs. When he pushes open the service door, thousands of stars twinkle down on us. They should be covered by the light of the skyscrapers like any city in my world, but here, they're not.

"Wow," I breathe as I step onto the roof.

"It's one of the best views you could ask for." Solomon steps to the middle of the roof and spreads the blanket out before taking a seat.

I lower myself beside him and fold my knees underneath me. "It's...it's amazing." I crane my neck, trying to take it all in.

"It is," Solomon says. Except he's not looking up.

Something warm stokes to life in my middle, and my gaze snags on his. Warm. Steady. If I lean forward...But then I blink and shove the impossible thought away. I can't fall for this boy. I can't. He's a Dream Guardian. From a whole different universe. And I'm going home. I force my gaze to the stars once more.

"What kind of beat would you give to this moment?" Solomon asks.

Heat creeps up the back of my neck and warms my cheeks. He remembers the sunset.

He nudges me with his elbow. "Come on, what kind of beat?"

"You really want to know?" I pick at a thread on the blanket.

"Always."

I huff a laugh and study the twinkling lights fixed in place by a Designer. Like all the glory of Heaven can't quite be contained, so a little bit leaks out for us to view from Earth. "Something slow. Peaceful."

Solomon nods. "Perfect."

A cool breeze sweeps past, awakening goosebumps on my arms. I shiver and hug my sweater tighter to my body.

Solomon glances over and slips his lab coat off and drapes it around my shoulders.

"Oh, you don't have to—"

"Never stop a man from being a gentleman, Gwen. Besides, you deserve to be treated with respect," he says.

My heart snags on those words, and all I can do is nod and whisper, "Thank you."

A comfortable silence settles between us as we watch the stars. Tension eases from my shoulders until I can breathe without restraint. "You were right. I needed this."

"Me, too, if I'm honest." Solomon's hand rests inches from mine.

It would be so easy to take it. My fingers itch to, but I resist and instead lift my hand to cover a yawn.

"Tired?"

I shrug and lower my hand.

"Here." He pats his shoulder.

I should refuse. Resist. But the moment is so safe and quiet, and exhaustion pulls at my body. So, I lower my barriers and lower my head to his shoulder.

"So, something quiet?" Solomon asks.

"Give me your hand."

He obeys, and I turn it palm up and tap out a slow beat.

"Like I said, perfect."

Once more, his gaze is turned to me.

We talk about Josie and the other fallen Guardian, Mc-Cormack. We talk about my family. Solomon regales me with tales of his early years as a Guardian. I trade him with stories from my childhood. And all the while, he doesn't let go of my hand, and I don't try to pull away.

After what seems like hours of stargazing, I try my best to rest in the bedroom, never really relaxing for more than a handful of minutes at a time. I remain there until my stomach starts growling. I doubt Solomon will be up for a trip to the café, so another round of dry cereal it is.

I ease down the hallway, take a quick shower, and step into the kitchen. Solomon is at the sink, rinsing a growing stack of mugs. Doesn't he know that much caffeine isn't good for a person?

He glances up, and that twinkle hasn't dimmed at all in his eyes. "Hey."

"Hey." I push my wet hair over my shoulder.

"Ready for another lesson?" He tips his head toward the espresso machine, grinning wickedly.

I open my mouth to say something, anything to distract him, but a spray of glitter explodes around me. The shards of sparkles converge into a whole, and then transform into a fresh scene. I'm standing in my kitchen. For one heartbeat, my breath catches in my throat. Could I be…home? I hardly even dare to think the word. But, no. Solomon is here too, tucked into a small alcove off to the side.

That's when the voices hit. Ah. Another memory-dream. It's a scene from this past spring. There's Macy and Beck sitting at the bar, Elijah at the sink. The sound of Tommy playing in the background proclaims his presence as well. The kitchen smells of burnt toast, and someone has definitely been chowing down some sickeningly sweet cereal, because the scent lingers in the air.

Elijah grabs three eggs from the fridge and begins to juggle them.

"Elijah!" I gasp, slamming my water glass to the counter.

He flashes a cheeky grin. "Relax, sis. They're hard boiled."

"Your brother is so dumb." Beck doesn't even bother looking up from her phone to deliver her eye-roll.

I shoot her a look. The kind that says she isn't family, so any negative comments about my people won't be welcomed here. But, of course, she's too engrossed with whatever's on her screen to notice.

Elijah sends the eggs spinning in an arc and then pretends to drop one.

"Not funny." I turn my glower on him. Of course, I know exactly how this ends, but the reaction comes out all the same.

Macy stifles a giggle with the back of her hand.

"Don't encourage him," I say.

But, ham that he is, my brother ramps up his performance with a series of tricks I'm sure he had to spend hours watching online in order to perfect.

"Cool!" Tommy springs up from the rug where he's got a miniature construction site laid out. "I want to try."

"Uh-uh." I block the way to the fridge. "I don't think that's a good idea."

He pouts, complete with a protruding lip.

I cross my arms and cock a hip. Two can play at this game. I raise an eyebrow, daring my little brother to up the stakes. Cue dramatic music. He fires back with a squinty-eyed glare for a solid three seconds before he huffs in exasperation, and his shoulders sag. "You're no fun."

And I'm just fine with that, thank you very much.

"Yeah, Gwen, you're no fun." Elijah mimics Tommy's tone and completes it with a pouty lip of his own. "Here, catch." He tosses one of the eggs at Tommy.

Tommy grins when he manages to catch the thing against his chest. And then there's a sickening cracking sound and...

Splat.

Runny goop slips down Tommy's t-shirt and drips to the floorboards.

"Oops." Elijah winces.

"Oh, you are so dead." I say before stepping around the mess to help Tommy pull the soiled shirt over his head. Too bad I can't actually carry through with a solid pounding, but don't stand out and all that still applies.

Elijah flashes a grin and holds up the last two eggs. "Okay, but *these* are hard-boiled."

Sure. I "believe" him. I jab a finger at the floor. "You get to clean that up."

Tommy sticks his tongue out at Elijah, who, mature as he is, sticks his right back.

I eye my youngest brother. "Don't think you're getting off the hook. Paper towels. Now."

"Aw." It's almost funny how in sync they are. Almost.

"You better not be making a mess in my kitchen," Nana calls from the family room where her soap opera is sure to be in full swing.

"We're not," we all say in unison.

"Whatever you have done, clean it up," the matron of our house commands.

Elijah salutes even though she doesn't have x-ray vision to see through the wall. "Yes, ma'am."

"Here, I'll help." Macy slides off her barstool and tears a length of paper towels from the stand and passes them to Tommy.

It's only now after the dream with the bees that I can see the slight tinge of pink that touches her cheeks when she smiles at Elijah. I'm such an idiot. How did I never notice before?

Solomon steps from the alcove he's tucked himself into. It's amazing, really, how he can hide himself so flawlessly that even I forget he's here.

"Something's bothering you," he murmurs near my ear.

I shrug and watch as the trio wipe the floor clean. Elijah must say something funny, because Macy laughs. Not the polite, fake one that's just a notch too high, which she uses around strangers, but the real one that ends in a snort.

"Tell me." Solomon nudges me with his elbow.

"Why do you think she never told me? About how she feels, I mean." I cross my arms and try to ignore the tightening in my stomach. "I thought we told each other everything."

Solomon leans back against the wall and crosses his ankles. "Maybe she didn't want you to know. Could be she thought it would make things weird. Or maybe she didn't think anything would come of it."

Yeah, but if that dream with the bees was any indication, that's not the case. Macy has hopes. Secret ones, but hopes all the same.

"Gwen—"

I wave him off before he can say more. "You're right. I shouldn't be so worried about it. When she's ready, she'll tell me." I punctuate the statement with a jerk of my chin. That's the only explanation I can think of. She's just not ready to fully admit her feelings. When she's sure, she'll tell me. I mean, I would have felt awkward about telling her if I'd had feelings for Luke or something.

Macy stands to throw away the soiled paper towels, and her foot slips. Then she's falling. I lunge forward and everything changes in a burst of black and white.

I squint, trying to force my vision back into focus.

Whiplash.

Mist swirls up around my ankles and climbs to my knees. Water laps at my feet. I'm balanced on a slick stone covered in moss, surrounded by a dark marsh. The place reeks of stagnant water.

"Gwen!" Macy comes into focus a few feet away, reaching out a hand for me. A dark rope of what looks to be tangled moss climbs up her left leg, covering first her knee, and then stretching up her hip. She teeters, arms flailing, as she struggles to maintain her balance. "Help me!"

My toes are at the edge of my own stone, and there is a wide expanse of algae-colored water between us. "Hold on," I call.

She nods, lip caught between her teeth. And yet her eyes shine with trust. I will not fail her.

I squint against the fog. There has to be a way to get to her. There…is that an outline of a stone? It's my one chance, though I'll be headed for one disgusting bath if I'm wrong. I stretch out a tentative foot. My boot touches something solid. Not a mirage then. I lunge, transferring my weight to the new stone.

"Hurry." Panic colors Macy's voice.

I look up from watching my steps.

Where Macy once stood mere feet away, she now stretch-es far out of my reach, that twist of mossy rope wrapped around her waist.

The Dream is not playing fair.

"Hold on, I'm coming." I pick my way across three more stones. Where is Solomon? He must be here somewhere, but with the thick fog there's no finding him.

"Gwen..." Macy's voice wobbles like she's fighting back tears.

I tighten my jaw and dash across five stones in a row, barely even checking my footing between each step. On the fourth, I teeter. On the fifth, my left boot slips, skidding across the surface of the stone. I squeal and rotate my arms in a desperate attempt to catch my balance. For one breath I'm sure I'm going to tumble head-over-heels, but then my footing steadies. Yikes. I take a gulp of air and raise my head.

"Gwen?" Macy is now almost thirty feet away, her form a mere silhouette against the fog. "You have to help me. Please, Gwen."

"I'm coming," I call. "I'm coming."

I lunge across another series of stones, and finally the distance is closing between us. When we're a mere few feet apart, I stretch my arm out as far as I can.

"Take my hand," I say.

Macy stretches, that vine creeping up her torso.

Our fingers are inches apart when a vine snags my ankle, yanking me backward. "No!" I cry.

Splash.

I tumble backward and land on my bottom in shallow water, Macy once more a shadow against the fog.

I slap a hand against the disgusting water, sending up a splash of pond scum.

"Gwen, save me," her call is little more than an echo in the distance

I growl and shove to a standing position, searching out the stone path once more. One, two, three, four…I lose track as I race across the marsh. My lungs burn and sweat plasters strands of hair to my temple, but I refuse to stop, even when a pang pierces my side.

"Gwen!"

I can see her now. The vine has reached her chest, twisting dangerously close to her neck.

I will not let the Dream win.

I push myself harder. Faster. Fire burns through my legs, my every muscle working to the maximum.

Almost there, almost there, almost there.

My ankle twists.

Splash.

I'm back in the shallow water near the shore once more. Tears prick my eyes, and I grab a handful of mud from the water's bottom and hurl it as far as I can.

"Gwen? Where are you?" This time it's Solomon's voice that is laced with panic.

I push myself up, disgusting water dripping from my clothes. "Here." I swipe some muck from my cheek. "I'm here."

"Stay there," he orders. Wherever he is, I still can't see him, and he doesn't sound exactly close.

"Okay, I—"

"Gwen, help me," Macy shrieks before she's cut off by a terrible gurgling sound.

"Macy." I crash through the water before I find the slippery stones once more. "Hold on, I'm coming." Oh, please let me get to her in time. "I'm coming, Macy."

"Gwen, stay where you are." Solomon's command is little more than a buzzing afterthought in my mind as I charge toward that terrible choking sound coming from Macy's direction.

"I'm coming, I'm coming," I shout until my throat burns, and my voice runs hoarse, just so she'll know she's not alone.

My boot slips. I crash down on one knee, but manage to pull myself back up before I can completely fall in the water.

"Gwen, wait." Solomon again.

Water splashes in the distance.

Macy.

I charge onward, my pulse hammering in my eardrums with every slap of my boots against stone.

She's there, flailing in the water, barely managing to keep her head above the surface. That vine has crept up her neck and is creeping toward the corner of her mouth. If it reaches her lips or nose...no, I won't even think about it.

"I'm here." I skid to a stop on the nearest stone and crouch, reaching for her. She extends her arm, but as the vine gives her a harsh tug, all she manages to do is spray me with the foul water.

"Gwen?" Solomon. Closer now.

"Over here." I stretch out farther, fighting to keep eye contact with Macy. "Grab my hand. Grab it, Macy."

She throws out a hand, but she misses my palm, and instead hits my knee. For one sickening moment, my stomach flips, and then *crash*, I'm back in the shallows. No, no, no.

"Macy!" I shove to my feet once again.

"Gwen." Hands catch me around the waist, halting me before I can go plunging down the path once more.

"Let go of me." I thrash against Solomon's grip.

"Listen." He doesn't break his hold.

"We have to help her. She'll drown—"

"Gwen, listen to me." Solomon pulls me tight against his chest, so tight all I can do is wiggle. "Listen."

I still, more to catch my breath than anything else.

"You'll never make it if you take the path. Think, how deep is the water?"

I want to resume fighting like a trapped lion, but instead I force myself to take a series of slow breaths. To *listen*. How deep is this water? Knee high. Wait, no, it can't be that simple, can it?

"Just go through the water. The stones won't work."

"How do you know?" I ask as he loosens his grip.

"This is a reoccurring nightmare Macy has. It took me longer than I'd like to admit, but I eventually figured it out. Go ahead." He motions in Macy's direction.

A terrible silence has fallen where she should be. Everything in me tugs toward the stones, but I squelch that urge and instead do as Solomon says. I wade through the muck. Sure enough, I meet no resistance, and we are at Macy's side just as the twisted rope of moss tugs her under. Solomon grabs one of her arms, and I snag her other. Together, we tug her to her feet. Solomon pulls his pocketknife from his lab coat, cutting away the moss, and Macy gulps in a breath.

The ground quakes, and then I'm falling. Down, down, down. Into deep blackness. I slam into the ground, and pain radiates through my tailbone. A full moon allows me to make out some of my surroundings. Bare trees spike from the ground, and tombstones jut up in random order.

I spin. More stones form a teetering line behind me. Giant footsteps thunder through the earth, sending my teeth clattering. A girl's scream rips through the air, pushing chills over my arms. This isn't going to be pretty. I scramble to my feet and nearly topple over the tombstone behind me. Somewhere, an owl cries out, adding further creepiness to the dream. The smell of recent rain drifts to my nostrils. There's an underlining aroma of something...else. It's pungent, and I hold my sleeve against my nose to keep it at bay.

I search the darkness for Macy or Solomon. Neither appear in my line of vision. Looks like I'm on my own for this one. At least for now, anyway.

The giant footsteps come closer. Two glowing, red eyes attached to a massive body loom above me. My breath catches in my throat. A gleaming smile stretches across the monkey's giant face. I stumble back, gaping at the creature. I'm trapped inside a nightmare with a monstrous version of Maria's stuffed sock monkey.

Sweat pools on my palms, and I hoof it backward to put some space between me and the Nightmare creature. The back of my knees crash against a tombstone, and I tumble to the ground. The impact steals my breath, and blades of wet grass stick to my hands.

"Gwen," Solomon roars my name somewhere in the distance.

Well, at least I'm not alone.

The monkey looms closer as lightning flashes across the sky.

My throat constricts, and I lie frozen.

The monkey swells, its mouth stretching, pulling at the seams holding it in place.

"Get up," Solomon says.

"Gwen." This time the voice belongs to Macy.

I crawl to my feet, but my legs tremble beneath me. I turn to flee, but it's like my feet weigh fifty pounds each. No matter how hard I push myself, I can't move quickly.

"Come on," Solomon urges, waving me toward him.

I focus on him and Macy huddled under a stone bridge.

Just a few more steps.

Rain bursts from the sky. Dousing me. Blurring my vision. I dash a hand across my eyes. Take another step. Another.

Almost there.

A giant hand wraps around my middle. Squeezing. Lifting me up, up, up.

"Solomon!" His name rubs my throat raw.

"Gwen." He's racing toward me, sword drawn.

The giant hand constricts around me like a noose. The pressure builds in my head. And then I'm being flung across the graveyard. For one beautiful moment, I'm free, and then my skull connects with a tombstone. Nausea floods me. The world twists and churns.

"Gwen." Solomon's voice seems to be coming from the other side of a wall. Muffled by the static roaring in my ears.

"S-S—" My eyes slip closed.

Chapter Thirty-Six

*B*eep. *Beeep. Beeeep.*

"You've got to open your eyes, sugar. I can't make you do it, the choice is yours."

Beep. Beeep. Beeeep.

"Hold on, honey. Deep breaths. Stay with me."

The voice of an older woman echoes through my head. The same one from before. The one accompanied by the incessant beeping that grates my ears.

Beep. Beep. Beeep.

"You need to fight, sweetheart."

Beep...

I suck in a sharp breath, and open my eyes. I'm floating in the sea of blackness once again. And then it's not dark anymore. Those ribbons of gold twist through the black, swirling and snapping until they collide. I close my eyes against the brightness and don't open them until the impression fades from behind my eyelids.

Pictures float in front of me.

Elijah with his baseball cap on backwards, draping an arm around my shoulders on the beach.

The twins swinging at a park.

Me with a driver's license, a grinning Beck at my side, her own license in hand.

Nana and Mom smiling in front of our Christmas tree.

There's a quick flash of something marred with fuzz around the edges. I squint trying to make it out. A folded flag. A coffin. It's gone in a whiff of smoke before I can truly make sense of it.

Then there's a picture of me smiling at Austin. Riding bikes with him. Him making me coffee. Holding hands and...there's one of me in a sundress, my hair blowing in the wind, standing on tiptoe.

My heart stops, and everything comes to a standstill.

I'm. Kissing. Austin.

This can't be real. Can it?

It's just a dream. Just a dream.

"I'm so sorry, Gwen. For everything."

I freeze.

The voice is Beck's, but it sounds far off. Distant. Almost like it's only an echo in my head. I hold my breath, waiting to see if I hear her again.

It's a different voice that comes through this time.

"It's going to be okay, baby. We'll get through this, we'll..." My mom's voice chokes off in a sob.

"Mom?" I try to reach for her. To focus on her voice and let it pull me closer to her, but it's like a vanishing string. The moment I try to grasp it, it's gone.

A bright light bursts in front of my eyes.

There's something different about this dream.

A heaviness weighs me down.

Why?

I step forward, tracing my hand along the green bleachers lining my high school football field. A rush of giddy excitement bursts upon me. I'm going to meet Austin. Flashes of our dates dance through my memory. How lucky am I to get the guy of my dreams?

Soft giggles drift from farther down the line of tiered benches. Austin and I are not the only couple looking to sneak a moment under the cover of the bleachers.

I smile and add a bounce to my step. Mom and I have already gone prom dress shopping. All I need is for Austin to ask me. Maybe that's his plan for today. I half jog the last few steps, and there he is, still in his football jersey. Warmth surges through my chest only to die away when my heart goes cold. His arms are wrapped around a girl with tight curls. I'm going to be sick.

"Beck?" I stumble backward, the feeling draining from my face. How can this be happening?

The couple who were making out only seconds before rip apart, breathing hard.

Tears burn my eyes. "Austin?"

Beck takes half a step forward, hand extended. "Gwen, it's not what you think."

"Oh, so you weren't kissing my boyfriend?" How could she? My chest heaves with the rapidity of my breathing.

She draws her hand back and twists it around her wrist where a new bracelet adorns her arm. Did Austin give it to her? A small gift box lies open on the gum strewn pavement. A wave of pain spears through my center.

Austin takes a step forward. "We didn't mean—"

"Didn't mean what? Are you trying to tell me you accidentally fell into each other's arms? Did you accidentally kiss her, too?"

His shoulders slump. "Gweny—"

It might as well be a slap. My tears are getting too thick to contain. One hot drop of saltwater escapes its prison and scalds a path down my cheek. "Don't you dare call me that." I dash the tear away because I do not want to cry over Austin Taylor.

"We didn't mean for this to happen," Beck whines.

"Well, obviously it did." Why am I still standing here? I turn away.

"We were going to tell you," Beck calls to my back.

"Yeah, and how did you think that would go?" More tears run down my cheeks to join the first. Crap. I swipe at my face. I. Will. Not. Cry. Over. Austin. Taylor.

"Gwen." Austin catches my arm and yanks me around to face him. "I'm sorry. Please don't be mad."

"Because you're totally the victim here." I jerk free and pivot on my heel.

"Gwen," Beck pleads.

I can't do this. I break into a jog, fleeing the scene. Tears surge down my cheeks, blinding me. I run until a stitch forms in my side, and I can't breathe. I fall against a tree and curl in on myself, sobs shaking my shoulders. Am I so unlovable that my boyfriend has to turn to my best friend?

Chapter Thirty-Seven

The pain ebbs to a soft throb. Like when I wake from a dream where seconds before I was crying. Only, I'm not awake. Without Solomon here, I have no idea how to leave. If I could, I'd be gone in an instant. I'd love nothing more than to have a girl's night with Mom and Nana. To hug the twins tight and read them a story.

I run a hand over my eyes and moan.

Why did the scene behind the bleachers feel more like a memory and less like a fabrication? I'd love to excuse it away as nothing but another trick of the Nightmares, but there is something too...pungent about it that won't quite let me shrug it away.

"Whose dream is this?" The words run through my head from my conversation with Beck on the beach.

The high school and football field fade away, and an open meadow takes their place. Birds sing in the surrounding woods, and wildflowers blow in the gentle breeze. Puffs of dandelion seeds trace their way through the bright blue sky.

Is it true? Has Solomon been lying to me this whole time? Pang stings my chest. He wouldn't do that. I have to believe he wouldn't.

But, where is he? My own voice inside my head asks.

I wrap my arms around myself even though it's far from cold. He'll be here.

"Poor little Gweny, what will you do without your Guardian?" The words from the Nightmare version of Macy echo through my head. She'd called Solomon *my* Guardian. What if there's more to her words than I'd thought?

Ugh, now I'm confused. I run my hands through my disheveled hair.

"I'm so sorry, Gwen. For everything." I replay the words that sounded like they came from Beck. Was that last dream really a memory? Did she try to apologize later? Or maybe this whole Dream thing is messing with my mind.

I drop my forehead onto my folded arms. I just want to go home.

Footsteps crunch over the grass, drawing my head up. Solomon approaches slowly, like he's afraid I'll spook.

I clench my jaw.

No more lies.

I stand. "Whose dreams are these?"

His face scrunches, his confusion clear.

"Whose Dream Guardian are you?" I'm shaking now.

He eases forward another step. "I told you. I'm Macy's."

"Yeah, that's what you told me. Is it true?"

Solomon hesitates. "Gwen—"

I jab a finger at his chest. "Don't lie to me. Don't you dare." Tears cloud my vision, and I blink fiercely to clear them away.

He watches me, expression growing sadder by the minute.

"Whose dreams, Solomon?"

His throat bobs, and he licks his lips.

A sob burbles in my chest, but I grit my teeth. Blast it, but I can feel snot gathering at the tip of my nose. "Whose?"

Finally, he holds my gaze. "Yours."

The one word might as well be a bullet to my chest. I reel back, hand pressed over my heart. He's been lying to me this whole time. This whole entire time. How is it possible that this hurts worse than Beck's betrayal?

"Gwen." Solomon snags my arm and turns me to face him, his grip far gentler than Austin's.

I shake my head, fighting the liquid burning my eyes. "Let go."

"Gwen, please. Let me explain." His words are soft. Coaxing.

I clench my jaw and glare at him. "Explain what? What's happening, Solomon?"

He slips his grip from my bicep to my hand and tugs, cajoling me into a sitting position. I duck my head and knot my free hand in the grass.

Solomon bends to catch my gaze. "There was an accident."

"Besides trusting you?" I wrench my hand free from his.

He flinches but doesn't look away. "You were in a car wreck."

My pulse spikes. "What are you talking about?"

The image of a news segment fills the space in front of us. A woman in a pink blazer talks about a teen girl in critical condition due to a drunk driver hitting her car. My senior picture flashes across the screen followed by one of the mangled mess that is supposedly my car.

"No." I shake my head. "No. Macy's brother was in an accident."

His smile is sad. "Macy is a figment of your imagination."

I can't breathe. He's wrong. He has to be. A shiver sweeps up my spine. "You're a liar."

He inhales deeply. "Gwen, please. You're in a coma. This—" Solomon indicates the surrounding area, "is all your imagination. Your way of coping."

"I don't believe you." Oh, but I do. Too many things make sense for this not to be true.

"I'm not lying." His fist clenches on his knee.

I get up and tap my palms against my hips. Drums. I need my drums. I swivel toward the boy still sitting at the base of the tree as I rattle off a beat against my thighs.

He watches me, mouth slightly parted like he wants to say something.

"What?" I cross my arms and hold my breath, waiting for some dramatic argument.

"I'm sorry."

What am I supposed to say to that? I don't say anything. Instead, I cover my face with my hand and sob.

Solomon stands and wraps an arm around my shoulders, drawing me close. I bawl into his chest and cling to his shirt like it's the final thread of reality. He rubs my back and presses a kiss to my hair. I cry until the sobs dissolve into shuddering breaths.

Solomon pushes me back so I can see his eyes, but he keeps his hands cupped around my biceps. "The truth is that I would do anything to protect you."

Despite my best efforts, a tear trails down my cheek.

"Anything." He strokes my face with his thumb, catching the drop of salt water.

I search his eyes. I want to believe. So badly want to not be alone in this mess of confusion. But how do I trust him when all he's done is lie to me so far?

Solomon leans closer, his face mere inches away. "Anything."

A small sob breaks through my shield, and a second wave of tears seep from my eyes.

Solomon drops his forehead against mine. "Can you trust me?"

My chin trembles. I should say no. Instead, I find myself nodding. Maybe I shouldn't, but I do.

"Thank you, Gwen." He places a kiss to my hands.

My throat tightens. "If this is my dream, if I'm just stuck in a coma somewhere, how do I wake up?"

He meets my eyes. "You just have to decide to."

I scoff. "Just decide to? It's as easy as that?"

"Well, not exactly. You've had many opportunities to wake up, but subconsciously, you've chosen not to."

"Yeah, well, can you blame me?" Even the small flash of memory of Austin and Beck with their lips locked is enough to bring heat simmering through my core.

Solomon shakes his head. "I think you're afraid to wake up, and I don't think it's because of some jerk boyfriend."

I knot my fingers in his lab coat and press my forehead against his collarbone. Why? Why would I be afraid to wake up? Because Solomon's right. As much as I'm mad at Austin and Beck, I would never want that to keep me away from my family. There must be something else. I concentrate on the blur of images from before. No. *Memories*. The pictures in my mind of my childhood with Macy and Luke are slowly replaced with ones of me and Beck, sometimes Elijah and the twins. But the problem is not with these. I nudge them aside. My mind fixes on one of a dark casket and a folded flag. No. No, that can't be right. I tighten my grip on Solomon's coat and squeeze my eyes shut, but the image only grows clearer in my mind, the memory invading. Pictures of Dad with each of us lined up on the stage. Nana, Mom, Elijah, the twins, me. All dressed in black, faces lined with tears.

I choke on a sob. "Dad. He's dead, isn't he? He won't be there when I wake up."

Solomon tightens his arms around me. "Yeah." He sounds choked up.

I shudder. "I don't want to face a world without him." Even with Solomon's arms around me, I feel so very, very small.

"You have to, Gwen."

A new thought grips me, and I hold his coat all the tighter. "What about you? You won't be there either."

Solomon swallows hard before stepping back, putting space between us. Tears shimmer in his eyes, and he cups my face with his strong, steady hands. "You have to wake up, Gwen. Because living in an imaginary world isn't really living."

Chapter Thirty-Eight

S olomon tugs on my fingers. "Come on."

"Where are we going?" I mop a sleeve over my face. Maybe I should be trying to make myself wake up this instant, but as much as Solomon is right, I'm not ready yet. I want to cling to this Dream world. Just for a little longer.

He smiles. "You'll see." He snaps his fingers, and soon we're standing in a large room.

A disco ball hangs above, casting dots of light around the space. Glass pillars line the marble walls with arches carved into their surfaces. Blue lights stain the lower half of the space in a becoming shade of turquoise. Yards of white gauze sweep the length of the gold, domed ceiling in elegant folds. The place is beautiful enough to belong in a palace.

When I turn away from the splendor of the room and face Solomon, he grins at me. He is handsome in a white suit, hair slicked into submission.

I laugh. "What is this?"

He shrugs, the tailored shoulders of his suit lifting. "Well, you missed Senior Prom, so I thought I should make it up to you."

My gaze travels down my sweater and jeans. "I'm not exactly dressed for it."

Now it's Solomon's turn to chuckle as he leans close to my ear. "This is your dream, Gwen. You can wear whatever you want."

I suck in a breath, and picture my dream prom dress. The one I couldn't get because it was too expensive. I open my eyes and peek at my outfit. I'm clad in a white dress which stretches long in the back and comes down to just above my knees in the front. The tiny sparkles catch in the light, making it appear as if my dress is made of starlight. Wow. Finally, this Dream stuff comes in useful.

I look up to find Solomon staring at me, mouth agape. I duck my head and twirl a loose strand of my curled updo. "Is it too much?"

He shakes his head. "No, you look beautiful."

Heat flames my cheeks, and I stare down at my glittery heels.

Soft music sweeps through invisible speakers.

Solomon bows over my hand. "May I have this dance?"

"Yes." The word comes out breathless.

He pulls me close, clasping my hand gently in his while placing the other on my lower back. I slide my free hand up to his shoulder, unable to pull my gaze away from his shining eyes. He swirls me around the dance floor, never missing a step, and to my surprise, neither do I. Even the heels I would kill myself in within the waking world seem perfectly molded to my feet. Solomon turns me under his arm, and I come back to him effortlessly. The music sweeps through the room, both sad and beautiful at the same time. It reeks of goodbye.

Moisture fills my eyes, and I blink.

Because waking up means leaving this boy behind. And despite my best efforts, I care.

Solomon smiles down at me, his gaze tender. I rest my head against his chest so he can't see my tears. He presses his cheek to my hair. A drop of water leaks between my lashes, and it soaks into his jacket. If only I could hold onto this moment and make it last forever. This is my dream. Maybe I can.

Or, then again, maybe not...

Flames shoot up along the walls, demolishing my perfect happily ever after. Heat sears through the thin layers of my dress and smoke fills the room. The gray haze clogs my throat. I try to suck in a clean breath, but end up coughing. My lungs burn with the poison.

Solomon grabs my hand and tugs me backward. The ring of fire sweeps around the room until we're cut off from all possible escape routes. My gaze locks on Solomon's. Panic reflects back at me.

And then the screaming starts. Nightmares, thousands of them, run at us. Coakley is in the lead, his lips twisted into a ferocious snarl. They race through the wall of flames as if the tendrils of fire are no more than a pesky puddle on a sidewalk.

I turn my wild gaze on Solomon.

"Come on." He grabs my hand and drags me toward one of the glass pillars.

A spark leaps from the flames and latches onto my skirt, crawling up and devouring the lower folds of my gown. The heat scalds my legs. I cry out. Solomon spins me around and rips away the burning cloth, delivering me from the inferno.

We're losing precious seconds.

He grabs my hand and tugs me forward. The heels that were my dream come true seconds ago morph into my worst nightmare as I flee my enemies. My ankles tilt this way and that as I run. My shoe catches in the grout, and my left foot caves. Pain spikes through my ankle. I crash sideways and sprawl over the marble tiles in a puff of silk and tulle. I push myself to a sitting position and, despite the waves of hair tumbling into my face, I reach for my stiletto and wrench it from my already swelling foot.

"Gwen." Solomon darts to my side, reaching to pull me up.

I latch onto his hand, but when he lifts me, a pain palpitates through my ankle. The blood drains from my face. I crumple, but Solomon catches me under my knees and hefts me into his strong arms.

I cling to his neck while he races away from the Nightmares reaching out to snag us. He skids to a stop in front of one of the glass pillars lining the room and reaches forward to yank open an invisible door. He shoves me inside. The second the door closes, its seams disappear, trapping me inside.

No. No. He has to come, too.

"Solomon?" I lean forward, fingertips pressed to the glass.

He's just going to another pillar. He must be.

But no, the Nightmares seize him, dragging him toward the flames. He struggles, but too many hands hold him. He can't break free.

"Solomon!" I beat at the glass.

The barrier doesn't so much as rattle under my drumming fists. He cannot leave me here alone. My heart shatters inside of me, the threads of hope for our impossible happily ever after unraveling at a rapid speed.

Coakley catches my eye, grin wide as he tugs Solomon backward. His revenge.

The flames shoot higher.

Pain swells in my throat as I choke on a sob. "Let him go." I can't lose him, too. I can't. "Please."

Coakley's eyes spark with satisfaction.

Solomon offers me a sad smile as a thousand wrinkled hands pull him backward. "It's time to wake up, Gweny."

No, no, I have to save him. A moment ago, I was able to control the Dream. Maybe I can do it now. I hammer the glass until my hand aches, but it refuses to break.

Coakley quirks a finger, beckoning.

He's mocking me.

"Enough. Leave him be!" I scream until my voice cracks, but no matter how frantically I search, I can't find a way to open the pillar.

"Solomon." I collapse to my knees while my heart shreds into a thousand miniscule pieces. I leave my palm pressed to the glass, willing him to rally. To defend himself as he's fought to protect me all this time.

The flames crawl up his pant legs and devour the man I've come to care for. A blaze engulfs the Dream, melting in time to the hoarse screams rubbing my throat raw. Tears scald my cheeks. I slam my palm against the glass. "No!"

"There's no way left for you to win," Coakley's muffled voice comes through the barrier between us as his eyes lock on mine.

He's wrong.

"Time to wake up, Gweny."

I squeeze my eyes shut and choke down a few deep breaths.

Time to wake up.

I open my eyes.

Chapter Thirty-Nine

S tiffness weighs my body down, and fog clogs my mind. Who are the strangers rushing around me in white coats and blue scrubs? My heartrate skyrockets, and I force my head to the side. Where am I, and why does it take so much dratted effort to *move*?

It takes me a good while, but with enough blinks, I drag the world into focus.

I'm lying in a bed, monitors and wires taped to me. The bright beam of a flashlight pokes at me, stinging my eyes. Machines beep. Chills dance up my arms and crawl under my thin gown. My leg aches, pierced with a fiery pain. I blink sluggish eyelids. They are so, so terribly heavy.

The next time I manage to peel my eyes open, the crowd of strangers descend upon me once again. A doctor and nurse perform a series of what they assure me are customary procedures, but they only make my eyes heavy. I do my best to cooperate, but the image of Solomon is seared into my mind. Tears pool in my eyes. One slips down the curve of my cheek.

"Well done, honey." A middle-aged nurse with faded blonde hair squeezes my hand the third time I manage to rouse. The world isn't nearly so fuzzy now. The faces far less scary. Even my eyelids don't weigh quite as much.

I scan the nurse for some sign. Something that will help me place her. My attention latches on the pink ballerina shoe pinned to her collar. From there, my gaze drifts down to her shiny name badge.

Macy.

My pulse quickens.

She pats my hand and moves on. "We've sent word to your family. They'll be here just as soon as they can."

I blink heavy eyelids, but another nurse pushes in front of me, demanding my attention.

One time, I wake when it is dark, and there's only the dull beeping of machinery to keep me company. There's an ache deep inside my chest. Not something that requires medical attention. No, this is something far deeper.

Because, no matter how I try, I can no longer recall Solomon's face. Over and over and over again, I try to pull up my memories of him, but there's only a faint recognition. That once upon a time, he existed. But, of course, he didn't. Because none of that was real. It couldn't have been.

And so, my chin crumples, and tears creep from the corners of my eyes and slip into my ears, because Solomon is gone.

X

Elijah pokes his head around the hospital door. His face lights up, and he steps into the room strewn with summer sunlight. "Hey."

Tears well at the sight of my brother's face. "Hi." I grimace at the sound of my voice. I may as well have a frog stuck in my throat and tissues shoved up my nostrils. My leg stretches in front of me, the skin not covered by my hospital gown crisscrossed with scar tissue.

"Mom, Nana, and the twins are on their way." Elijah eases further into the room, hands shoved deep in his pockets.

Internally, I wince. All I've wanted since waking up is to hug my family close, but I guess that's the problem with being life-flighted to a specialty hospital. It's farther from home. At least it's close to Elijah's college.

I nod in response to Elijah's statement. I'm not sure I could even manage to push words through my aching throat. My nose stings at my effort to hold back the mess of emotions swirling through my body. Because Dad is gone. Elijah didn't say one word about him. I guess I've clung to the hope that maybe, just maybe, that funeral was all in my dreams. But no, the gaping hole in my chest is the kind only torn by the absence of a loved one.

My brother crosses to my bed and pulls me against his chest in a light hug. I latch onto him, and for a moment, we both cry.

My brother pulls back and lowers himself to a chair.

"What happened, Elijah?" I bump hair away from my forehead. No matter how hard I fight to conjure my memories, the events remain elusive, trapped somewhere in the back of my mind. Forgotten. All I have is what Solomon told me, but I can't be sure any of that is real.

Elijah rubs his palms together. "After everything that happened with Austin and Beck, you got in your car and left school early. There was a drunk driver who ran a red light and t-boned the car. It's been a couple months."

No memories well up to confirm his words, but I dip my chin in acknowledgement. Beck. My best friend. A sting of pain burns through me, but I blink away the hurt. "Dad?" Because I need him to confirm it out loud.

Tears well in Elijah's eyes. "Listen, it's normal to be confused. They say your memory might be foggy for a while. Gwen, Dad's been gone since right before Christmas."

Right. "I know," I whisper. Swallow the lump in my throat. "What about Luke?" His name feels wrong and misplaced on my tongue, but I have to ask. To know. His name is the first knot in my tangled reality.

Elijah's brow furrows. "Luke? Who's Luke?"

A knock sounds against the door, and Elijah shoots me a hesitant look before moving to open it. Seconds later, the whole family piles in. Mom cries, the twins shout their joy only to be quickly hushed, and Nana cradles me close, a flow of loving Spanish washing over me.

The doctors perform tests and scans, all designed to show them I'm alive, awake, and all brain functions are good to go. Each test comes back with optimal results. My family is currently staying across the street in an apartment rented for them by anonymous saints from our church. So many blessings, and yet, a very real piece of me is gone. Lost with a boy in a silly, white lab coat.

The next day, Elijah returns early in the morning. Not that I mind. I could do with more company around here that doesn't involve any pokes or jabs. He has to move aside bundles of flowers and gifts to make space to sit in the small hospital room. With each movement of the flowers, puffs of their strong aroma drift through the air to mix with the pungent aroma of lemon cleaner the hospital staff seem to favor.

A knock sounds on the door.

No doubt the rest of the family or another nurse coming to poke and jab me.

"Come in," my brother says.

A second man about Elijah's age steps into the room, wearing a white lab coat, coffee cup in hand. "Parked the car." A British accent colors his voice.

My cheeks heat, and I pull my soft blanket up to my neck. I can't look very good after being in bed for such a long time. I rub my thumb against the edge of my blanket before reaching to fidget with my earrings. Only, the metal studs have been removed. I drop my hand to my lap.

Elijah, seemingly unaware of my embarrassment, gestures toward the guy standing near the door. "Gwen, this is a friend of mine. He's been putting in observation hours here at the hospital. You're his coffee break date." He winks, and heat shoots through my cheeks.

His friend offers a shy smile and keeps his head ducked. "It's a relief to finally see you awake. The name's Solomon." He peeks at me then, and our eyes connect.

My breath catches in my throat.

Solomon.

Impossible.

The haze of my dreams and the reality of this boy standing before me collide. He's here. He's not the same. He can't be. And yet...there's something so right about his presence.

My heartbeat thunders in my chest, and my heartrate monitor goes off, beeping frantically, but I can't pull my gaze away from the boy in the lab coat. My pulse kicks up a beat, sparks dancing up and down my arms, making my hands shake. Nurses are running into the room, but I don't care. I simply sit there, grinning like an idiot.

Because I'm finally wide awake.

Epilogue

S olomon holds the door for me, ushering me inside *Dashiell*'s booming atmosphere. He keeps one hand at my back, mindful of my limp and teetering balance. Progress, the doctors call it. I prefer the word challenge.

"Take it easy," Solomon says.

I stiffen and slide a glance up at him. "What?"

"You think you have a game face, but I can see everything going through your mind." He taps his temple.

I laugh and elbow his side. "Creep."

He laughs, too, and we move to the line in front of the counter. The hum of machines combined with the chatter of baristas shouting orders back and forth greets us. Part of me still expects to find Austin working the register, but with graduation, both he and Beck have moved on. And a tiny bit of me still aches with the way we've left things, but neither have tried to reconcile now that I'm awake, though I'm told Beck visited me in the hospital. Once. Now, she's blocked my number. But that's okay. Sometimes you have to let go.

Solomon tugs my hand, pulling my attention back to the present.

"Okay, so if you know me so well, what am I going to order?" I cock a brow.

"Easy. Peppermint tea."

My jaw drops, and I shake my head. "How?"

"It's what you've ordered the last three times." He flashes a cheeky grin.

Someone has been paying attention. A flurry of taps and beats shoot through my veins. A keeper, my dad would have said. Still, I can't let the guy's ego get *too* big. "Okay, but how do you know I'm not in the mood for something else this time?"

"Are you?" His expression is dubious.

"Therapy went well today, so I think I deserve a reward." If well means I almost died of exhaustion, which seems to be my PT's definition.

"A reward?"

"Yeah, a little adventure." As in, maybe a spray of whipped cream.

The girl ahead of us swivels away from the line, two steaming mugs in hand. I try to sidestep out of her path, but my knee buckles. Solomon steadies me and helps me move to the side.

"Does that mean I get to order for you?" He asks when the jingle of the bell announces the girl's exit.

Oh, snap. He knows how to up the stakes. I hesitate, searching the menu overhead for some excuse. All that reflects back at me are the many, many coffee names I don't have a clue about what they mean.

Solomon weaves his fingers through mine, sending a wave of warmth through my middle, and guides me up to the counter. "Don't you trust me?"

Our gazes meet and hold.

For a moment I swear I see a world of skyscrapers and Guardians reflected in his eyes, but then it fades, replaced by the flesh and blood boy in front of me. The one who gives piggyback rides to the twins, who meets me on his lunch breaks, and takes me out for tea after physical therapy. "Okay."

He shakes my hand, jiggling my entire frame. "Just okay?"

I laugh and give in. "Yes, I trust you."

A love song croons from the speakers, the beat and lyrics perfectly capturing the flutter of my pulse, the way my heart jumps a little, as if trying to get closer to his.

The barista has to clear his throat to break the spell.

Great, we're *that* couple.

But Solomon struts forward without even a hint of embarrassment. "Remember, you trust me."

Funny, the more he reminds me, the less sure I get. "Don't go crazy."

"Never." He squeezes my hand and rattles off an order that leaves my brain spinning.

"A what now?" I ask as the barista passes him a receipt.

"It's a surprise." Solomon slips his wallet into his pocket all without letting go of my hand.

I bite my lip and scan the menu for any hints.

"Aw, come on, Gonzales. Live a little." Solomon drapes an arm over my shoulders.

"Fine." I sigh and settle in to my "adventure."

Except when the drinks arrive with fluffy whipped cream and drizzles upon drizzles of caramel sauce, drool forms in the corners of my mouth.

"Ooh..." The sound releases before I can stop it.

"Your beverage." Solomon passes one to me.

I pause to give it a sniff. "It's coffee."

"Try it."

Well, I did promise to trust him...I take a sip, and the layers of sweetness slip down my throat. Refreshing. "Wow."

"Told you."

I stare at him, warmth sizzling through my middle. Maybe I don't hate coffee. Maybe it just matters who I drink it with.

Solomon slips his hand around mine and squeezes.

Yeah, I'd take reality over a dream world any day.

DG

Acknowledgments

First and foremost, I can't start my acknowledgements without thanking my Lord and Savior. Without You, this book never would have happened. Thank You for walking through this process with me every step of the way, answering the many, many prayers surrounding this writing process, and for opening the doors that let this book come into the world.

A very special thank you to my amazing family for championing me all these years and encouraging me to never give up. I don't have enough words to thank you all for reading the countless drafts, for all the dinner time brainstorming sessions, and just being there to listen through the hurt of rejections and the excitement of the highs.

Thank you to all of my friends and loved ones for your support and excitement over this writing journey. You'll never know how much your words of encouragement have impacted me over the years.

Thank you to the amazing team at Quill and Flame Publishing House for your beautiful work and wonderful support. Thank you AJ for taking a chance on a debut author and helping bring my dream to life.

Thank you to Megan Gerig for always supporting, always having a listening ear, and always being available for a brainstorming session or a critique. I couldn't have done this without your friendship. If anyone is looking for an editor, Megan is your girl. She's absolutely brilliant.

Dempsey, you won't remember, but thank you for all the nap time writing sessions. You were always there to lend a helping hand and were always sure someday somebody would help make the book on my computer one we could hold in our hands.

Thank you to Sara Ella who critiqued the first ten pages of R.E.M. and for your amazing feedback and kind words. Thank you for encouraging me to start submitting to agents and editors. You were right. ;)

And to every author who has ever taken a moment to answer my many, many questions throughout this writing journey, thank you. Every reply to an email/message, every comment or like on social media, means the world to me. Thank you for your support and encouragement.

I would be remiss if I didn't take a moment to thank the amazing authors who agreed to endorse R.E.M. You made this debut author's dreams come true.

Thank you to Bryanna Reeser for providing the amazing character art. You truly brought my characters to life.

Special thanks to Daniel Schwabauer and the wonderful team at the One Year Adventure Novel. Without your curriculum and community, I may never have realized how much I love writing and may never have pursued publication. And without the 2017 Student Novel Contest and my OYAN friends who pushed me to enter, I'm not sure R.E.M. would have ever seen the light of day. Thank you.

And to my readers. Thank you for picking R.E.M. up. For giving this book of mine a chance. If you enjoyed your read through, please consider leaving a review so more readers can discover this world of Dreams and Guardians.

The Author

Ashley Schaller is an award winning author who prefers tea over coffee, will never say no to puppy snuggles, and proudly wears the title of "Dog Mom". When not writing, she can often be found reading her next favorite book, taking long walks, baking, obsessing over owls (but only the cute cartoon ones), or learning new crochet patterns. As a writer, she seeks to create stories that glorify God. Stories that entertain, but you never have to worry about the content. To connect with Ashley and stay updated on all things books

and writing, follow her on Instagram @ashleyschaller-
author or find her at https://ashleyschaller.wordpress.com

Find Ashley on Instagram at: @ashleyschallerauthor

Quill & Flame

Find other Quill & Flame titles at www.quilland-flame.com or
@quill.and.flame.publishers on Instagram.
Stay tuned for more short stories as well as future releases from Quill & Flame Publishing House.
Join Quill & Flame Book Tours by emailing quillandflame publishinghouse@gmail.com.

Find other Quill & Titles releasing soon!

Making Magik: A Magik Prep Academy Anthology January 2023

Fortified by V. Romas Burton February 2023
Of Flame & Frost by AJ Skelly March 2023
By Light & Love by Anna Augustine April 2023
R.E.M. by Ashley Schaller May 2023
Hearts by Brittany Eden June 2023
Heart of the Sea by Moriah Chavis August 2023
By Blade & Blood by Anna Augustine September 2023
Shadowcast by Crystal D. Grant October 2023
Magic & Mistletoe: A Quill & Flame Christmas Anthology
December 2023